Maya Corrigan
A Parfait
Crime

Kensington Publishing Corp.
www.kensingtonbooks.com

KENSINGTON BOOKS are published by

Kenington Publishing Corp.
119 West 40th Street
New York, NY 10018

All Kensington titles, imprints, and distributed lines are available at special quantity discounts for bulk purchases for sales promotion, premiums, fund-raising, educational, or institutional use.

Special book excerpts or customized printings can also be created to fit specific needs. For details, write or phone the office of the Kensington Sales Manager: Attn.: Sales Department. Kensington Publishing Corp., 119 West 40th Street, New York, NY 10018. Phone: 1-800-221-2647.

The K and Teapot logo is a trademark of Kensington Publishing Corp.

First Printing: November 2023
ISBN: 978-1-4967-3459-4

ISBN: 978-1-4967-3460-0 (ebook)

10 9 8 7 6 5 4 3 2 1

Printed in the United States of America

A PARFAIT CRIME

Val went to the kitchen at eight the next morning to make coffee and warm up day-old muffins. With her assistant manager handling the café, Val planned a leisurely day of gardening, reading, and spending time with Bram later. She might fit in some baking too.

The doorbell interrupted her thoughts. It would surely wake Granddad, whose bedroom was near the front door. She hurried to the hall.

She was surprised that the doorbell ringer was Chief Yardley. He came to the house now and then to visit Granddad, but only once before had he shown up this early. And that was to break the news that a woman they knew had been killed in an apparent accident.

Why was he here now?

"Good morning, Chief." She opened the door wider for the barrel-chested man to come in. "You're just in time for coffee."

"I could use some coffee . . . and some help from you and your granddaddy."

Granddad had emerged from his bedroom at the end of the hall in time to hear the chief's comment. "Good morning, Earl. What kind of help do you need?"

"I want to hear what happened at the spa's open house." He turned to Val. "You were right that I should have stationed an officer there, though I don't know that it would have changed what happened. A dead body was found there this morning . . ."

Books by Maya Corrigan

Published by Kensington Publishing Corp.

Dedicated to the Queen of Crime, Agatha Christie, whose books and plays have given pleasure to countless readers and inspired many authors to write mysteries.

Chapter 1

Val Deniston turned down the setting on the burner and watched the blue gas flame ebb under the casserole pot. But rotating a knob wouldn't get rid of the other fire on her mind this evening—the blaze her boyfriend, Bram Muir, was fighting.

Still in training as the newest member of Bayport's volunteer fire department, he'd gone with the crew to minor fires they'd extinguished within minutes. But this one was apparently more serious. He'd promised to call her when he was on his way back. He'd already been at the fire for over an hour, and she still hadn't heard from him.

Granddad came into the kitchen from the dining room. "The table's set. How's the *coq au vin* coming along?"

"I'm at step five of Julia Child's recipe, setting the *coq* on fire."

"Just don't set the cook on fire." He grinned.

"That's a serious concern. The first time I flambéed something, my eyelashes got singed. I was hoping Bram would be here to prevent that or something worse from happening when I ignite the cognac." Worse would be burning down the Victorian house she'd shared for the last two years with her widowed grandfather.

"Your hair will catch fire sooner than your eyelashes. It's curling down your forehead and springing out on the sides." Granddad opened the door to the pantry closet, took out his chef's hat, a toque with *Codger Cook* on it, and gave it to Val. "You can borrow this."

Val shoved her cinnamon-colored curls under the hat. Her mother had given Granddad the toque as a gag after he wangled a job as the local newspaper's recipe columnist, calling himself the Codger Cook. When he pulled off that ruse, he could do little more than heat up canned soup, grill burgers, and cut down on the ingredients in Val's recipes. But by sticking to easy dishes and doggedly persisting, he'd become a decent home cook, though far from a chef. Tonight he was making a parfait for dessert, layering raspberries and cream into glasses.

"Parfait is your perfect dessert, Granddad. Easy to make ahead, pretty to look at, and . . ." Val waited for him to add his culinary mantra.

"Only five ingredients," he responded. "How many ingredients in *coq au vin?*"

"Closer to fifteen than five. I'm about to torch our dinner."

Granddad reached for the fire extinguisher on the wall. "I'll take care of any flare-ups with this."

But not without ruining the French dish she was

making to give Bram a taste of what awaited them in Paris next month. "Please don't, unless I yell for help." She poured the cognac and ignited it, keeping her face averted. Once the flames subsided, she added more ingredients to the pot and adjusted the heat to a simmer. "You can hang up the fire extinguisher, Granddad."

The doorbell rang. Val looked up from poking the chicken to test for doneness. "That could be Bram." He might not have had time to call ahead.

"Or his mother." Granddad hurried to the hall.

Bram's mother had become a regular visitor since she'd moved back to Bayport six months ago. Dorothy Muir had grown up here, returned as a widow, and opened a bookstore. Bram had come along to help her set up Title Wave, an apt name for a bookstore near the Chesapeake Bay's tidal waters. She was thrilled when he decided to stay rather than return to Silicon Valley. Instead of honchoing tech start-ups in California, he had the challenge of making a brick-and-mortar start-up successful. His mother's shop was now Granddad's favorite haunt when he wasn't testing recipes for his column, fishing in the Chesapeake Bay, or watching classic movies.

When he brought Dorothy into the kitchen. Val noticed a change in the usually cheerful woman. Dorothy managed only a tight smile. She must be worried about Bram.

Granddad took a bottle of wine from the fridge. "Can I pour you a glass of white wine, Dorothy?"

"I'll have wine with dinner." She checked her watch and rubbed her neck under her shoulder-length silver hair. "I'd like some ice water for now."

Granddad brought her the water and put the appetizer tray on the kitchen table, where she sat. "This should tide us over for a while."

"But don't hold up dinner for Bram." Dorothy stabbed a cheese cube. "He wouldn't want us to do that."

When dinner was ready, Granddad sat at the head of the long table in the dining room with Val at the other end. He ate with gusto. Dorothy picked at her food as she kept glancing across the table where her son was supposed to sit.

Granddad caught Dorothy's eye. "Bram has good folks looking after him. Our volunteer fire-fighters have years of experience."

True, but Val wouldn't relax either until she heard from Bram. Time to change the subject for her own peace of mind, and for Dorothy's. "How are your play rehearsals going, Granddad?"

Dorothy turned to him. "I'd like to hear about that too, Don. I hope I didn't pressure you into doing something you aren't enjoying."

Val suspected Granddad would do whatever Dorothy requested, like it or not. She'd coaxed him and Bram to take roles in a Readers Theater performance, a dramatic reading of an Agatha Christie play, *The Mousetrap*. If Granddad had suffered any qualms about making his stage debut, they vanished when he found out he wouldn't have to memorize his lines.

He speared a piece of chicken. "I'm not sure how the show will turn out, but we all love rehearsing at Jane Johnson's house. She serves an afternoon tea that would rival one at the Ritz. Finger sandwiches, scones with clotted cream and homemade jam, and parfaits. I got the recipe for one her parfaits. That's gonna be our dessert tonight."

Dorothy buttered a piece of French bread. "Jane's remarkable. Not just a good cook and a tireless organizer, she volunteers at the homeless shelter in Treadwell and at the Bayport library. She's in her early forties so she has a lot of energy."

Val suppressed a smile. Dorothy had just started a new career as a shop owner, and she was in her sixties. "You have tons of energy too."

"Compared to the whirlwind I was when I was younger, I've slowed down."

Val sipped her wine. "How did you get to know Jane?"

"She and the cast members from the retirement village are in the mystery book club I started at the shop. Then they formed an offshoot club to read Agatha Christie's books. The Readers Theater was Jane's idea to raise money for the shelter."

A good cause, Val thought, but an unusual way to raise money for it. Her best friend, Bethany, was in the Christie book club and in the Readers Theater cast, but Val hadn't heard much about the play. "Does Jane have theater experience?"

"She had roles in high school plays, but no recent experience." Granddad sopped up gravy with a piece of French bread. "Millicent Rilke has acted in and even directed some Readers Theater shows. No one else has performed for an audience lately. We'll see how that plays out."

"Are you worried someone will get stage fright, Granddad?" He certainly wouldn't. Since moving in with him, Val had seen him assume a number of roles, though not on a stage. He'd managed to convince people he was a food guru, a private eye, and even a ghost-buster, making up the script as he went along.

Dorothy spoke up. "Reading a script probably cuts down on stage fright."

"But you gotta know how to put feeling into your lines. The Dernes, the retired couple in the cast, need to work on that. He reads with no emotion, and she reads with too much."

A phone on the sideboard played a tune. Dorothy put down her fork. "That's Bram's ring."

Val popped out of her chair to get Dorothy's phone for her and watched her reactions to the call. When the worry lines disappeared from Dorothy's forehead, Val released the breath she'd been holding. The idea that Bram might be hurt had scared her. In the six months she'd known him, he'd become such an important part of her life that she had trouble imagining it without him. Now she could relax . . . or maybe not. The tension had crept back into his mother's face.

Dorothy listened for a few moments and then nodded. "Yes, I'll tell them."

Granddad, too, must have been studying her expression. As soon as she hung up, he leaned toward her. "Is anything wrong?"

Dorothy hesitated. "Bram just got off the fire. He's going to shower and change into the spare clothes he keeps at the firehouse. He says he's fine, but his voice didn't sound like it. Something's bothering him that he didn't want to tell me on the phone."

Val wasn't surprised he sounded different. Seeing a raging blaze would upset anyone. Having to put it out made it even more stressful. Maybe Bram was reconsidering his decision to volunteer as a firefighter.

She dawdled over her dinner, leaving half of it for later so Bram wouldn't be eating alone. When he arrived, she read in his face what his mother had heard in his voice. He usually broke into a dazzling smile when Val opened the door for him, but tonight his lips were pressed together. His wavy brown hair, wet from his shower, was slicked back instead of tumbling over his forehead in a carefree way. His grim expression made him look older than thirty-five, though most of the time he looked younger than his age.

Val hugged him. Rigid at first, he soon relaxed and then held her tight.

He released her and inhaled deeply. "It smells wonderful here. Breathing in smoke from a house fire is nasty."

"Here you can breathe in chicken cooked in wine and garlic."

"Only chocolate chip cookies in the oven can beat that." They went into the dining room.

Bram hugged his mother, greeted Granddad, and sat down. Val dished up Bram's dinner from the pot on the stove and reheated what was left of her meal. By then Granddad and Dorothy had finished their dinners and were sipping the last of their wine.

Granddad gave Bram time to take a few bites and then said, "Where was the fire you were on?"

Bram answered without looking up from his plate. "On a country road outside Bayport." He consumed his food steadily and silently.

The fire was obviously not a topic he wanted to discuss. To prevent more talk about it, Val asked Dorothy one question after another about the bookshop—which new books were selling well, which would she recommend, what the book clubs she hosted at the shop were reading this month.

Bram finished a glass of wine and poured another. After sopping up the last of his gravy with bread, he saluted Val. "Kudos to the chef."

Val was happy to see even a ghost of a smile from him. Food and wine had worked their magic and relaxed him. "We have two chefs tonight. Granddad made a dessert."

After clearing the table, Val put on the teakettle. Granddad took the parfaits from the fridge and arranged them on the silver tray he'd recently polished. She was glad the tray and Grandma's china were no longer gathering dust as they had for a few years after her death. Ever since Dorothy's return to Bayport, Granddad entertained more often, showing off his new culinary skills.

Val poured the tea while he delivered the champagne flutes filled with layered red-and-white parfait.

He sat down. "It's a raspberry and cream parfait, same as Jane made for us last week."

Bram recoiled, and his face turned pale.

Val's first thought was that eating his dinner too quickly had given him indigestion. "What's wrong, Bram?"

"The fire was at Jane's house." Bram sounded hoarse. "Most of the damage was in the kitchen. That's where we found her. Too late to save her."

Val's stomach clenched. No wonder her mostly

upbeat boyfriend was depressed. In his first big test as a volunteer firefighter, he'd battled a blaze that had killed a woman he knew. "I'm so sorry, Bram."

He sighed. "Me too. I met Jane only a few weeks ago, but I liked her a lot."

Dorothy shuddered. "What a terrible way to die."

"If it's any consolation, Mom, the fire chief thinks she was dead before any flames got to her." Bram coughed as if smoke still irritated his lungs. "My first assignment when I joined the volunteer fire department three months ago was to check smoke detectors for people who requested that. I personally checked Jane's. They were working."

Val grasped the point he was making. "So if she was conscious, she'd have run out of the house when the smoke alarms went off."

Bram nodded. "Only an autopsy can tell for sure if she was dead before the fire started. Anytime a body is found at a fire scene, the medical examiner, the homicide detectives, and the arson investigator are called."

"Arson!" Granddad ripped off his wire-rimmed glasses, making the white tufts that curled around his ears stick out. "The fire mighta been set to destroy evidence of another crime—burglary or even murder."

Val recognized that scenario from a case that had been in the news recently. "Covering up a crime isn't the only explanation for the fire. Jane could have died of a stroke or a heart attack while she was cooking. Then the food could have burned, starting a blaze."

Granddad folded his arms. "Jane was in her early forties. People that age might die of heart attacks or strokes, but it's not common. And just 'cause she was in the kitchen doesn't mean she was cooking. It's a big room with a sitting area and a large table. Eight of us sat at that table yesterday to read through *The Mousetrap*. Her killer mighta sat there today."

Dorothy shook her head. "But who'd want to kill Jane? She was cheerful and kind, a lovely person."

Bram cleared his throat. "We only saw Jane's public face." He stopped and looked down, as if deciding how much more to say. "Behind closed doors, her life might have been unhappy." He paused again and took a deep breath. "In the storeroom adjacent to her kitchen was a chest freezer the size and shape of a coffin. It had only one thing in it—a dead body."

Chapter 2

Granddad gaped at Bram. "Lordy, lordy. While we rehearsed a play with a dead body in it, a corpse was in the next room."

Questions popped into Val's head. "Whose body was in the freezer, and how did it end up there?"

Bram shrugged. "No one seems to know. I heard the man had been on ice for a while, possibly for years."

After a long silence, Dorothy said, "Hmm. 'Fire and Ice.' That's the name of a poem by Robert Frost."

Val had heard Bram say of his mother, *Once an English teacher, always an English teacher.* "What's the poem about, Dorothy?"

"I can recite it. It's only a few lines long. 'Some say the world will end in fire, /

Some say in ice. / From what I've tasted of desire / I hold with those who favor fire. /

But if it had to perish twice, / I think I know enough of hate / To say that for destruction ice /

Is also great and would suffice.' " Dorothy sighed. "Desire and hate are behind a lot of violent deaths."

Val wondered if desire or hate had led to Jane's death. No one spoke for a moment.

Granddad broke the silence. "Jane told me she never wanted to move away from that house. She had a good reason to stay put. If she had the freezer carted off, moved to a new location, or left there, the body was bound to be discovered."

Dorothy frowned. "You're assuming she knew about the body. But someone else might have dumped it there when she wasn't around—a maintenance worker, a neighbor, even a stranger passing by."

Unlikely, but so was the idea that Jane had died of natural causes, as Val had assumed until she heard about the freezer's contents. "The fire, Jane's death, and the body in the freezer are probably related."

Bram put down his wineglass. "Yes, but how are they related?"

Granddad stroked his chin. "Jane musta known something about the frozen guy's death or even caused it, maybe by accident. She couldn't handle the guilt, so she started the fire. Then she took a fast-acting poison like cyanide."

Dorothy shook her head. "Jane isn't the sort to commit suicide, but even if she were, the timing makes no sense. Bram said the body had been in the freezer a long time, so why would she decide to kill herself now? She was rehearsing for a show she'd worked hard to put together."

Val thought of a reason. "Maybe the Christie

play touched a nerve in her and brought on remorse. It's been a few years since I saw *The Mousetrap*, but I remember that the murder victim had a connection to a death in the past. Was Jane playing the part of the victim in the show?"

"Nope," Granddad said as the doorbell rang.

Val crossed through the sitting room to the hall and opened the door to her best friend. Bethany O'Shay huddled under an umbrella with multicolor dinosaurs on it, a design chosen to appeal to the first graders she taught. Still in her twenties, a few years younger than Val, Bethany often wore bold patterns in vivid colors. Tonight the umbrella was the only cheerful thing about her. Her usually bouncy, strawberry-blond hair hung down listlessly, and she looked on the verge of tears.

She closed the umbrella and came inside. "I have terrible news."

Bethany must have heard about Jane. As a member of the Agatha Christie book club and *The Mousetrap* cast, she'd known Jane longer than Bram or Granddad had.

Val hugged her friend. "I'm really sorry. Bram told us what happened. He was with the firefighters at her house."

"Ryan called me with the news. He's on duty tonight and responded to the emergency call."

Bethany's boyfriend, Officer Ryan Wade, was the youngest member of the Bayport Police Department. She'd coaxed him into joining the Readers Theater cast, so he knew Jane from the rehearsals. He must have been as shaken as Bram was by the scene at Jane's house.

"Dorothy and Bram are here." Val led Bethany to the dining room. "We were just talking about the fire."

Granddad pulled over a chair for Bethany between Val and Dorothy. "How about some parfait and tea or coffee?"

"The parfait looks delicious, but I've already had dessert. I wouldn't mind some tea, though." Bethany sat down as Val brought her a cup and saucer from the china cabinet. "Before I left home to come here, I phoned Millicent and told her about Jane's passing. The first words out of Millicent's mouth were: 'Oh, dear. Who's going to take Jane's place in the cast?' How heartless can you get?"

Val remembered that Millicent was directing *The Mousetrap.*

Dorothy patted Bethany's arm. "What sounded like a cold response could have been a defense mechanism. For all we know, Millicent is crying her eyes out now. She probably didn't have words to deal with the shock of Jane's death."

Bethany stirred her tea. "If so, I'm glad I didn't give her another shock by talking about what was in Jane's freezer. That'll be all over town soon enough. Millicent's going to tell the other cast members who live at the Village about the fire."

The Village was the shortened name of the retirement community near Bayport. "How many cast members live there?" Val said.

"Four. Millicent and her sister Cassandra, who's the stage manager, and Nigel and Nanette Derne. Millicent wants us to get together for a rehearsal as planned on Monday afternoon, but it's still up in the air where the rehearsal will be. She's going to try to reserve a conference room at the Village."

"No, let's meet right here." Granddad gestured around the room. "This table's as big as the one in Jane's kitchen. I'll keep up the tradition she started and serve afternoon tea."

"That's really nice of you, Mr. Myer." Bethany turned to Val. "I was hoping you'd take over Jane's part. You had catering jobs on our first two rehearsal days, so you couldn't join the cast then, but how about now? The rehearsals should be easy to work into your schedule. We usually start at three thirty. By then, you're done at the café."

Val much preferred sitting in the audience to being onstage, even if the performance involved only reading from a script. "Can't you get someone else to take Jane's place?"

"You're almost the same age as the character in the play," Granddad said. "Jane was a bit old for the role."

Bethany put down her teacup. "She was going to wear a wig with a ponytail so she'd look younger. Bram was cast as her husband. The show will work better with you in the part, Val. And it's not much of a stretch for you and Bram to play newlyweds."

Val felt as if Bethany was nudging her toward that role, not just in the play, but for real. To avoid the appearance of angling for the position either way, Val hedged. "Why don't you try to find someone else to take over the part?"

Bethany grimaced. "There isn't enough time to do that. If we don't find a substitute for Jane immediately, Millicent will take over that role."

Granddad chuckled. "Bethany's right. Millicent's

ultimate goal is total domination. She'd rather put on a one-woman show than mess with the likes of us amateurs."

Dorothy chimed in. "She'd need more than a ponytail to make her look like Bram's wife."

Val was relieved that Dorothy was bantering with them about the play rather than brooding over Jane's death.

Bethany sipped her tea. "Millicent's already playing one role in addition to being the director. We don't have enough males in our cast, so she's playing a young man."

Granddad dipped a spoon into his parfait. "She doesn't do a bad job of it."

Bram turned to Val. "You'd be good in the role Jane had. We can get you up to speed fast. If Bethany, your grandfather, and I do a read-through with you tomorrow, you'll be ready for Monday's rehearsal. Not that we're trying to pressure you." He smiled like a little boy begging for a piece of candy.

Val didn't have a shield to protect her against that smile. "Give me some details about the character you want me to play."

Bethany put down her cup. "Her name is Molly. She and her husband have bought a large older home to turn into a guesthouse. Neither of them has ever run a business."

Granddad pointed across the table at Val. "Just like you, when you first came here from New York and got the contract to run the athletic club café."

Luckily for Val, a café was easier to manage than a guesthouse, and the working hours were shorter.

"So I should channel my slightly younger self to play Molly."

"Almost the whole cast is channeling themselves." Bram said. "Ryan doesn't have to do much acting as a young policeman. Nigel Derne, who was in the military decades ago, is playing the square-shouldered major."

Granddad looked up from his parfait. "My character is a shrewd older man with a flair for the dramatic."

Val laughed. "Typecasting if I ever saw it. What about your role, Bram?"

"I play a man who's only slightly more bumbling than I am in real life." Bram flashed a self-mocking grin.

Dorothy smiled. "You don't bumble when it comes to business."

But Val knew Bram was somewhat inept in other matters. The man who'd made a fortune in tech start-ups was plagued by indecision in his personal life. He'd told Val about his on-again-off-again engagement that ended for good when he broke it off a week before the wedding. The guilt over how he'd treated his fiancée had made him commitment-phobic. Val wondered if he'd ever get over it.

Bethany said, "So I can call Millicent and tell her you'll be in the show?"

Time for Val to commit. She nodded. Though nervous about her acting debut, she couldn't disappoint Bethany, Bram, and Granddad. And the full-cast rehearsals would satisfy her curiosity. Val was eager to hear how Jane's friends would react to her death and the corpse in her freezer.

Chapter 3

By Sunday afternoon Val had gotten over her reluctance to be in the Readers Theater cast. With her grandfather, her best friend, and her boyfriend in the show, it might even be fun, and it certainly would be a change of pace. She set drinks on the dining room table—water glasses for everyone, coffee for Bram, and tea for anyone else who wanted it. Bram moved a spare chair next to him so Val could read from his script. Bethany sat down across from them and poured tea for herself. Granddad took his usual seat at the head of the table.

Bethany stirred her tea. "You won't have to share a script for long, Val. Millicent's going to drop yours off. I think she also wants to check out the setup for the rehearsals here."

"And check out me too," Val muttered. "We'd better get started on the reading."

Granddad said, "But first, what's new on the Jane front? Did you talk to Ryan, Bethany?"

"Yes, but he didn't have much news to share. The police don't yet know who the frozen man is."

Granddad raised one of his furry white eyebrows. "I heard rumors after church this morning that she killed the man and committed suicide."

Bethany put down her glass with a bang. "No way. I was in the same book club with her for almost a year. When people talk about books, you find out a lot about their values, especially when those books are about crime and punishment. Jane got mad whenever a character escaped justice, like when Poirot let a killer commit suicide instead of facing trial and execution. For her, suicide was a cop-out. She wouldn't have killed herself or anyone else."

Bram nodded. "My mother said the same thing."

If their only contact with Jane was in a book club and a play rehearsal, how could they know what she would or wouldn't do? Val put down her cup. "Comments about books are just words. Actions tell you what people are really like."

Bethany spooned some parfait. "Then look at Jane's actions. She did a lot of fundraising and volunteer work. She believed in social justice, not just criminal justice."

With nothing more to say about her predecessor in the show, Val was anxious to start rehearsing her lines. Working as a cookbook publicist in New York and as a café manager and caterer in Bayport hadn't given her any practice speaking to an audience. "Why don't we move on to *The Mousetrap*?" She hoped to go through a good chunk of it before Millicent showed up.

Bram pointed to her cup. "Finish your tea first.

You and I have the opening lines in the play. Once we start reading them, we can't pause for a sip." He downed his coffee.

Granddad adjusted his bifocals. "Jane's relatives might shed some light on her marriage and the man in the freezer. Did Ryan say if the police had reached her next of kin, Bethany?"

"Yes. Her nearest relative is a nephew who lives in Washington State. He always called Aunt Jane around the holidays. Otherwise, they didn't have much contact. He said Jane had split with her husband a few years ago. He had a funny name. Witterly? No, Witterby. The nephew didn't know how to contact her ex."

Val swallowed the rest of her tea, slid Bram's script toward her, and positioned it between them— a visual hint to get down to work. Better than nagging.

Granddad turned to Bethany. "You've been in the same book club with Jane for a couple of months. Did you notice signs that she was worried lately? Was she acting out of the ordinary?"

Bethany frowned in concentration. "Now that you mention it, yes. She'd always been relaxed and cheerful. For the last week, though, she seemed tense. It started right after she went for a job interview. She'd been doing temp work, and she wanted something steadier."

Granddad sipped his coffee. "Where was her interview?"

"At the spa that's opening outside town. Do you remember the name of it, Val?"

"The Med Spa and Wellness Center." It wasn't far from the athletic club where Val managed the café. For the last month she'd driven past the huge sign announcing the spa's opening.

The doorbell rang.

"I'll get it." Granddad stood up. "That must be Millicent."

So much for reading the play before the director showed up. Val went into the sitting room to greet Millicent and her sister as Granddad brought them in from the hall. He introduced her to the Rilke sisters. Val figured they were both in their late sixties.

They couldn't have looked less alike. Millicent exuded energy in a cranberry-red jacket over black slacks and top. The jacket's bright color drew attention away from her thickening waist and hips. Her wavy hair, mostly white with streaks of brunette, was so perfect that Val wondered if it was a wig.

The beanpole Cassandra wore a baggy gray sweat suit. If she hadn't stooped, she'd have towered over her sister. Her oversized, dark-rimmed glasses contrasted with her short gray hair. It looked as if it had been cut with a mower that skipped a swath here and there. After mumbling a hello, she peered at the books on the shelves surrounding the fireplace.

Meanwhile, her sister surveyed the sitting room with her head thrust forward as if she was sniffing out noxious odors or checking for cobwebs. The house must have passed muster because she handed Val a copy of the script.

"Would you like some coffee or tea?" Granddad said.

Millicent shook her head. "We really must get on the road. We're due at a friend's house by—"

"*I'd* like tea." Cassandra turned away from the bookshelves.

Pleased that Cassandra wasn't under her sister's thumb, Val silently applauded, though she'd have preferred the Rilke sisters leave. With them there, she might have to sit through a rerun of *Whatever Happened to Saintly Jane?*

Once they were seated, with Millicent at the end opposite Granddad, and Cassandra next to Bethany, Val steered the conversation toward the upcoming show. "Could you tell me how the Readers Theater production will work, Millicent? Are we going to stand in front of a microphone to read our lines?"

Millicent waved away the idea. "The microphones will be on the stage floor near the footlights. You'll each sit on a stool to speak your lines. The stage will be bare except for eight stools. They'll be in a semicircle so you can see one another and partially turn toward the person you're speaking to."

Cassandra leaned toward Val. "You'll be conversing a lot. You have more lines than anyone else. Don't feel bad if you lose your place and miss your cues. Jane had that problem."

Bethany shook her head. "She lost her place the last time we rehearsed. Before that, she had no trouble. She was really preoccupied ever since she applied for that spa job."

Cassandra nodded and said something Val couldn't hear because Millicent talked over her sister.

"We'll all miss Jane, but the show must go on," Millicent said brusquely. She tapped her watch. "Cassandra, it's time we left."

"The gossip at the Village about Jane is awful." Cassandra swirled her tea, paying no attention to her sister. "They're saying she killed her ex-husband, stuffed him in the freezer, and committed suicide because she was eaten up with guilt."

Granddad straightened in his chair. "Did you know her ex?"

Millicent shook her head. "She divorced him before she moved here."

Cassandra said, "She would have never taken her own life even if she killed him, which I don't believe she did. She often said people who do wrong have to face the music to be at peace with themselves and pay their debt to society. No, she didn't commit suicide. She was murdered."

Millicent rolled her eyes. "Jane died by accident in a fire. My sister reads too many mysteries. She thinks Bayport is an English village in an Agatha Christie book, with a killer around every corner."

"Bayport does have a rather high body count, as the two of you know." Cassandra fixed her shrewd gray eyes first on Val and then on Granddad. "You should take up Jane's case. Justice mattered to her. Her killer shouldn't go free."

Val glanced at Granddad. Cassandra had presented him with exactly the kind of challenge he relished.

Granddad crossed his arms. "Why are you so sure Jane was—?"

"We need to leave now." Millicent stood up.

Cassandra nodded. "I've done what I came for."
She marched to the door.

"Don't pay any attention to her," Millicent hissed.
"Cassandra gets bees in her bonnet. See you all tomorrow at the rehearsal."

Val walked them to the door, and then returned
to the table. "What do you make of the sisters?"

"Cassandra's a bit zany, but she's also sharp,"
Bethany said. "She's done her homework on you
and your grandfather. That's how she knows you've
uncovered the truth about several suspicious deaths
in the past."

"Homework," Bram repeated. "I see Cassandra
as someone who always did her homework when
she was a kid, while Millicent had more important
things to do."

Bethany frowned in disapproval. "And Millicent
copied her sister's homework, I suppose."

"If she did, she was smart enough to throw in a
couple of mistakes so her cheating wasn't detected." Bram said. "Millicent's good at creating il-
lusions."

Val glanced at him. He, too, had a flair for illusion, performing as an amateur magician. "I wonder if she was creating the illusion that her sister's
judgments weren't reliable. When Cassandra brought
up the spa, Millicent drowned her out. Did you
catch what Cassandra was saying about the spa,
Bethany?"

"It sounded like '*the spa's the key.*' What could this
mean?"

No one had an answer.

Granddad stroked his chin. "The burning question is why Millicent tried to shut her up."

Bram shrugged. "Could be knee-jerk sibling rivalry, going back to childhood. They're so different. One of them was good-looking, outgoing, and probably more popular, and the other was plain, quieter, and more observant."

"Which of them should we believe?" Granddad said. "Tomorrow, before or after the full-cast rehearsal, we need to separate the sisters. See what we can get out of Cassandra when her big sister isn't there to shush her."

Bethany turned to him. "Millicent's not the big sister. Cassandra's older by a few minutes. They're fraternal twins."

"What else can you tell us about them?" Granddad said.

"Cassandra's a retired librarian. She never married. Millicent and her husband are separated. Back in the day, he was a columnist for the Baltimore newspaper that folded. She taught high school, ran the theater program, and played a lot of roles in Baltimore theaters."

Val wondered what part Millicent was playing now. "You said Jane's reactions to books showed that justice was important to her. Any insights into the sisters from their reactions to books?"

Bethany laughed. "Their reactions to killers differed from Jane's. She was offended if a murderer wasn't brought to trial. But the sisters talked about where the murderers had slipped up and how they could have avoided detection."

Granddad's eyebrows rose. "Reminds me of *Arsenic and Old Lace*. Two charming but batty old women pulling off perfect poisonings."

Val was used to his habit of finding parallels between current events and old movies he loved watching, but this one wasn't a good fit. "Millicent and Cassandra don't strike me as either charming or batty. Cassandra's a bit eccentric. Both of them are canny. Millicent would rather not believe that Jane was murdered. Maybe she pushed back against that idea to make sure the play wasn't derailed by a murder investigation."

"Or because she has something to hide." Grand-dad finished his parfait. "I'm busy tomorrow writing up the recipes for my column and making parfaits for our rehearsal in the afternoon. But on Tuesday I'll see what I can dig up on Jane's ex-husband."

Remembering Granddad's off-base theories about other murders, Val foresaw an unexpected outcome. "Maybe you'll find out he's sunning himself in Arizona and the body in the freezer isn't his."

"Nah. Wanna bet he's been resting in a colder spot?" He didn't wait for anyone to take the bet. "Can you delve into the spa angle, Val? Try to find out why Millicent kept her sister from talking about it."

Val had no idea how to approach this assignment. "I've never even been to any spa. Is the new one open yet?"

Bethany shook her head. "But Chatty's been there a few times. Ask her about it."

Chatty Ridenour worked part time as a massage therapist at the athletic club where Val managed the café. "How could she have been to the spa when it's not yet open?" Val thought of an answer to her own question. Maybe, like Jane, Chatty had gone there for a job interview. "Is she going to work at the spa instead of the club?"

Bethany hesitated. "She told me this in confidence, so don't spread it around the club until it's final. She wants to split her time between the spa and the club."

"And collect twice as much gossip," Val quipped. Their friend's given name, Charity, had been shortened to Chatty, for a good reason. Chatty hunted scandal like a cadaver dog sniffed for a corpse. But, unlike the dog, who signaled the presence of a dead body by sitting down quietly and waiting for a reward, Chatty rewarded herself by spreading her news all over town.

Val couldn't have asked for a better source of information. "I'll talk to her tomorrow at the club. Now can we please read through *The Mousetrap* and tackle real mysteries later?"

Chapter 4

On Monday morning, as Val cleared up after breakfast at the café and was making quiche for lunch, she thought about yesterday's reading of *The Mousetrap*. It had gone well, despite her jitters. She would get the hang of it after a few more rehearsals. But the dialogue between her and Bram troubled her. The couple running the guesthouse had married after a brief acquaintance, knowing nothing of one another's pasts. Under the pressure of being snowbound with strangers, including a murderer, the trust between man and wife broke down. It crossed each of their minds that their spouse might be the murderer.

Though less than half a year had passed since Val had met Bram, she couldn't imagine they'd ever behave like the couple in the play. She was certain Bram could never kill anyone, nor would he suspect her of murder. But they had one big thing in common with the pair in the play. Wrapped up in the present, they'd spoken little about their former lives and loves. With both of them in rehearsals for the next two weeks and the play the following weekend, they wouldn't have much time alone before leaving for Paris. In a way, they themselves were caught in *The Mousetrap*.

Val had just poured the egg mixture into the quiche crust when her friend Chatty Ridenour came into the café. With no distinguishing facial features, the middle-aged Chatty made herself memorable by her skill with makeup and fashion. Chatty's lipstick, earrings, eyelids, and scarf were all rose pink.

She sat down at the counter across from the food-prep area. "I'm glad I caught you alone before the hungry hoards arrive."

Val was glad too. Now she wouldn't have to track down Chatty to ask about the Med Spa and Wellness Center. Val poured her friend a mug of coffee. "Would you like a muffin or a sandwich?"

Chatty glanced at her watch with its rose-pink band and shook her head. "Not enough time to eat. I have to set up for my aromatherapy client who's coming at noon. So let's dish while we can. Your grandfather is such a pal of the police chief, I figured you'd have details about the dead man in the freezer."

As usual, Chatty wanted to pick up new gossip before sharing the rumors she'd already collected. Val put the quiche into the oven and came up with a response that wouldn't involve naming Bethany's police officer boyfriend as an inside source. "Chief Yardley's out of town, so I don't have any details. Last I heard, even the police don't yet know what relation the man on ice had to Jane Johnson.

It's probably not her ex-husband. They divorced years ago."

"Good thing I didn't repeat the story that she killed her husband." Chatty stirred sugar into her coffee. "It's weird. I heard Jane Johnson's name for the first time last week. And now she's dead."

Where had she heard Jane's name last week? Val took a stab at the answer. "Did you meet Jane at the new spa?"

Chatty gave her a sharp look. "I didn't actually *meet* her, but who told you I was at the spa? Must have been Bethany. Honestly, no one in this town can keep a secret."

An ironic complaint, coming from the woman who'd never kept a secret in her life. "Is it true you'll be giving massages at the spa?"

Chatty nodded. "The Med Spa's owners did a good job of repurposing the old motel into offices and treatment rooms. My massage area will be much bigger, and it has windows."

Val always had to fight claustrophobia when she went into the tiny room where Chatty worked at the club. More space and windows were huge incentives for her to switch jobs. "Congratulations. I hope it works out for you, but I'll miss seeing you here."

"I'll continue here part-time as long as I can. I like perks like free tennis courts and fitness classes. Demand for my services at the spa won't be great at first. It takes a while for a new business to get off the ground."

And it was taking a while for this conversation to get back to its starting point. "Did you hear Jane's name mentioned at the spa?"

"No. I talked to her on Thursday. I'd just signed a contract to run a massage concession at the spa. The receptionist had called in sick, and other staff members were taking turns filling in for her. To show I was part of the team, I offered to cover the reception desk and answer the phone while the marketing manager took a lunch break."

And what did Jane say on the phone? Val rejected asking so direct a question. It sounded like an invasion of privacy. Better to coax Chatty into volunteering the information. "I heard Jane was applying for a job at the spa."

Chatty's perfectly drawn eyebrows rose. "I don't know anything about that. They certainly have positions to fill. She called last week to make an appointment with the cosmetic dermatologist, Leeann Melgrem. She and her husband, Ron, own the spa. Jane specifically said she wanted to meet only with the doctor, not a nurse, not the doctor's assistant." Chatty sipped her coffee. "Do you know how old Jane was?"

"In her forties."

"She must have been trying to make herself more attractive. A lot of women in their forties go to cosmetic dermatologists for laser resurfacing, filler injections to plump out their wrinkles, or thread lifts."

"I've never heard of a thread lift. What does that involve?"

"The doctor uses a needle to insert barbed thread under the skin in your cheeks and around your neck and then pulls the thread tight to give your face a lift."

"Eek!" Val clutched the sides of her face, recoiling at the idea of barbed threads under it. "That sounds like a medieval torture. Why would anyone want that?"

"Your face doesn't sag enough for you to want it . . . yet. The day will come. A thread lift costs less than a surgical facelift, and it doesn't hurt as much. But it also doesn't last as long, a few years at most."

Hoping to steer Chatty back to Jane, Val took a moment to fill the blender with fruit and yogurt for smoothies. "Did you make the appointment for Jane?"

"Uh-huh. A printout of the doctor's schedule was on the desk, so I penciled in her name for Tuesday afternoon. That's the first day the doctor's seeing patients in the spa. I wrote in another appointment before I had to leave and let the answering machine take over. Then Jane's appointment *mysteriously disappeared.*"

Val was used to Chatty making tidbits of gossip as dramatic as possible. "What do you mean, it disappeared?"

Chatty glanced at her watch and gulped down some coffee. "I left the doctor's schedule next to the keyboard so the receptionist could add the appointments to the online calendar. I called the receptionist the next day to make sure that had been done. She hadn't noticed the schedule. When she unearthed it, she saw two names on it. Someone had erased the name in the time slot where I'd put Jane."

Val shrugged. "She probably rescheduled."

Chatty shook her head. "The receptionist said there was no appointment for Jane in the system.

She must have changed her mind about seeing the doctor and called back to cancel. Maybe she broke up with the person she was trying to look younger for."

Val could explain Jane's change of mind without inventing a romantic partner for her. "Here's another theory. After researching filler injections and barbed threads, she decided against turning her face into a pincushion."

"Hey, millions of people pay big bucks for needles in their faces." Chatty drank the last of her coffee. "My explanation for why Jane cancelled her appointment can account for what happened to her. The guy she threw over got furious and set her place on fire."

Neither of their theories explained Jane's stress after a job interview at the spa or Cassandra's comment that the spa was the key. "I wonder what type of job Jane was applying for. What positions are open at the spa?"

"Several need to be filled quickly. The soft opening is Wednesday and Thursday. The owners typically try to fill two positions for the price of one. For example, the computer techie is also the maintenance guy. When the director saw my résumé, he asked me to be the massage therapist and the makeup artist, but I refused. I couldn't do both and keep working here. Besides a makeup artist, they're still looking for a medical receptionist and someone to do medical billing."

Not having met Jane, Val couldn't guess which of those jobs she might have wanted, but learning about the setup and the people at the spa would be helpful. "I would love to visit the spa in the next few days, before they open to the public. Can you get me in, Chatty?"

"In a heartbeat, if you're willing to manage a café there instead of here."

Val was willing to *say* she might be a café manager to get inside the spa. "I'm not sure, but I'd like to talk to them about it." If nothing else, she'd find out about the interview process.

Chatty drank the last of her coffee. "When I go there this afternoon, I'll mention you to Ron, the spa director. Are you free to meet with him later today?"

The full-cast reading of *The Mousetrap* was on Val's schedule for today. She had no idea how long that would take. "How about tomorrow afternoon instead? I'll finish here at two, so any time after that would be fine."

"That works." Chatty slid off the counter stool. "I'll swing by here at two and take you over there. See you then."

Chapter 5

When Val got home from the café, she found Granddad in the kitchen making the nibbles for the rehearsal tea break.

She put on her apron. "Can I give you a hand?"

"Yup. We're having ham biscuits instead of tea sandwiches. I'll slit the biscuits, and you add the ham. The parfaits and the cranberry scones are done. I was gonna make clotted cream for the scones 'til I found out it takes twelve hours. Nothin's worth that much time."

Val opened the fridge and spotted the small container she was looking for. "Let them eat whipped cream. I'll help you with the biscuits and then whip the cream. By the way, I'm going to visit the spa tomorrow afternoon." She filled him in on her conversation with Chatty.

"Even if you don't find out anything about Jane at the spa, you might end up running the café there."

"Not interested. I like my customers." Several of

them were good friends, and Val wasn't sure she'd have as much in common with the spa crowd and, like Chatty, she didn't want to give up free access to the club's facilities. "I'm looking forward to seeing the spa though. Chatty said the owners did a good job of converting the old motel for their purposes."

Granddad chuckled. "Instead of the Bayport Motel, we used to call it the Bates Motel, after the one in *Psycho.*"

Startled, Val looked up from assembling ham biscuits. Over the last two years, Granddad had coaxed her into watching every Hitchcock film from his video collection. She'd enjoyed most of them but found *Psycho* too creepy for her taste. "Why was the Bayport Motel called that? Not because of a gruesome murder there, I hope."

"No murder that I know of. The setup is the same as in the movie, a basic strip motel with a big old house behind it where the owners live. The house in *Psycho* is on a hill behind the motel, but the one here is on the downslope toward the river."

"Huh. I never noticed a building behind the motel."

"You can't see it from the road anymore because the trees grew tall enough to hide it. It's an old farmhouse. The family working the land fell on hard times and let the place go to seed." He grinned.

Val smiled at his pun. "How did the farm end up with a motel on it?"

"After the Chesapeake Bay Bridge went up in the 1950s, folks from Washington and Baltimore started coming to the Eastern Shore for vacations.

The family decided they'd make more money off of tourists than from farming. They sold most of the acreage for money to build the motel. They never—"

The doorbell interrupted him.

Val looked at her watch. "The cast is arriving already? It's fifteen minutes before the rehearsal."

"Gotta be the Rilke sisters or Nigel and Nanette Derne. They compete for who can come earliest. Let 'em in and keep 'em company while I whip the cream."

Val opened the door to a man and a woman. She guessed the Dernes were in their early seventies, a few years younger than Granddad. Tall and thin, Nigel dressed like a professor in a sweater and jacket. But he stood straight-backed as if he were in a military uniform. His hair was sparse on top, and his gray mustache was pencil thin.

His wife, Nanette, was about Val's height, five-foot-three, and wore a banana-yellow pantsuit with a violet turtleneck. Her outfit matched the pansies Val had planted along the walk. Nanette also wore heavy makeup, which didn't completely hide patches of greenish skin along the sides of her face down to her jaw—small bruises in late-stage healing. Not the kind of damage you'd get from running into a door, falling flat on your face, or domestic abuse. After talking to Chatty this morning, Val would bet those facial bruises came from needling rather than Nigel. His wife had taken pains to look younger.

Nigel shook Val's hand. "Good of you to fill in for poor Jane."

"I'm glad to help." Val led them from the hall into the sitting room.

Nanette plopped down in the middle of the sofa. "I could have easily filled in for Jane. I'm cast as the murder victim, so I have nothing to say after Act One." She had a hint of a Southern drawl, pronouncing *I* like *ah*.

Nigel sat down next to his wife. "You have the best lines before you're killed off. And be glad this is Readers Theater, or you'd have to lie as still as a corpse onstage." He chuckled.

The brief exchange between Nigel, with his stiff upper lip, and his wife, with her pouting lower lip, convinced Val that Millicent had typecast them in their roles—the polite, mild-tempered army major and the demanding, carping older woman.

Val perched on the side chair, hoping the others in the cast would arrive early so she wouldn't be stuck making small talk with the Dernes for the next quarter hour. "I'm looking forward to the rehearsals and the show. I've never done anything like this before."

Nanette shrugged. "That's true of most of us. It's no big deal."

As Val racked her brain for a response, Nigel leaned toward her. "Were you acquainted with Jane?"

"No." Val wondered whether he was making idle conversation or really wanted to talk about Jane. "My friends and my grandfather spoke highly of her."

He nodded. "As did everyone who knew her. She was—"

"What do you do besides keep house for your grandfather?" Nanette's interruption suggested she'd heard enough about Jane.

Val had come across the phrase *keeping house for* in novels from previous centuries. It didn't apply to her situation. "My grandfather and I share the housekeeping. I manage the café at the Bayport Racket and Fitness Club, and I cater small dinner parties."

"Your grandfather's fortunate to have you with him. I wish our grandson . . ." Nanette trailed off. Her combativeness gone, she looked on the verge of tears. "He used to be close to us, but now—" When she broke off, Nigel grasped her hand. She reached across her body and encased his hand between both of hers.

Val gazed at their hand sandwich, the first sign of tenderness she'd seen between them. Though seemingly incompatible in other ways, sorrow over their grandson appeared to bond them together.

Wishing she could melt away, Val was relieved when the doorbell rang, giving her an excuse to leave the sitting room.

The Rilke sisters came in. Cassandra carried a straw tote bag, an odd accessory for her gray sweat suit. Millicent held a large binder and spare scripts. She'd replaced yesterday's cherry-red jacket with an electric-blue one.

Val started toward the dining room. "Would you like to sit at the table? We can have coffee and tea and snacks while we wait for the others."

Millicent shook her head. "We always take tea at intermission after Act One. And I'd rather wait until the other cast members arrive before going to the table." She lowered herself into Granddad's easy chair.

Cassandra turned her back on her sister and the Dernes to study the bookshelves along the fireplace wall.

"Yoo-hoo," Bethany called from the front door, and then came into the sitting room. "Ryan asked me to tell you he has some things to finish after his shift. He should be here in thirty minutes or so. We can start without him, can't we?"

Millicent pursed her lips. "I suppose so, since he doesn't come on until late in the first act. We'll start when Bram comes." She turned to Val. "And when your grandfather's ready."

Val took that as a hint to hurry Granddad along. She went through the dining room to the kitchen to see if he needed help, but he had everything under control. The ham biscuits and scones were on platters. The parfaits were on a tray in the fridge along with the whipped cream.

"I finally have a use for this thing your mother gave me as a birthday gift." He held up a large, insulated stainless steel teapot. "It'll keep the tea hot for hours. The coffee machine is set to brew in forty minutes."

"Is that how long it's going to take to get through the first act?"

"Yup. If Millicent doesn't stop us too much to give pointers. She usually speeds up once she smells coffee."

"She wants to start as soon as Bram arrives. If you don't need me, I'll go back to the sitting room."

Val went through the butler's pantry and into the dining room. Hearing Bethany mention Jane and not wanting to interrupt, Val tiptoed through the dining room and stopped just short of the archway into the sitting room. From there, she could see the Dernes and Millicent, but not Cassandra and Bethany, who were on the other side of the room.

Nigel shifted on the sofa. "This is the first time our group is meeting without Jane. Any news about a memorial service for her?"

No one responded.

Bethany broke the silence. "I believe she has a nephew in California. I guess it's up to him. Or maybe her ex-husband will do something, but the police haven't located him yet."

"Ha. They'll have to look where the birds are flying," Cassandra said.

Until now Val had assumed Cassandra was slightly weird, but that comment was peculiar even for her.

Bethany followed up on it. "What do you mean by '*where the birds are flying*'?"

"Jane's ex is a competitive birder. He's even gone on the so-called Big Year, trying to see or hear more species of our feathered friends than any other birder. You can't list birds you've located in other years, so you have to travel for most of the year. I don't know that he ever won the Big Year, though he tried several times."

Val had seen the movie *The Big Year*. One such year would strain a marriage. But to keep striving for the longest bird list, with the slate wiped clean every January, would be like the situation in *Ground-*

hog Day, only it would be Groundhog Year. That would doom any relationship.

Nanette *tsk*ed. "An expensive obsession."

"He found a way to make it pay," Millicent said. "After winning prizes for his bird photography, he sells his photos as artwork. His expenses are deductible. An article about him in the *Baltimore Sun* said he was traveling the world, building up his lifetime bird list. Even if he could be located, he wouldn't let Jane's funeral interfere with counting another bird."

Cassandra added, "At first, we heard rumors that Jane had killed her ex-husband and put him in the freezer because he divorced her. We told the gossips that she divorced him because he was bird crazy. So they came up with a new theory. One of Jane's neighbors said a man had visited her a few times when she first moved into the house, but they never saw him after that. The gossips are sure he was her lover."

Val saw no reason to eliminate the husband as the man who'd visited Jane. He might have wanted to reconcile with her.

"So she had a boyfriend!" Nanette glanced at her husband. "Then she got rid of him."

Nigel harrumphed. "I hope you're not implying she stuffed him in the freezer. Couples break up all the time. Nothing sinister there."

"She probably just got tired of him," Cassandra said. "Or maybe he wanted to move to another state, and Jane wouldn't do that. She loved Maryland. We all do. None of us has strayed far from Baltimore."

Millicent sat forward in the easy chair. "No reason to leave. Maryland has mountains in the west, the ocean on the east, and the splendid bay in the middle. Sites from the Revolution, the War of 1812, the Underground Railroad, the Civil War. Everything's an easy drive away."

With an expressive voice and her gesturing from west to east, she might have been auditioning for a Maryland tourism ad. She'd also steered the conversation away from Jane. Val was convinced the sisters were closer to her than they'd let on. At some point, she'd told them all about her husband. She hadn't done that in the Agatha Christie book club, or Bethany would have heard the story too. How long a history did the Rilke sisters and the Dernes have with Jane? And did they know anything about the man in the freezer?

Chapter 6

Val had lingered in the dining room for the last few minutes, but now she edged into the sitting room, intent on learning more about the Rilke sisters and the Dernes. "Were the four of you friends when you lived in Baltimore?" Judging by the silence in the room, she'd posed an awkward question.

"Acquaintances," Millicent said. "That's what we were, wouldn't you say? We got to know each other better after we moved to this area." She looked around the room for support. Her sister and the Dernes nodded.

Bethany spoke up. "Jane used to live in Baltimore too. Did any of you know her there?"

Bravo, Bethany. Exactly the question Val wanted to ask them, but it sounded more natural coming from someone who'd been in their book club along with Jane.

The sisters studied the floor. Nanette locked eyes with her husband.

Nigel cleared his throat. "We crossed paths with Jane. Didn't really have much to do with her until we all ended up here."

It sounded as if they'd avoided her or she'd shunned them. Or maybe they simply didn't want to reveal the depth of their friendship with a woman who had a body in her freezer. As long as the four of them were together, they'd stonewall. Val might have a better chance of finding out how they were connected to Jane if she, or Bethany, could speak to Cassandra without her sister.

The tapping on the front door signaled Bram's arrival. With a knock followed by three short taps, he mimicked Morse code for the letter *B*. He delighted in codes and puzzles, magic tricks, and biking—cheap pastimes compared to championship birding.

As Bram entered the sitting room from the hall and Granddad from the dining room, Millicent stood and called the rehearsal to order.

Val's heart had always beaten faster at the moment a theater curtain rose and she anticipated a new world unfolding before her. Now, instead of watching from the audience, she would be part of creating that world. She was about to find out how a play came together. Excitement chased away her fear of failure.

Millicent stood in the archway to the dining room. "For this rehearsal, we're going to pretend the sitting room is where the audience will be. Today we'll mimic the stage setup but with the chairs around the dining room table instead of stools in a semicircle as they'll be on stage. In the theater, you'll be backstage until your character makes an entrance. You'll then take your seat and remain there for most of the play."

Nanette piped up. "I can't be onstage after I'm murdered. Can I go sit in the audience?"

"No, you should stay backstage." Millicent couldn't have missed Nanette's pout and added, "You'll want to be there so you can come out and take a bow at the end." The pout disappeared.

"Val, you'll be the first to enter and sit downstage stage right." Cassandra pointed to the chair where she wanted Val. "And Bram will sit opposite you, downstage left. Go ahead and take your places."

Val sat down. "Excuse my newbie ignorance. Based on where you put me, right and left must be from the actors' perspective, not the audience's. And downstage is closest to the audience. Is that right?"

Cassandra nodded. "The terms come from the Renaissance period, when stages were slightly sloped down toward the audience. Actors literally went down when they walked toward the audience and climbed up when they went in the other direction, upstage."

"Returning to the seating," Millicent said, "I'll be the first guest to arrive and take my place next to Bram. The rest of you will fill the seats as you enter one by one."

When everyone was in position, Bethany sat between Val and Granddad. The empty chair next to him was for Ryan. The Dernes filled in the seats on Millicent's side.

Cassandra moved the remaining chair close to the sideboard. "In our rehearsals so far, we've worked only on the dialogue. But today I'll add the sound effects. When we move our rehearsals to the theater, we'll have a sound technician, and I'll be backstage. Before anyone comes onstage, the audience hears ominous noises."

She played the audio on her laptop computer—the "Three Blind Mice" tune, a piercing scream, and a radio announcement of a murder. Then it was time for Val to speak her lines.

Millicent stopped the reading after Val had exchanged a few lines of dialogue with Bram. "You need to let your emotions shine through, Val. Molly is nervous because the first houseguests are due to arrive and a snowstorm is brewing. She's upset that her husband's been gone all day. She's had to do all the work to get the house ready for guests. Put yourself in her shoes and read those last few lines again."

Remembering Granddad's comment about Millicent stopping the reading to give pointers, Val threw all the annoyance she could muster into the lines she reread.

Millicent still wasn't satisfied. "Dial it back a little now. There's tension, but submerged tension. Molly doesn't want to nag her new husband. Later in the play, you'll add suspicion to the mix as you each consider whether your spouse could be a murderer."

Once Val found the right combination of affection and irritation, the reading went quickly, with only a brief pause when Ryan came in. He sat down at the far end of the table between Granddad and Nigel.

Cassandra played sounds—a doorbell signaling

the arrival of each houseguest, "radio" announcements about a murderer on the loose, and the recurring tune of "Three Blind Mice." Once she was late with a sound because she was looking up at the ceiling and putting in eye drops, earning a frown from her sister. Val resolved not to miss any cues.

Act One ended with the discovery of the murder victim and a scream by Val. Everyone agreed that she needed to practice her scream and that it was time for a tea break.

As the sweets were passed around and cups filled with coffee and tea, Millicent described the stage business that would liven up the Readers Theater production. "There's a snowstorm outside when the characters arrive at the guesthouse. For the London production that's been running for six decades, there's a snow room backstage where the actors get covered in white flakes before going on stage. For our low-budget production, Cassandra will sprinkle artificial snow on each of you as you come on stage and toss out some snow to suggest it's blowing in as the door to the outside is opened. That'll be good for a few laughs."

Bethany said, "The more laughs, the better. This play has a grim plot, but at least the dialogue's amusing. Everyone has funny lines, except Ryan." She winked at him.

"Yep. The script says I'm the 'stern and hard-boiled' policeman." Showing he could act the part, he frowned and sounded gruff. When his face relaxed and he ran his hand through his short blond hair, he looked barely older than a college freshman. "I wish Christie had given me a few witty lines."

"You're investigating murders in the play, so you have to be serious." Cassandra put down her teacup. "And you're doing the same for real, right? Looking into the fire at Jane's house and the body in her freezer?"

Ryan shook his head. "I'm a patrol officer, not a detective. My job the night of the fire was to start the ball rolling, calling in medical and crime scene personnel. Now it's up to the crime lab and the criminal investigators."

Granddad piped up, "But you must have heard if they've made progress identifying who was in the freezer."

Ryan took a moment to respond, his head turning slowly toward the people across the table from Val. "The police have a good idea who the man is. They'll make the identification public before long."

Val was sure he'd been watching for a reaction to his words, but she couldn't tell which of the cast members he'd focused on—Millicent, Nanette, Nigel, or possibly Cassandra, who'd moved closer to the table for tea and sweets.

Millicent drummed her fingers on the table. "We'll start on the second half of the play in a few minutes. Finish your coffee and tea, take a bathroom break if needed, and get yourself into character. You are trapped in a guesthouse with an unidentified murderer. You have no way to contact the outside world. Every one of you has a secret you want to cover up."

Val looked around the table. How many cast members had a secret to cover up in their real lives?

An hour later, Millicent summed up the session, explaining what parts of the play had gone well and which were still rough. She gave each cast member specific dialogue to practice before the next rehearsal on Wednesday, which she said would start at four because an appointment might delay her.

Cassandra hurried to the hall bathroom as soon as her sister stopped talking.

Val whispered to Bram, "Would you please keep Millicent occupied here? I want to catch her sister alone."

From the hall that ran past the bathroom, Val could see the front door and who was leaving. Nigel and Nanette left first, followed by Bethany and Ryan.

When Cassandra came out of the bathroom, Val pretended she was going into it, and then turned around as if she'd just thought of something. "Yesterday you said you wanted the mystery of Jane's death cleared up. When we were talking about her job interview at the spa, you said, 'The spa's the key.' What did you mean by that?"

Cassandra looked down the hall as if checking for an eavesdropper. In a voice barely above a whisper, she said, "Jane recognized someone there who'd gotten away with a crime and belonged in jail."

Val gasped and took a moment to digest this surprising news. Given the strong sense of justice everyone said Jane had, she just might have been tempted to right a wrong. Would the person who'd avoided punishment have tried to prevent Jane from exposing a crime? Val suspected that question had occurred to Cassandra as well. "Did Jane tell you the name of the person she recognized or give you a description?"

The older woman bit her lip, avoided eye contact, and said nothing.

Millicent came into the hall from the sitting room. "Ready to leave, Cass—?"

"Yes." Cassandra hustled toward the front door, opened it, and gestured for her sister to go first. After almost closing the door behind them, Cassandra poked her head in again. "See you at the next rehearsal, Val."

Was that a promise to reveal what else Jane had said? Maybe, but Val was going to check out the spa before the next rehearsal. Her visit would be more productive if she knew the identity of the person Jane had recognized or the kind of crime that person committed.

Val found Bram and Granddad in the kitchen.

Bram looked up from loading the dishwasher. "Sorry I couldn't delay Millicent for long. She was anxious to leave. Did you have a chance to talk to her sister?"

"Briefly." Val told them what she'd heard from Cassandra. "Millicent interrupted us before Cassandra could name the person Jane saw at the spa who belonged in jail. When I was with the sisters and the Dernes before the rehearsal, they dodged questions about how they knew one another and

Jane in Baltimore, like they were embarrassed to talk about it."

"Or afraid to." Granddad dumped the leftover coffee. "Could be that Jane and the other four saw a crime go down and needed to get out of town. That might be why they all left Baltimore."

Val smiled. Granddad's theory resembled the plot of one of his favorite movie classics. "They didn't go far or change their identities like the characters in *Some Like It Hot.* Hard to believe that the five of them witnessed a mob hit and that a gangster is hiding out at a spa."

Granddad gave her a withering look. "An outwardly respectable person mighta committed a crime and threatened them if they went to the police. When you go to the spa tomorrow, keep an eye out for someone like that."

Bram wheeled around. "You're going there tomorrow? I thought it wasn't open yet."

"It's not." Val explained the arrangements she'd made with Chatty.

He frowned. "Don't bring up Jane while you're there, in case what Cassandra said is true. A criminal Jane recognized at the spa might have recognized her too."

"And decided to eliminate her?"

"It's possible, and if you start throwing her name around, you might be next. I'm not trying to be overprotective, just prudent."

"He's right, Val," Granddad said.

"I wasn't going to mention Jane. I'll just try to find out who might have seen or talked to her the day she was there for an interview." Val wiped down the counters. "But the best sources of information are the Rilkes and the Dernes. Like the characters in *The Mousetrap*, they all have something to hide. Did they act aloof toward Jane during last week's rehearsals?"

Bram chuckled. "Not Nigel. He was more attentive to Jane than his wife liked. The only aloof one was Nanette."

Granddad nodded. "Can't blame her. Her husband was ignoring her in favor of a woman decades younger."

So Nanette's bruised face might be the result of trying to shave off a decade or two and lure Nigel back. She should have tried to change her personality instead. "Was Jane making a play for Nigel?"

Bram shook his head. "She did nothing to encourage him."

Granddad stroked his chin. "The Nigel–Nanette–Jane triangle is a sideshow. It has nothing to do with the man in the freezer, how he got there, and why Jane left him there. We can't figure those things out until we find out more about Jane. I'm going to dig up what I can on her tomorrow. Right now, I'm going to meet Ned for pizza. You want to join us?"

Bram and Val looked at each other, and both shook their heads. She occasionally tagged along to Granddad's weekly pizza dinner with his old friend, but not tonight.

"You two enjoy the evening." Granddad headed out of the kitchen.

Bram wrapped his arms around Val. "I believe we'll enjoy the evening."

"Mmm. Let's start right now." Dinner could wait, and so could further talk about murder.

Chapter 7

On Tuesday afternoon, Chatty gave Val a ride from the athletic club to the spa. Val gave no hint she hoped to scope out the people who worked there. She doubted it would be obvious which of them Jane believed had committed a crime. But finding out who'd met with her would at least narrow the field. That shouldn't take long. With the sun shining, a light breeze, and a temperature around seventy, Val was anxious to plant her tomato seedlings in Granddad's vegetable garden.

She turned to Chatty. "Tell me the names of the staffers I might meet at the spa."

"You'll interview with Ron Melgrem, the head honcho. Brown hair, red beard."

"That's unusual. Do you think he dyed his hair or his beard?" Maybe so he'd be harder to recognize?

Chatty shook her head. "If a guy has a recessive gene for red hair, his beard can turn red. Usually happens after he hits forty."

"Does Ron interview all job applicants?"

"He does all the initial interviews. Anyone he likes gets a second interview. Mine was with the marketing manager, Sabrine, because my job involves dealing with customers."

So probably Jane had met with Ron, but possibly not with Sabrine. "Who would do a second interview for other types of jobs?" Val said.

"Applicants for computer and maintenance jobs meet with Patrick Parenna, who's in charge of that stuff. He'll also serve as eye candy for the women coming to the spa. For jobs on the medical side, Ron's wife, Doctor Leeann Melgrem, does the follow-up interview. I've never met her, but she's supposed to be at the spa today." Chatty pulled into a graveled lot near the road. "This is the new parking lot. They replaced the parking spaces and the walkway in front of the motel rooms with an addition to the building."

From the parking lot, the one-story former motel was barely visible through the trees and shrubs. But once they left the parking lot behind, Val could see more of the building.

She was stunned by the sprawling building's glassed-in façade. The addition resembled a greenhouse, with low shrubs and blooming tulips planted outside along the foundation. "Wow. The motel has died and gone to heaven." As they approached the entrance at the center of the building, Val saw that the addition running the length of the building was less than six feet deep. "What are they doing with the extra space in the front?"

"It's a hallway leading from the reception area in the center to the wings fanning out from it." As they went inside the addition, Chatty pointed to the right. "I'm in this wing with the skin, hair, and nail rooms, plus the sauna, the indoor hot tub, and a relaxation chamber with a floatation tank. The rooms just inside the other wing are offices, and beyond them are the medical treatment spaces."

They went straight ahead to the reception area. With gleaming marble floors, it looked like a cross between a high-end hotel lobby and a medical-practice waiting room. The chair cushions were thick and the greenery plentiful—potted fig trees, bamboo palms, and cane plants. A young woman with a large watering can was moving from one plant to another. Seeing no one at the check-in desk, Val guessed that the receptionist doubled as an indoor plant caretaker.

A tall woman carrying a steaming paper cup came out of a room off the lobby and approached them.

Chatty introduced Val to Sabrine Gillette, the marketing manager. About Val's age, she had golden-brown skin, cropped dark hair, and the features of a model, but not the requisite rail-thin body. Sabrine had curves where they should be.

She smiled broadly. "Nice to meet a friend of Chatty's. You're getting a sneak peek at our facility today, but I hope you'll come to our open house on Saturday, Val. And bring your friends and neighbors." As she glanced over Val's shoulder, Sabrine's eyes hardened for an instant before her smile returned. "Let me know when your massage area is all set up, Chatty. I can't wait to see it."

Val shifted her position, half-turning to look at

what might have caused the change in Sabrine. Two men stood talking just outside the reception area in the building's hallway. The red-bearded one clutching a stack of mail had to be Ron, the spa director. Did Sabrine loathe her boss, or was the other man, whose face Val couldn't see, the object of her glare?

Sabrine said goodbye and hurried toward the wing with the offices, skirting around the men without speaking to them.

Chatty pointed to the men. "That's Patrick Parenna, the maintenance guy, talking to Ron. We can wait here until Ron is finished. I don't think they'll talk long. They aren't great pals."

Sabrine wasn't a great pal of one or possibly both of them. Val pointed to the young woman with the watering can. "Is that the receptionist?"

"Uh-huh. With all the greenery here and along the hall in both wings, the spa should get a plant service to care for them, not pile more work on her."

Val watched the woman disappear into the office wing. The reception desk wasn't just unattended, but out of her view. Val thought about the appointment Chatty had penciled into the doctor's calendar for Jane. While the receptionist was watering plants in the wings, anyone at the spa could have erased Jane's appointment.

"Oh, good. Ron's free," Chatty said. "I'll introduce you to him. When you finish talking to him, come to the massage room."

Ron pumped Val's hand enthusiastically. She estimated he was in his early forties. A good-looking

"For that many guests, I'll need an assistant." If Bethany was free, she'd probably join Val.

"Include the cost of an assistant in your proposal." Ron reached into a desk drawer for a paper with closely spaced type. "Would you please look this over? Our lawyer insisted that any contractors we hire sign a form like this. The caterers for the open house signed it. Basically, it states that responsibility for the safety of the food and drink you serve rests with you, not the spa. I don't expect anyone to become ill because of what you serve, but if that happens, we can't be held liable since we have no control over the food." He came around the desk, handed Val the contract, and returned to his chair.

She skimmed the small print. She wouldn't sign the contract until she'd studied it more carefully, something to do after planting tomatoes.

She stole glances at Ron as he sifted through his mail, sorting it into two piles before opening it. Jane had surely met him when she came for an interview. Was he the person she thought belonged in jail? Nothing in his demeanor suggested he was a typical lawbreaker, but he could be a white-collar criminal. Val watched as he slit open a small envelope, pulled something out of it, and froze. The color drained from his face.

Wow. What could have caused that reaction? Val rolled her chair closer to the desk. Ron was cradling a playing card in his hand. She glanced at the small envelope he'd taken it from—no return address, just a printed mailing label addressed to him at the spa. The envelope lay flat on the desk.

It wasn't thick enough to have other playing cards in it. The one he was holding must have a special meaning for him to turn pale at the sight of it. Maybe he was a gambler who owed debts, and the card was a reminder to pay up.

He hastily put the card in his pants pocket, but not before she glimpsed a corner of it. It was the ace of spades.

"The contract looks fine to me." Val held it up. "But I'd like to take it with me. I have a friend who's a lawyer, and she usually looks over any contracts before I sign them."

"Totally understandable. She won't find any problem with it. It's standard stuff." A knock on the open door made him and Val look toward it. "What's up, Patrick?"

The six-foot-tall man at the door had thick dark hair and rugged good looks. The T-shirt clinging to his shoulders and biceps proved he put in a lot of time with weights. Techie, maintenance man, and eye candy, all rolled into one.

"Sorry to break in." Patrick smiled apologetically, giving Val a glimpse of his straight white teeth. "The sensory deprivation chamber is ready when you can spare an hour to try it out."

At first Val assumed he was making a joke, but neither man looked amused. Maybe that was the relaxation chamber Chatty had mentioned. Val wouldn't find it relaxing to be deprived of her senses.

Ron frowned. "We're calling it the *mind-enhancement room*, remember? I'll join you there shortly." He waited until Patrick disappeared and turned to Val. "Patrick's been adjusting the variables in our floatation tank. You should book a spa day and try it out. No other spa around here has one. You spend an hour alone, floating in warm water in a darkened, soundproof room. Without any distractions, your mind and body relax. It's the closest thing to being weightless without going into outer space."

Space was endless, while a dark and soundless room was a prison. With mild claustrophobia, Val wouldn't last ten minutes in that room. "That sounds like a unique experience." She folded the contract and put it into her tote bag. "Assuming I have no problem with the contract you gave me, I'll email you a proposal tomorrow for the smoothie bar."

"Call me if you have any questions." Ron handed her his business card. "We've mailed open-house invitations to prospective customers, but we couldn't send them to everyone in the area. Would you mind taking some with you and setting them out for your café customers? Feel free to give them to your friends too." He reached into a drawer and pulled out a two-inch-high stack of cards the size of wedding invitations.

"I can do that."

He tucked them into a manila envelope and gave it to her. "We want as many people here as we can round up."

Val could guess who'd received an invitation in the mail—people living in the waterfront estates lining the Chesapeake Bay and its tributaries, the target demographic for a high-end spa.

She stuffed the envelope in her tote bag, and Ron walked her to the door. They shook hands as a woman in a white lab coat hurried down the hall toward them, carrying a floppy, wide-brimmed hat.

"Here comes my wife, Leeann. I'll introduce you two."

Unlike everyone else Val had seen at the spa, Ron's wife wasn't good-looking. She had a thin face, sunken eyes, and a tiny mouth. Her complexion, though, was amazing—the color of buttermilk, as smooth as a baby's. Had she ever been out in the sun?

"Leeann, this is Val Deniston. She's going to make smoothies for us at the open house."

"I'm Doctor Leeann Melgrem." She held out a bony hand for Val to shake. "I'm so pleased Ron found you. Smoothies will give our open house a special touch." She turned to her husband. "I have a break in my schedule and hoped we could stroll through the garden. It's a lovely day."

Ron shook his head. "Patrick's having a problem getting the temperature and salinity right in the floatation tank. He wants me to try it out. Why don't you show Val the landscaping and how we're going to use the outdoors during the open house?"

Val couldn't tell from Leeann's impassive face if she was miffed at Ron for not walking with her or if Botox had frozen her facial muscles.

Val piped up, "I was admiring the garden when I walked in. I'd love to see more of it." Also to learn more about the spa owners and staff, where they'd lived and worked, anything that would help narrow down who among them might have crossed paths with Jane.

"I'll be glad to show you around." Leeann's voice was as expressionless as her face.

She took sunglasses from her lab-coat pocket, put them on, and donned her floppy hat, ready to face her archenemy—sunshine.

Chapter 8

Val envisioned a leisurely stroll in the garden during which she could nonchalantly ask Ron's wife nosy questions. Instead, Leeann gave her a long-winded tour of the property, leaving no plant unnamed.

When she'd finished with the flora, Leeann described the party tent that would be set up for the open house. "The food and drinks will be in the tent. We'll have tables and chairs there and spread around the lawn. Entertainment will be in the building. After a short video about the spa, I'll give a presentation. So will Sabrine, our marketing manager. Did you meet her?"

Val nodded and began to form a question about Sabrine, but Leeann continued. "The beauty therapists will be in their treatment rooms to interact with the guests. And, of course, we'll have free samples in each room as an incentive for the guests to check out the facility."

So *entertainment* meant sales pitches to Leeann.

Val recalled the motel pool as sitting on a concrete slab in the middle of the lawn with no shade, no shrubbery near it, and no screening from the road. Now flowers surrounded a fountain with a six-foot-high water plume. "You've taken out the pool that was here. This area is really attractive now, with the azaleas and tulips blooming around it."

"It does look nice. The landscapers are returning tomorrow to put in flower beds along the path leading to it." Leeann backed away from a buzzing insect. "We'll have to get this place fogged on Saturday or the mosquitoes will chase our visitors away."

Val couldn't imagine anything ruining an evening at a "wellness" spa more than an insecticide haze. Outdoors the smell would disperse quickly. Inside the tent, it might stick around longer. Hoping Leeann would be as talkative about other topics as she'd been about the garden, Val nudged the conversation in a new direction. "What gave you the idea to open a spa in this location?"

"The property has a wonderful house on it. The owner wouldn't sell it to us without the motel, which we didn't want on our doorstep. Demolishing the motel would have cost a mint. Ron had the brilliant idea to repurpose it as a med spa, a place where both of us could work and not have to commute." She pointed toward the office wing of the spa. "Let's circle around to the other side of the garden. From there, you can view the house down near the water."

"I'd like to see it." Val would also like to find out where Ron might have run into Jane in the past. "Has Ron worked at spas previously?"

"No, he was a manager in different types of businesses before we got married."

Val waited in vain for her to say more about her husband's background. "How did you two meet, if you don't mind my asking?"

"On a matchmaking website. Trust me, that's vastly superior to blind dates and bar pickups." Leeann glanced at Val's left hand. "I see you're not wearing a ring. If you're interested, I can recommend a good dating app." She scrutinized Val's face as if trying to figure out how to improve on it.

"Thanks, but I'm in a relationship." Heading off a possible pitch from Leeann for facial fillers or threading, Val said, "Are you and Ron from this area originally?"

Leeann shook her head. "Ron was an army brat, so he lived in a lot of different places. I grew up in Northern Virginia. My family used to stop here on the way to the beach. I was always sorry to leave the Chesapeake Bay for the Atlantic Ocean with its sand, waves, and no shade."

"Are you hiring mainly locals to work at the spa, or are you casting a wider net?"

"We're hiring the best we can find, wherever they come from. My assistant grew up here. We worked together at a former dermatology practice. Sabrine, our marketing manager, is from Washington, D.C. We've known each other for years. I can't remember where the other staffers hail from. How about you? Did you grow up here?"

"Like Ron's father, mine was in the military. I spent summers with my grandparents in Bayport, worked in New York for ten years after college, and then moved here two years ago. I run the café at the athletic club down the road." As they rounded the corner of the spa building, a two-story white house came into view. It had six gables, a wrap-around porch, and a million-dollar view of the water sparkling in the sun. "Your house is stunning. The style is Victorian, but it looks new. When was it built?"

Leeann's small mouth widened slightly into something resembling a smile. "It's a real Victorian, built in the late nineteenth century as a farmhouse. The owners didn't keep it up. The house had termite damage, and every system needed replacement—plumbing, electricity, heating and air-conditioning. After we bought the property last fall, Ron hired contractors to do the major work, which took months. Once they were done, the house just needed a face-lift."

And that was Leeann's specialty. "When did you move in?"

"Just last month, though we bought it in the fall, a wedding present to ourselves. I guess you could say we're still on our honeymoon. We delayed moving in to avoid being here during the construction." The doctor glanced at her watch. "I've got a patient coming in five minutes." She pulled a key card from her pocket, used it to open the spa's side door, and said over her shoulder, "Good talking to you, Val."

Not so good listening to you, Leeann. While the doctor had offered no insights into the spa staff, she'd revealed what was important to her. Leeann strived for perfection, eliminating the flaws in a garden, a house, or a patient's looks. Had she found perfection in a husband, or was she doing a makeover on him too?

* * *

Val's phone dinged as she pulled into the driveway. A text told her that her evening tennis team match had been called off because of rain in the forecast. The local weather site told her that light rain would start in the next hour and end a few hours later. Perfect for the tomato plants if she could get them in the ground quickly.

Granddad was in his recliner with his eyes closed and his bifocals halfway down his nose.

He stirred as she tiptoed by him. "I'm not sleeping, just resting my eyes. How did it go at the spa? Did you find out who interviewed Jane?"

"She could have spoken to any of the managers, depending on what kind of job she was applying for. The director, Ron, conducts the initial interviews and passes any applicant he likes to one of the managers for a follow-up."

"Did you get a job offer?"

"No, but I got a gig for the spa's open house on Saturday. Apparently, Ron is allowed to hire a caterer for one event without asking for a second opinion." She described the plans for the open house. "Ron gave me a bunch of announcements about the open house to leave at the café and give to my friends. Here's yours." She pulled the manila envelope containing the announcements from her tote bag and gave one to Granddad.

He adjusted his bifocals. "With the heavy paper and embossed printing, this looks like an invitation to the White House. Tell me about the folks you met at the spa."

"I spent the most time with the Melgrems." Val

described them in detail and added the little she knew about Sabrine and Patrick.

When she finished, Granddad said, "Did any of them strike you as a lawbreaker who got off scot-free?"

Val had asked herself the same question on the drive home. "I'd rule out Leeann. Her pursuit of perfection would probably keep her from breaking the law."

"Unless she wanted to commit the perfect crime." He grinned.

This wasn't the first time he'd suggested that plotting the perfect crime was the motive behind a mysterious death. This time, at least, he was joking. Val believed that someone could commit a perfect crime, but not that it would be a motive for murder, especially not for Leeann Melgrem. "Leeann's next step after finding the perfect man, the perfect house, and the perfect job would be raising the perfect child, not committing the perfect crime. If I had to pick an incognito criminal at the spa, I'd go for either Ron or Patrick."

"Why?"

"Sabrine's cheerful expression turned into a look of loathing when she spotted them together. It made me think one of them could have preyed on her in some way." Or maybe both of them. Val headed for the stairs. "I'm going to change into my gardening clothes."

"Don't you want to hear what Jane's neighbors said?"

"Yes, but I want to get the tomato plants in the ground before it starts raining. You can tell me about Jane's neighbors while I do that."

"Okay. I'll move the plants closer to the vegetable bed and meet you there."

Five minutes later, Granddad handed her a tomato plant to put into the first hole she'd dug. "Jane's house is on Horseshoe Lane, a country road that used to run along fields and farmhouses. Her closest neighbors are the Finnegans, a retired couple. They said Jane moved in about three years ago. They saw a man visit her shortly after she moved in, but they didn't see him after that."

"Were Jane and the Finnegans friends as well as neighbors?"

"They didn't have much to do with each other, but they weren't unfriendly. They visited back and forth now and then. They brought her vegetables from their garden, and she'd bring over things she baked." He handed Val the next plant. "They knew the whole history of Jane's house. An elderly couple who owned it for decades passed away six years ago within a month of each other. Their nephew inherited the place and put it on the rental market. Docksteiner was his name."

Val looked up from planting. "Was he the person who sold Jane the house?"

"Yup. The only time the neighbors met him was when he and his wife came after the renter moved out three years ago. They stayed a few weeks to oversee some maintenance, and then they sold the place to Jane. The Finnegans said the house never went on the open market."

"Maybe the Docksteiners didn't list it with an agent because they knew Jane, and she wanted to buy it." Val looked up at him. "Did the Finnegans tell you the first names of the Docksteiners?"

Granddad nodded. "Howard and Missy. They kept to themselves. Howard looked unwell. The Finnegans thought a woman who visited the Docksteiners a few times might have been a nurse checking on him. When Missy was packing up the car, the neighbors came over to ask about Howard. She said he'd gone ahead to Arizona. He had friends there, and the warmer weather would do him good. Jane moved in a couple of weeks later."

"I'm ready for the next tomato." Val took the plant from him. "Did you look up Howard and Missy Docksteiner online?"

"I looked, but I couldn't find either one. I tried Melissa in case Missy was a nickname, but no dice. Then I checked the property records for the house. Howard Docksteiner was the sole owner when Jane bought it. I figured he mighta married Missy after he inherited the place from his elderly aunt, and Missy's name never got on the deed."

"Or they were living together without being married." Val held up her hand for another plant. "How old were the Docksteiners?"

"The Finnegans guessed she was in her sixties. He looked ten years older."

"Maybe the Docksteiners died. Oh, wait. If they had, wouldn't you have found an obituary online?"

"Not necessarily. There's no legal requirement to write an obituary or a death notice."

Val patted down the dirt where she'd just planted. "That does it for this row. You can water these plants lightly in case the rain forecast is wrong. I'll plant the rest of the tomatoes on the other side of the bed." She stood up and stretched her legs, glad to take a break from crouching. "Did the neighbors notice anyone around Jane's house on Saturday?"

"They can't see her house from their property because of the trees between the lots. That's the bad news. The good news is, they can see who's driving by. Their house is just past Jane's after you turn onto Horseshoe Lane from the main road."

Val knelt down to plant the next row. "So anyone driving to see Jane wouldn't go past the Finnegans' house."

"That's right." Granddad put the remaining plants within Val's reach and watered the ones she'd already put in the ground. "Most of the cars they see from their windows belong to people with houses farther along on the lane. On Saturday evening, before the fire broke out, Mrs. Finnegan saw a car that didn't belong to the folks who live on Horseshoe Lane. It went past their house and then came back two minutes later. That was before the fire broke out."

"Probably the driver had taken a wrong turn and didn't realize it at first. Did you ask the neighbor to describe the car?"

"Yup." Granddad turned off the hose. "She pointed at my car."

"They saw your car? No way. You were here with me making dinner."

"She saw a similar car—a full-size sedan, a darker color than mine, either black or deep gray. She didn't have any idea what make it was. It was going pretty fast when it went by the first time, but slower after it turned around and came back. I figure the driver mighta been going to visit Jane, overshot her house, and didn't want to miss it a second time."

A reasonable theory, but not provable, unless someone had spotted had the car turning into Jane's driveway. Val loosened the roots of a plant, set it in the hole she'd dug for it, and filled in the soil around it. "So far you've talked to Jane's neighbors and researched the previous owner of her house. What's next on your agenda?"

"Going online and looking up the folks you met at the spa."

"Good idea. I'll write down their names when we go inside." She looked up at the sky. The clouds had thickened. She dug the holes for the last two tomatoes. "A weird thing happened during my interview with Ron."

She told Granddad about the envelope with the playing card in it and the spa director's reaction to it.

Granddad stroked his chin. "How old is Ron?"

"Early to mid-forties, I'd guess. But he has a wife in the business of making people look younger, so he might be as old as eighty." She winked at Granddad. "Does it matter how old he is?"

"Yup. A man in his forties might have learned the meaning of the ace of spades from his daddy."

Val concentrated. Though her head was full of trivia, none of it related to playing cards. "I don't know what the ace of spades means."

"I'll bet Ron does. It's the death card."

Chapter 9

Val tried to figure out why the ace of spades had such a bad reputation. "Is it the death card because you can use a spade to dig a grave? Of course, that's true of any spade, but the ace is the thirteenth card in the suit, and thirteen means bad luck."

"Who knows how a superstition starts? It was in an *I Love Lucy* episode ages ago. Lucy's having her fortune told, turns over the ace of spades, and is terrified to hear it's the death card. She thinks her husband's trying to kill her and goes to silly lengths to stop him."

"Ron doesn't seem the type to watch *I Love Lucy* reruns." Unlike Granddad, who got a kick out of them. "How else could he have found out about the ace of spades?"

"The superstition got some fuel during the Vietnam War. American soldiers heard that the guerillas they were fighting, the Viet Cong, believed the card meant bad luck or even death. Some lieutenants contacted an American playing card company and asked for decks containing only the ace of spades. The troops ended up with thousands of decks. They scattered the aces in the jungle and left them on the bodies of the dead Viet Cong. Guys who'd been over there told me the ploy didn't psych out the enemy." Granddad chuckled. "The Vietnamese probably thought it was a strange American ritual."

"Leeann mentioned that Ron was an army brat. It's possible his father served in Vietnam or heard stories from guys who did. No matter how Ron learned of it, the person who mailed him the ace expected him to interpret it as a bad omen." Val felt the first drops of rain as she put in the last plant. "I feel sorry for Ron. He received a threat, but it was so well disguised that he'd have trouble convincing the police to investigate it."

Granddad gathered up the hose when the drops turned to drizzle. "I won't have to water that last bunch of tomatoes."

They hurried inside.

Val jotted down the names of the spa staffers so Granddad could search for them online. He went into the study while she stayed in the kitchen. She read slowly through the contract Ron wanted her to sign and had no issue with it. Then she called Bethany and asked for her help at the spa's open house.

"I'd love to do that," she said. "How did you end up with this catering job?"

"Chatty took me to the spa." Val briefly described the place and people she'd met there. "I was hoping to find out what job Jane had applied

for, but I didn't. Did she ever mention what kind
of work she did before she moved here?"

"Not that I remem—" Bethany broke off. "Oh,
wait. I do remember. She referred to her job at a
book club meeting a few weeks ago. We were dis-
cussing a Christie mystery that had a doctor in it.
One woman said it was unbelievable that any doctor would act so immorally. Jane disagreed, saying
ethics wasn't a concern in the last doctor's office
where she'd handled the accounts."

Maybe she'd applied to be a medical billing spe-
cialist, one of the jobs Chatty had said still needed
to be filled at the spa. If Jane had interviewed for
that or any other position on the medical side of
the spa, she'd have met with both Ron and
Leeann. That didn't mean either of them was the
person she believed had evaded the law. While at
the spa, she could have encountered Sabrine and
Patrick, as Val had today, or even other staff, job
applicants, and landscapers preparing the grounds
for the open house.

After getting off the phone, Val took out the ingredients for salmon with pesto, one of Granddad's favorites. She was about to cut the salmon in
two pieces and freeze half of it when Bram called
to ask about her visit to the spa.

"No one there jumped out at me as a possible
criminal, but one odd thing happened. Are you familiar with superstitions about the ace of spades?"

"When I do a magic trick and ask the audience
to think of a card, a quarter of them will choose
the ace of spades, with the queen of hearts in second place. But that's statistics. What's the superstition?"

Val told him about Ron's reaction to the ace mailed to him and Granddad's theory about the superstition. "He'll give you the story behind the ace if you have dinner with us. We have plenty of salmon."

"I can't. I just grabbed a quick sandwich before a Critical Incident Stress Debriefing. Whenever there's a fatality at a fire, the firefighters and EMTs who were there have a meeting with a counseling team to help them handle traumatic stress."

"I'm happy to hear they're doing that." Val reminded herself to watch for any signs of lingering stress he might have. Bram had looked traumatized the night of the fire. Though he seemed his old self by the next day, appearances could be deceiving. "Talk to you tomorrow."

Granddad was hunkered down at the computer until Val called him to dinner. As they ate at the small table in the kitchen, he filled her in on his research.

"I found lots online about Leeann Melgrem, where she studied and where she practiced. For the last five years, she's worked in a large dermatology group with offices in Easton and Chestertown."

"Did she ever practice in Baltimore?" Where Jane had also lived and might have worked at a doctor's office with unethical practices.

"Nope. Now we get to what wasn't online. The only information I could find about Ron Melgrem is from the last six months, and it all relates to the spa."

"That's odd." Val didn't doubt Granddad's researching skills. After taking an investigation course, he could dig up online sources better than she could. "If Ron was a manager in different companies, as Leeann said, he'd have an online presence. They met through a dating app and got married last fall. Hard to believe she didn't vet him before getting serious about him. Not being online would be a red flag."

"Married last fall. Huh." Granddad sipped his wine. "She's been practicing medicine as Leeann Melgrem for the last fifteen years. She didn't change her last name when she got married. What are the chances that two people with the same last name marry each other?"

"Remote. I could believe it if their names were Jones or Miller, but Melgrem . . . no. Maybe Leeann wanted to keep her name for professional reasons, so he adopted hers."

"Why? Lots of married folks have different last names these days."

"True. But a new surname would explain why you couldn't locate him online. How do we find out what name he might have used before marrying her? Are marriage records public?"

Granddad's forkful of salmon stopped halfway to his mouth. "Yup, but you gotta know where to find them. In Maryland you can't look up marriage licenses online. You hafta know the county or city where the marriage took place and contact the records office there. For all we know, Ron and Leeann tied the knot in Las Vegas."

"More likely they had a destination wedding somewhere exotic." Val thought of her friends who'd bucked surname traditions after marriage. "I knew couples in New York who combined their surnames when they got married. From then on, they both used the double-barreled name. Ron shed his name entirely. Why?"

"He had a long name that was hard to spell or pronounce? He had a name with a bad vibe like Greedy or Putin?" Granddad smiled. "Or else he didn't want to be found."

"Exactly. When I saw how the ace affected him, I thought immediately about gambling debts. The card could have been a warning from loan sharks who've tracked him down."

Granddad shook his head. "Loan sharks send goons to deliver physical warnings. Whoever sent the ace of spades was messing with Ron's head. Here's what I think is going on. Ron's hiding a criminal past, and Jane recognized him at the spa. She could have mailed the letter with the ace of spades on Saturday afternoon, and it would have arrived today. Maybe Ron recognized her too, was afraid she'd blow his cover, and stopped her from doing it."

"By killing her and setting her house on fire?" Val saw a big hole in Granddad's theory. "If he knows she's dead because he killed her and set her house on fire, why did he turn pale when he saw the ace of spades? He thought it was a message from the great beyond?"

"Nope. He's scared someone else recognized him and sent that card. Maybe he'd like to eliminate another threat, but he doesn't know where it's coming from."

Val swirled the wine around her glass. "Ron's a possible suspect in Jane's death, but the case against him is like a house of cards. Its foundation is a remark by a woman who devours murder mysteries and who her own sister says is detached from reality. You need more than the ace of spades and Ron's name change to support the roof. We don't even know how Jane was killed or if she was murdered." But Granddad had a direct line to someone who'd be the first to know that information, his longtime friend, Bayport police chief Earl Yardley. "Are you thinking about sharing your suspicions with the chief?"

"Not yet. He'll say the same thing you just did. And he doesn't like me interfering in his cases."

But if it turned out that Jane had been murdered, Val wouldn't hold back what they'd learned. She'd make an appointment with the chief.

Val didn't need to make an appointment with Chief Earl Yardley. He strolled into the café at eleven on Wednesday morning. She'd just served two women berry smoothies when she spotted the gray-haired and barrel-chested chief coming into the café alcove. He sat down at the eating bar. With few customers in the café, she'd have time to talk to him.

She greeted him and gave him a mug of coffee.

He sniffed it contentedly. "The brown sludge I get at police headquarters isn't in the same league as this."

She pointed to the glass-covered display of sweets. "Would you like a muffin or a scone?"

"Sure, I'd like one, but the doc says I should lose a few pounds." He patted his round middle and sipped his coffee. "I hope your granddaddy's well.

We had a great time together on opening day at Camden Yards."

"He always enjoys going to baseball games with you. And this time the Orioles won." In recent years the two men had revived a tradition begun when the chief was still a teen. After his father died, Granddad had served as a dad substitute, cheering young Earl's efforts on school teams and taking him to Orioles games. "Granddad's keeping busy rehearsing for the Readers Theater production. Officer Ryan Wade must have told you about it."

"Yes. He had to adjust his duty schedule to work around rehearsals. He said you took Jane Johnson's place in the cast." The chief added some sugar to his coffee. "What's your take on the older folks in that group?"

Surprised by his question, Val wondered if the chief believed the senior members of the cast had something to do with Jane's death. "I assume you heard what Ryan knows about them, so I'll tell you what I found out when he wasn't there. The Rilkes and the Dernes lived in Baltimore before they retired here. When I asked if they'd known Jane there, they clammed up. They were like actors who'd lost their scripts, all of them waiting for a cue before they spoke their next lines."

"It's not easy to talk about a friend who died in a terrible way, especially if she had a body in her freezer."

"But Nigel Derne talked about her a lot, though not about their Baltimore connection. Jane's death hit him hard, I think because he was attracted to her. Whenever he brought up Jane, his wife changed the subject. She even tried to poison his memory of Jane, suggesting she'd killed the man who was in the freezer. Nigel pushed back hard on that."

The chief put down his mug. "Ryan said Nanette's jealousy was obvious at the first rehearsal. Let's say she goes to Jane's house and finds her dead. Does Nanette seem like a woman who'd set the place on fire?"

Val thought a moment before answering. "Maybe to cover up her tracks after killing Jane. But if I'd murdered my rival and burned down her house, I wouldn't diss her once she was gone. I'd be singing her praises so no one would suspect me."

"Hard to do if your husband's devotion to the other woman continues even after her death." The chief cradled his mug. "What did Cassandra and Millicent Rilke have to say about Jane?"

"Cassandra insists Jane was murdered and mumbled that the new spa was the key to the murder. She tipped me off in private that Jane saw someone at the spa who'd gotten away with a crime, implying that this criminal had killed her. Millicent says her sister's steady diet of mysteries makes her imagination run wild." Val spotted two older men coming into the café, regular customers who stopped by for coffee after their workout. "I can tell you about the people at the spa, but not until I wait on the two guys who just came in."

"The spa and Cassandra Rilke's murder theories aren't at the top of my list." The chief looked longingly at a muffin. "The autopsy report on Jane Johnson isn't final. The medical examiner hasn't pinned down the cause of death, but they've found no sign of trauma or anything that suggests foul play."

Val was taken aback. She kicked herself mentally for going to the spa in search of a criminal based on nothing but Cassandra's imaginative scenario about Jane's death. At least Val had gotten a catering job out of the visit. But the chief must have had a reason to ask about the Rilkes and the Dernes, if not because of Jane's death, then maybe because of the fire at her house or the body on ice.

The chief drank the last of his coffee.

"You want a refill, Chief?" When he shook his head, Val figured he'd leave shortly. She wouldn't have time for more than one more question. "Do you know yet who the man in the freezer is?"

The chief stood up. "Still working on identifying him, but we know who he isn't. We located Jane's former husband in Ecuador. As soon as he spots the bird he traveled there to see, he'll fly back home and help in any way he can."

Cassandra and Millicent had described Jane's birding ex-husband to a T.

Before leaving, the chief warned her against sharing anything he'd told her until the police made the news public. Not that he'd told her much.

As he exited the café, a trio of women in yoga togs came in, followed by a foursome who'd just finished playing tennis. As the café filled up, Val was too busy serving lunches to think about what the chief had said.

Bram called her as she was driving home.

She pulled over to the side of the road. "How did the debriefing go last night?" She hoped the discussions intended to relieve firefighters' stress hadn't increased it.

"The meeting was better than I expected. And actually helpful. For the last few days, I've wanted to see Jane's house again, but I was afraid I couldn't handle it. After last night's counseling session, I'm sure I can." He paused. "Would you be willing to go there with me?"

"Of course." He might need moral support when he returned to the fire scene. And she was curious to see where Jane had lived, even if not much was left of her house. "We can go there before the rehearsal since it's not starting until four. I'm on my way home now."

"Can you swing by the bookstore and pick me up?"

"See you in five minutes."

She pulled back onto the road. Why did Bram want to go back to the fire scene? The counselors at the debriefing might have emphasized the need for closure after a traumatic event. Or was Bram pulling a Sherlock, searching for a telling detail the professional investigators had overlooked?

Chapter 10

With Bram in the passenger seat, Val drove along Horseshoe Lane, a winding road with newly planted fields on one side and houses on the other. Mature trees and shrubbery between the lots gave residents privacy from their neighbors.

They'd gone past half a dozen houses when Bram said, "Take the next driveway on the left."

Val turned onto the gravel driveway and braked. In front of her were the remains of a one-story white wood house with its windows boarded up. More of the place was standing than she'd expected. The middle of the house and its front porch looked intact. Driving closer, she saw the fire had burned through part of the roof on the left side and consumed most of the right side of the house. The carport bordering it had little damage.

Bram stared at Jane's home and took deep breaths. He pointed to the left side of the house.

"My team was assigned to fight the fire there. Guys from larger fire departments dealt with the bigger blaze on the kitchen side. Last night at our debriefing, I heard some details from them that I wanted to check out." He opened the passenger door.

"I'll go with you." Val got out of the car. They walked slowly down the driveway toward the carport. A silver compact was parked inside it. "Is that the car Jane drove?" When Bram nodded, Val said, "It doesn't look as if the fire got near it."

"Yeah, we got lucky. The fire in the kitchen spread toward the living room instead of the carport. Fighting the flames would have been harder with a car on fire. On the other side of the house, the small room Jane used as a study was destroyed. Not just the books and papers, but also the desk and shelves. We were able to put out the fire in that room before it spread."

Val had assumed that any damage had come from a single blaze fanning out from the kitchen. A fire there could have been accidental, but with a second origin point, the conclusion was obvious. "This has to be arson."

"Yes, and the investigators found proof of that." Bram studied the house but didn't try to look inside. "The fire pattern suggested an accelerant was used in the kitchen and the study, but not in the living room, bedrooms, or the storage room."

Val knew an accelerant made a fire burn and spread faster. "So the arsonist brought enough gasoline to pour around two rooms but not the whole house. Or else the arsonist had a reason to make sure those particular rooms burned."

"That's my take, though I don't know for certain it was gasoline. It could have been something else—kerosene, turpentine, butane. The arson investigator's report is still in the works." Bram pointed to a boxy structure taking up part of the space in the carport. "That's the storage room. It's an addition to the side of the kitchen." He walked toward it.

Val followed and saw that the door to it was padlocked. "Did the police put on the lock to keep nosy people away?"

"No, the lock was there. The police used a bolt cutter to get into the shed and to open the freezer, which also had a padlock on it."

"Sturdy locks make a lot of sense here. Otherwise, someone in search of ice cream would get a huge shock. But why did the police open the freezer?"

Bram shrugged. "I think they were looking for drugs, guns, or any sign of illegal activity that someone might have wanted to cover up with a fire. The door to the kitchen was also padlocked on the storage room side. When we had our last rehearsal in Jane's kitchen, Nanette tried to open that door, looking for a bathroom. What do you make of that third padlock?"

Val saw no other door in the carport besides the one to the storeroom. "It tells me that Jane didn't use the storage space much." Val walked out of the carport to verify the location of the house's front door. "With the lock on the inside of it, she'd have to go out her front door, carrying whatever she wanted to stow, walk around the house to the car-

port, and open the padlocked door into the storeroom. Of course, she had a reason not to go into
the storeroom at all—the body in the freezer."

"If she knew about it. Maybe she rented out the
storeroom to bring in some money. Her renters
might have owned a freezer that wouldn't fit in
their house and offered to pay Jane extra for the
electricity it would use."

"That theory explains the padlocks." And it
would get saintly Jane off the hook for hiding a
dead body. "What do you suppose happened the
night of the fire?"

"Maybe the people renting the storeroom came
by, looked in the kitchen window, and saw Jane
dead on the floor. Here was a chance to sever any
connection they had to the dead body. They set
the kitchen on fire so it would look like Jane had
accidentally started it while cooking. They then
started another fire in the study to destroy any
records of the rental agreement."

Val had her doubts. "Why didn't they burn the
storeroom where the body was?"

"It wouldn't have looked as much like an accident as a kitchen fire."

"There's a storage rental facility just outside
Treadwell. Why not use that instead a room attached to someone's house?"

"Most storage units don't have electrical outlets.
No way to plug in the freezer."

Val couldn't deny that Bram's scenario explained the oddities about the fire scene. The
bushes bordering the driveway rustled. She turned
to see a man and woman emerge from the shrub-

bery at the side of the driveway. They must have come from the house next to Jane's. Probably the neighbors Granddad had interviewed.

The couple, gray-haired and pleasantly plump, were in their sixties. They both wore bulky, hand-knitted sweaters and roomy jeans. And they both eyed Val and Bram warily.

Val smiled to put them at ease. "Are you the Finnegans?" When they nodded, she continued. "You talked to my grandfather, Don Myer, earlier today. This is Bram Muir. He's one of the volunteer firefighters who was here Saturday night. He wanted to see the damage by daylight."

The couple relaxed and stepped closer to them.

Mrs. Finnegan thanked Bram profusely. "If you and the other firemen weren't so quick to come, our house might have looked just like this one. Isn't that true, Jim?"

"That's right. I was the one who called in the fire. We didn't see flames, but there was an orange glow that looked suspicious. Lucky we spotted that."

"I'm sorry you lost your neighbor," Val said.

"It was such a shock." Mrs. Finnegan held her hand to her heart. "We'd have rushed right over to help Jane, but we didn't think she was home."

"What gave you that idea?" Bram said.

"I saw her car parked in the driveway. She usually put it in the carport." Mrs. Finnegan pointed to where the car now stood. "Sometimes she'd stop in the driveway first to take groceries inside. It's a shorter walk to the front door than from the carport. On Saturday—"

Her husband broke in. "You didn't *see* Jane Saturday evening. And I didn't see her car in the driveway."

Mrs. Finnegan's lips pursed. "I got a good look at it when I was setting the table in the dining room and *you* were watching TV in the living room. By the time we sat down to eat, the car wasn't there anymore. Jane must have come out and moved it from the driveway into the carport when I wasn't looking."

The nerve of her! Val hid a smile. Did Mrs. Finnegan have nothing to do except look out the window at cars? "My grandfather said you saw a dark sedan on the road a short time before the fire broke out. Was that before or after you noticed Jane's car in the driveway?"

"Before. The sedan went by as I was making salad. My kitchen window faces the road."

So she combined domestic chores with car spotting. Val glanced at Bram. He was peering through the wooded area separating Jane's house and the neighbor's.

Then he turned his gaze on the carport. "Jane's car doesn't have any features that set it apart from similar cars. Are you sure the one in the driveway was hers, Mrs. Finnegan?"

Before she could respond, her husband did. "From our side window, Jane's driveway is mostly hidden by trees. And my wife can't tell one car from another."

Val studied the couple. He might as well have shouted, *My wife is an unreliable witness.*

Mrs. Finnegan glared up at him. "I can describe a car's color and size even if I don't know the make and model."

Her husband ignored her. "We'd just sat down at the table when fire lit up the area. Is the cause of the fire known?"

"Not yet." Bram shook hands with the Finnegans. "It was good talking to you, and I'm glad you called in the fire or it would have been harder to put out."

Val said goodbye to the couple. They disappeared into the shrubbery as she climbed into the driver's seat.

Bram checked his watch. "We still have an hour before the rehearsal. Would you drop me off at the shop? I'll spell Mom so she can have her afternoon tea."

"Okay." Val pulled out of the driveway. "The silver car Mrs. Finnegan saw might have belonged to the arsonist rather than to Jane."

Bram buckled his seat belt. "Yes, but that isn't as helpful as it could be. I'd estimate a quarter of the cars around here are silver or light gray, including plenty of compacts like Jane's."

"The car's description won't help locate the arsonist, but if there's a suspect with a similar car, it would be additional evidence." That wasn't enough to cheer up Bram. Talking about something other than the arson might help. "How's your house coming along?"

He'd spent the last two months tearing apart an older house in need of a lot of work. "Parts of it are almost ready for your second visit."

"I can hardly wait." Val had cringed when he first showed her the place. "What have you been doing there lately?"

For the rest of the drive to the bookshop, he detailed the latest repairs he'd done and the setbacks that made rewiring take longer than expected.

Back in town, Val found a parking space along Main Street near Title Wave. "I'm going to stop in and say hi to your mother." Dorothy was the best person to ask the question that had occurred to Val after talking to the chief this morning.

A dozen people were in the shop, most of them browsing for nonfiction in the back and for recently published books in the front.

Dorothy sat on a high stool at the checkout counter. "Bram, would you please help the young man who's in the business and economics section? He's looking for the best book on starting a business. I said my son might be able to recommend one."

Val watched Bram thread his way through the shelves. "He's the expert on start-up businesses, and you're the expert on mysteries, Dorothy. Do you remember any book in which a victim appeared to die a natural death, but it was really murder?"

"That happens in an Agatha Christie. Supposedly by accident, the murderer cut the victim with something rusty and then, under the guise of giving first aid, rubbed the discharge from an infected wound into the victim's cut."

"That's nasty. The victim was infected and died?"

"Death by septicemia, blood poisoning. There was another Christie mystery where a character was injected with typhoid. Injections leave traces on the skin."

"Unless the body is burned," Val muttered.

As Bram joined them at the counter, Dorothy said, "Did you notice anything significant at Jane's house?"

He told her about the locks on the storage room and his guess about her having a renter.

Dorothy said nothing for a moment. She pressed her lips together, as if holding back her first reaction. "Hmm. How did Jane and the storeroom renter find each other?"

Bram shrugged. "Probably online, where everyone advertises these days."

His mother looked skeptical. "Jane wouldn't have wanted a stranger renting part of her house. Padlocks or not, that person would know when she was home and when she wasn't. A man might take a chance like that, but most women wouldn't."

Val agreed with Dorothy's logic, but she viewed it from a different angle. "Maybe Jane rented the storage room, not to a stranger, but to someone she trusted."

"That's a possibility. As a volunteer and fundraiser, she'd gotten to know quite a few people around here." Dorothy stepped down from the tall stool behind the counter. "Now that you're here, Bram, I'm going to get a cup of tea." She walked toward the back of the shop.

Bram turned to Val. "Got any candidates for the role of storeroom renter?"

An image of the watchful Finnegans popped into Val's mind. "Jane might have rented the room to her neighbors. She'd have wanted to stay on good terms with them."

"It's convenient for the Finnegans. Their freezer would be nearby in case they ever needed something from it." Bram grinned.

The young man he'd helped to find a book came to the checkout desk with three books under his arm. Val waved to Bram on her way out the door. "See you at the rehearsal." It might give Val a chance to coax some unscripted lines from the older cast members.

Chapter 11

Val joined Granddad in the kitchen and sniffed the aroma wafting from the oven, a heady mix of butter, sugar, and chocolate. "Are you baking chocolate cookies or brownies?"

"Brownies. I also made cucumber sandwiches for the cast's teatime. A lotta trouble for something without much flavor." He opened the oven door, peeked at the brownies, and closed it again. "What have you been up to?"

Val gave him a rundown on her visit to Jane's house, telling him Bram's theory about the padlocked storeroom and her latest idea that Jane's neighbors might have rented it. "Maybe they're the ones who had a body to hide. Mrs. Finnegan described the cars that were in the vicinity of Jane's house just before the fire started. She told you about a dark sedan that drove by her house, and she told Bram and me about a silver car parked in Jane's driveway. Were those cars really there, or did Mrs. Finnegan make them up to steer us away from the truth?"

"Like Cassandra pointing us to the spa as the key to Jane's death?"

"I told the chief about that when he stopped by the café this morning. The spa didn't interest him at all. Neither did Cassandra or Millicent, but he did ask about Nanette's jealousy of Jane." Val poured herself a glass of water. "The chief also shared some big news. The police located Jane's ex-husband, alive and birding in South America."

"That's not gonna get rid of the rumors that she killed a boyfriend and stuffed him into the fridge. The Finnegans said a man visited Jane a few times after she moved in, but not recently."

"They'd have a reason to invent a male visitor for Jane if they're the ones who put a man in the freezer." Val opened the fridge to grab an apple. A platter of cucumber sandwiches looked ready to serve, as did parfaits with chocolate shavings on top. "You've been busy today. What kind of parfait did you make?"

"It's single servings of tiramisu in a parfait glass. And yup, I've been busy—and not just in the kitchen. Yesterday I couldn't find anything online about the couple who sold Jane the house, Howard and Missy Docksteiner. I figured Missy was a nickname for Melissa, but today I had another idea. I entered a different full name for Missy and got a hit. Guess what name worked."

Val wouldn't play his guessing game. His habit of promising big news and delaying it irked her. "I give up." She bit into her apple. He'd tell her before long.

He hunted for oven mitts, eased them on, and removed the brownies from the oven. She'd eaten half her apple before he satisfied her curiosity.

He set the baking pan on a rack. "I found a Millicent R. Docksteiner in a list of contributors to a theater fundraiser in Baltimore."

Val thunked her head. She should have thought of Missy as a possible nickname for Millicent. "So Millicent Rilke was the woman Jane's neighbors knew as Missy. She was married to Howard Docksteiner, who sold his house to Jane."

"That would explain why the house wasn't advertised for sale. Jane bought it from people she knew—Millicent and her husband."

"Right, but did she buy it with or without a freezer in the storeroom? With or without a body in the freezer?"

Granddad shrugged. "It's harder to move a freezer than to let it be. The Docksteiners mighta sold the house for a lower-than-market price on the condition that Jane rent them the storeroom. It sure would be nice to know when those padlocks were put on. The Finnegans might have noticed when."

"Be careful what you say to them. We can't rule out that they rented Jane's storeroom to keep a body on ice. If they suspect you're on to them, they might buy another freezer just for you." Val grinned at him, though she was only half joking. She glanced at her watch. "Rehearsal starts in fifteen minutes. I want to change out of my café outfit before then. You need any help from me?"

"Nope. Still gotta make coffee and tea, but that's—" The doorbell interrupted him. "The early birds are here. When I'm finished here, I'll come out and join them in the sitting room."

Val hurried to the front door and let Millicent and Cassandra in. The spa's open-house invitations, which Val had forgotten to take to the café this morning, were on the hall table.

Cassandra stared at the invitations, frowning. "Look at this, Millicent. The spa's having an open house this Saturday."

"Would you like to go?" Val handed each of them an invitation. "I was hired to run a smoothie bar for the event and ended up with a pile of invitations to distribute. Take some extras if you have friends who might like to attend. I have to run upstairs for a few minutes. Make yourself comfortable in the sitting room."

She was halfway up the stairs when the doorbell rang again. She turned to face the hall.

Millicent looked up at her. "No need for you to come down." She opened the door for the Dernes.

Val continued up to the second-floor landing. She stepped away from the staircase and paused where she wouldn't be visible from below but could hear what was said.

"Here's an invitation to an open house at the spa." Cassandra's voice carried up the stairs. "Millicent and I are going to it. You want to come along?"

"Absolutely not!" Nanette Derne emphasized each syllable. "I wouldn't go near that place."

Val was surprised at that reaction. Nanette struck her as the one who'd be the most curious about the spa, where she might come out looking younger—once the bruises healed.

Nanette continued. "There's no reason for Nigel to go back there. He went to the spa's VIP night last Wednesday. They invited the entire county council."

Nigel cleared his throat. "Why are you two going there?"

"To look a killer in the eye," Millicent said. "That's why we should all go."

Val was taken aback. Two days before, Millicent had stopped her sister from talking about the spa and blamed Cassandra's overactive imagination for the idea that Jane was murdered. Now Millicent was talking about a killer at the spa. What had changed? For one thing, the audience was smaller. The four friends from Baltimore were talking among themselves, not in front of the other cast members.

"Don't even think about going to the open house, Nigel," Nanette said. "Nothing good will come of it. Let's sit down and talk about something else."

Val strained to hear what they were saying, but their voices didn't carry from the sitting room. As she changed into jeans and a light sweater, she tried to make sense of what she'd heard. Jane had told her old friends that she'd seen someone at the spa who'd gotten away with a crime. Was that crime a murder? Was the person Millicent called a killer responsible for Jane's death? Why didn't she go to the police if she believed a killer would be at the spa's open house?

Val noted that Nanette and Nigel hadn't disputed Millicent's conclusion about a killer at the spa.

For the first time, Val found herself agreeing with Nanette. Nothing good would come of looking a killer in the eye.

Ten minutes later the cast was seated around the dining room table, except for Millicent.

She remained standing. "The script tells you when your character comes onstage. Cassandra, our stage manager, will position you so you're ready to enter on cue. You'll sit down on a chair-height stool and angle yourself toward the audience." Millicent took her seat and demonstrated the angle she wanted, pretending the sitting room was the audience. "When the script says you exit the stage, you'll swivel and turn your back to the audience so they know you're not part of the scene." She turned her body away from the sitting room. "Any questions?"

Bethany raised her hand. "Should we always face the audience rather than the person we're speaking to onstage?"

Millicent shook her head. "While you're reading from the script, you'll be projecting toward the audience. After a few more rehearsals, you'll know your lines well enough to look up from the script and toward the person you're addressing, at least occasionally."

With fewer rehearsals than the other cast members, Val wondered if she'd be able to do that. "I have a question too. We enter one by one at the start of the play. According to the script, all the characters enter and exit multiple times. Do we ever exit, or do we remain in our seats the whole time?"

"Good question, Val. All of you except the murderer's victim will exit the stage before the final scene in Act One. We want the audience to gasp in fear when the stage lights go out and the murderer strikes."

Cassandra added, "Most of the cast will exit again in the second act, when the culprit attempts another murder. We won't practice the exits until our first rehearsal in the theater next week."

Reading through the first act went faster than it had the last time. The cast didn't stumble over their lines, and Millicent stopped the action less often to give pointers on their delivery. Even so, the tea between the acts was a welcome break.

Once they all had their cups and plates filled, Bethany said, "What should we wear for the performance, Millicent?"

"Choose something from your closet that reflects your character's age and personality. You and Nanette often wear bright colors, but for the parts you're playing, you'll both want to dress in more subdued and conservative clothes."

They tossed around ideas for what each of them might wear until it was time to continue the rehearsal.

As Val cleared the table, Ryan spoke up. "I thought you'd all like to know that the police have located Jane's ex-husband in South America."

Cassandra sniffed. "Birding, no doubt. This

should put an end to the rumor that Jane stuffed him in the freezer."

Val picked up Ryan's empty plate and cup. "Any leads on whose body was in there?"

"The police have a pretty good idea who the man is." Ryan trained his gaze on Millicent at the opposite end of the table. "They'll announce his identity as soon as they have positive proof."

The wide-eyed looks Cassandra and Millicent exchanged told Val that Ryan had given them surprising news. Unwelcome news too, given what she'd learned about the previous owner of Jane's house. Howard Docksteiner, Millicent's husband, had looked unwell the last time the neighboring Finnegans saw him three years ago, and now he was nowhere to be found. They'd also reported that a woman had visited the Docksteiners during the weeks before Jane bought the house. That could have been Cassandra, coming to help Millicent clear out the house and dispose of her husband's body.

Val glanced at the sisters. They were pushing seventy, but neither looked frail. The two of them could have lifted a medium-sized man into a freezer. Val could think of no reason why they'd do that, though, unless Howard hadn't died of natural causes. Afraid that her face might reveal her thoughts, she hurried to the kitchen with the dishes and warned herself not to jump to conclusions.

The second half of the rehearsal erased any doubts Val might have had about the effect of Ryan's news on the Rilkes. Cassandra was late playing half of the sound effects. Millicent lost her place in the script and missed her cues several times. She'd never previously done that. When the rehearsal was over, she hustled Cassandra to the front door.

Ryan headed back to work at the police station, and Bram slipped out a minute later. His mother was running a book club meeting at the Title Wave this evening and needed him to manage the shop until closing time.

Bethany went into the kitchen to help Grand-dad with the dishes. That left Val to walk Nanette and Nigel to the door. As she opened it for them, she noticed a full-sized sedan at the curb, a darker one than Granddad's. It matched the car Jane's neighbor had described going past her house shortly before the fire started.

It was worth finding out whether the Dernes had been near Jane's house on Saturday. Maybe they'd noticed something that would help the police figure out what had happened there. Val decided to talk to Nigel about it, but not the defensive Nanette, who overreacted to every mention of Jane's name.

As Val left the hall and went into the sitting room, Bethany came toward her. "I wish I had time to talk, but I have to feed and walk Muffin before choir practice."

"A quick question before you go. Have you ever seen Nigel without Nanette?"

"No, but I've seen Nanette without Nigel. She comes to every pet-a-pet session at the Village, and he never does. She's fond of dogs, especially Muffin." Bethany smiled. "Who wouldn't love Muffin?"

Someone who didn't care for spoiled dogs? Nonetheless, Val found Bethany's cute spaniel irresistible. She also saw an opportunity. "Are you taking Muffin to the Village this week?"

Bethany nodded. "Saturday at one o'clock. If you want to catch Nigel alone, why don't you come with me? He and Nanette don't live in an apartment, but in a cottage at the Village. I've seen him gardening in their front yard. Theirs is the third cottage from the main building."

Val could fit in a visit to the Village on Saturday afternoon. Her prep for the open house that evening wouldn't keep her busy all afternoon. "Sounds good." A perfect setup, but would it be fruitful?

Val joined Granddad in the kitchen. The dishwasher hummed as he wiped down the counters. He'd reached the same conclusion Val had. The man in the freezer was Millicent's husband, Howard Docksteiner.

"We should tell Chief Yardley what we discovered about Millicent's connection to Jane's house," she said.

"He's ten steps ahead of us, Val. Ryan said the police have already identified the man in the freezer, and they'd know who his wife was. I'm guessing that when Millicent checked her phone after the rehearsal, she found out the police had called her." He hung up the dishrag. "By the way, a man's coming here in a few minutes who might hire me."

"To do what?"

Granddad shrugged. "I'm not sure. He heard I was good at getting to the bottom of things and was familiar with the community. I didn't catch his name."

"I was going to use the computer in the study. I'll take the laptop upstairs if you want to meet your prospective client in the study."

"Don't bother. It's more comfortable in the sitting room. Just close the doors to the study."

When the doorbell rang five minutes later, Val was trying to shut the French doors separating the sitting room from the study. They were usually open, needed to be planed, and didn't close tightly. While she checked the cost of the fruit, vegetables, and flavorings she'd need to make smoothies for a large crowd, Granddad's voice drifted to her from the sitting room. As soon as the other man spoke, she sat upright. The voice belonged to Ron Melgrem. What did the spa director want from Granddad?

Chapter 12

Val moved her chair away from the desk and closer to the sitting room. The gap between the French doors allowed her to hear Granddad and his visitor clearly. Ron introduced himself as the director of Bayport's Med Spa and Wellness Center.

"How did you happen to call me?" Granddad's question didn't reveal that he'd ever heard of Ron.

"I gave a talk about the spa at the retirement village two weeks ago. A man who lives there passed me your business card, in case I needed someone to look into problems in a discreet way. He said you know a lot of people in Bayport, and you've even solved some crimes here."

"You must have talked to my old friend Ned, but he didn't say that just 'cause he's my friend. What he told you is one hundred percent true."

Val smiled. No one ever accused Granddad of being humble. Though he mostly spoke the truth, it wasn't always the whole truth. In this case, he'd left out the role that Val and the police had played in solving those crimes.

Ron continued. "The Village had a reception with refreshments for my presentation there. The punch they served made me really sick. Since the spa employees with me were fine, I assumed I had a stomach bug. But other stuff has happened since then that makes me think someone in Bayport has it in for me."

"When was the reception?'

"The weekend before last."

Before Jane died, Val noted.

"What else happened after that?" Granddad said.

"Threats by mail. Envelopes with nothing in them except one card from a deck. The first one was a tarot card of the grim reaper. It came in the mail Tuesday of last week. Yesterday, I got the ace of spades in an envelope. I've heard it's called the death card. I'm worried about what will happen next."

Val saw a pattern, or at least the start of one. Like the tarot card, the ace of spades had arrived on a Tuesday. Would Ron receive another ominous card on the same day next week?

Granddad took a moment to respond. "The cards could be just a prank, not a threat."

"That's not all that happened. Someone ran me off the road. If that was a prank, it was a dangerous one. I had to brake really hard to avoid hitting a tree. I still have whiplash from it."

Val remembered Ron rubbing the back of his neck when he'd interviewed her.

"When and where were you forced off the road?" Granddad said.

"On my way home after the reception at the Village. It was on a two-lane country road around here. I was so rattled I can't even remember which one. I thought it was a shortcut."

"Did you report the road incident to the police?"

"No. I couldn't describe the car that forced me off the road. It all happened too fast. My car wasn't damaged. It started up with no problem. So I got it back on the road, found my way home, and tried to soak away the pain in a hot tub."

Val crept over to the window and checked the cars parked on the street. There was only one she didn't recognize—the red sports car parked in front of the house. Ron was lucky that his small, low car wasn't damaged when it went off the road. She returned to her eavesdropping spot.

"Local folks know the roads and sometimes pass other cars when they shouldn't," Granddad pointed out. "But I understand why the cards in the mail on top of the punch and the car episode make you wonder if you're a target. What do you want me to do?"

"I'd like you to keep an eye out for trouble at the spa's open house on Saturday evening."

Val stiffened. Did Ron have any reason to expect a problem on Saturday? And was Granddad the right person to handle it? He must be thinking it over because he didn't rush to accept the job.

After a moment, he said, "If you're really concerned, you should let the police know. They might send an officer or two to make sure nothing goes wrong."

Ron groaned. "I don't want that. Having police around would change the mood. The spa's a place to relax. We're trying to convey a sense of harmony and security. I thought of hiring plain-clothes security guards, but I couldn't find any on short notice."

So Granddad was the last resort. That's why Ron had asked for his help.

"How many folks are you expecting?" Granddad said.

"More than a hundred. Less than two hundred."

"I can't watch that many people on my own. My granddaughter, Val, will be there making smoothies for the crowd. She can keep her eyes peeled, too, but—"

"I didn't know you and Val were related. She seems a pleasant and competent young woman."

Val would have preferred "gorgeous and brainy," but she appreciated any compliments.

"She sure is," Granddad said, "but she'll be stuck in one spot. I'll need assistants who can roam around, if I can get them on such short notice."

"Bring as many people as you need to get the job done. When you've lined them up, call or email me with the terms. Can you do that by tomorrow?"

"Yup. I got a question before you go. How did you get the drink at the Village? Did you ladle it yourself from a punch bowl?"

"No, a woman handed me a cup of it."

Aha. Val gave Granddad points for confirming that Ron's drink could have been spiked.

"Can you describe the woman?"

Ron laughed quietly. "She looked like most of the people I saw there, a white woman with gray hair. We didn't talk to each other. I don't remember any distinguishing traits."

"Would you recognize her if you saw her again?"

"Doubt it."

Granddad quoted a price that sounded high to Val, but Ron accepted it. As the two men said their goodbyes, Val moved her chair back in front of the desk. Instead of working on her shopping list for the smoothie bar, she thought about the punch Ron had drunk. Probably he'd had a stomach bug, but possibly Cassandra, Millicent, or Nanette had added an extra ingredient so the punch would sicken him. Val could think of only one reason they'd do that—they knew or suspected he was the person who'd gotten away with a crime. But that was Jane's battle, so why would the others care about it?

Once Ron left, Granddad came into the study and sat down on the sofa across from the desk. "You listened to me talking to my client, didn't you?"

Val swiveled her chair around to face him. "With my acute hearing, I couldn't avoid it."

Granddad rolled his eyes. "Is the spa director paranoid, or is someone really after him?"

Val shrugged. "Who knows? His car might have gone off the road because the punch made him dizzy or he'd had a few stronger drinks before the reception. Fear of not passing a sobriety test would explain why he didn't report the incident to the police. And just because the punch disagreed with him doesn't mean it was spiked. The only thing we know for sure is that the tarot card and the ace of spades spooked him, maybe because he has a guilty conscience."

"What's he guilty of?"

"Millicent seemed to believe there was a killer at the spa. She might have meant Jane's killer."

"Let's say Jane recognized him as the criminal who got off scot-free. But another person also knew about Ron's past and decided to make sure justice was done. The chickens are comin' home to roost for Ron, and that's why he's nervous."

Val thought of another explanation. "What if Ron isn't the criminal Jane recognized? He could be the latest target of the person Jane said had escaped justice." Val wasn't surprised when Granddad shook his head. They rarely accepted each other's theories without question. "Okay, it's less likely than your theory, but we can't yet rule it out. A killer on the loose, Jane dead, an arson covering up how she died, and Ron threatened. How do those things fit together?"

"Ron's in the middle of it, one way or another. Because he's using a different name, he's not easy to research online." Granddad's face lit up. "I haven't had a chance to do a deep dive into the other folks who work at the spa. Maybe one of them has some dirty laundry or a hidden connection to Jane. If not, we're left with Ron by process of elimination."

"People don't usually air their dirty laundry." The Dernes and the Rilke sisters had kept their connection to Jane a secret too, dodging Val's questions about how they knew her. "Cassandra claimed Jane's death was related to the spa, and Millicent's going there to look a killer in the eye, but neither has mentioned the name of the person they suspect. Why don't you hang out around the Village tomorrow and try to get Cassandra alone? She's the one who blurts out secrets. I'll bet she knows who Jane recognized at the spa."

"Good idea, Val. What's on your to-do list for tomorrow?"

"Dropping off the contract relieving the spa of liability for the smoothies I serve. While I'm there, I'll check if Chatty has ferreted out any secrets about her colleagues in the last two days."

Granddad stood up. "I'll call Ned. Maybe he noticed who served the punch when Ron was at the Village promoting the spa. And I'm gonna ask him to be a lookout with me at the open house. I'd like Bram to come, too, if he's willing."

"I'm sure he's willing." Last month he'd tailed and protected someone in danger, and yesterday he went to Jane's house looking for clues. He wanted to solve the mystery of her death as much as Granddad did.

Val pulled into the spa's parking lot shortly after two on Thursday. Dozens of cars were in the lot, many more than when she'd been there on Tuesday. Val remembered this was one of the soft opening days Chatty had mentioned, when the staff would check that every part of the business ran smoothly.

She scanned the cars, looking for any resembling the ones Jane's neighbors had seen. No sedans like Granddad and Nigel drove and no silver compact cars. SUVs and midsized sedans dominated the lot. Ron's red sports car wasn't there either. Val walked to the end of the lot, peered through the trees at the Melgrems' house, and saw it had a garage, probably where Ron parked his car.

As she retraced her steps, a silver compact backed into a parking space. The shine on the car suggested it had been washed and polished recently. Approaching it, she noticed a dent in its fender.

Patrick Parenna climbed out of the driver's seat, looking as attractive and squeaky clean as his car and without any obvious dents.

Val reminded herself how common silver cars were. She had no reason to think that the car belonging to the spa's computer and maintenance manager was the one Jane's neighbors had seen in her driveway. Even so, Val couldn't pass up this chance to find out more about him.

Chapter 13

"Hey, Patrick," Val called out. "I'm Val Deniston. Ron introduced us on Tuesday."

Patrick smiled. "I remember. You were there for an interview, right? Are you joining our spa team?"

"Just as an extra hand for the open house." She glanced at his dented bumper. "I'm curious about your car. I was thinking of buying one like it. Is it this year's model?" When he nodded, she continued. "And it already has a dent. That's too bad. A car I had was dented like that. Someone hit it in a parking lot and drove off. Did that happen to you?"

Patrick's jaw clenched. "No, I made the mistake of lending my car to someone, who's going to foot the repair bill. Are you leaving the spa or just arriving?"

"I'm on my way in. I wanted to talk to you about the open house." She walked along the path with him. "I was hired to make smoothies in the tent.

I'll need electricity near my booth to run the blenders. Leeann said you could arrange that."

"No problem. It's easy to set you up near the electrical line. This is the first I've heard of a smoothie bar."

"Leeann thought the spa should offer some healthy options in addition to what the caterers were providing."

"*Whatever Leeann wants*," Patrick crooned, "*Leeann gets*." He must have noticed Val's surprise and grinned at her. "It's from a musical."

Though he could carry a tune, Val still found it odd that he'd broken out in song. "I know the musical—*Damn Yankees*. Lola was the name of the character who got what she wanted." She'd sold her soul to the devil in exchange for beauty. Dr. Leeann Melgrem clearly hadn't done that . . . at least not yet.

"*Damn Yankees* isn't well known in our generation. You must be a fan of musicals."

"My grandfather roped me into watching it. He collects classic movies and loves baseball. *Damn Yankees* hits his sweet spots." They were approaching the sprawling motel-turned-spa, and Val had yet to find out anything about Patrick's background. "Did you work at a different spa before you took this job?"

"No. I had my own business, recording and producing audio for ads, online training, and occasionally books. I even did some voice-overs myself."

Val could believe that. He enunciated clearly and had a resonant voice. Why would he switch to an occupation so different from his previous one? Val had made a radical change too—from cookbook publicist to café manager—but she'd waited until her thirties to have that early midlife crisis. Patrick looked as if thirty was still a few years away. "What made you take this job?"

"Sitting at a console in a windowless, sound-proof room got old. You can't have windows when you're recording because street noises might break into the audio. Once the spa's running smoothly, I'll have time to get out on the bay and fish."

Apparently, his previous position didn't come with nearby fishing opportunities. "You weren't working in this part of Maryland before?"

He shook his head. "In the D.C. area."

"How did you hear about the spa job?"

"From a friend." His eyes narrowed. Nearly a foot taller than she was, he looked down at her from his imposing height. "You ask a lot of questions. Sounds like you're interviewing me for a job."

"Just curious."

After a moment, he said, "Are you familiar with this song? *Curiosity, they say, killed the kitty cat one fine day.*"

If he'd simply said "*curiosity killed the cat,*" she'd have felt intimidated. Couched in a melody, the words didn't bite as much, though possibly they were meant to. "I never heard that tune before now."

He jerked open the door to the lobby and waited for her to enter ahead of him. "Have a good one, Val."

The conversation that had started with a warm smile ended on a frosty note. Because she'd asked one question too many?

She looked around the lobby. Three men and four times as many women sat in well cushioned armchairs scattered around the spacious room. Most thumbed their phones, and a few filled out forms attached to clipboards. They must be waiting for their treatments. The marketing manager, Sabrine, was walking around chatting with them and snapping photos.

She waved to Val and approached her. "Would you mind posing for a picture at the reception desk?"

Val imagined herself in an ad for the spa, which might imply endorsement of the place. "I'd rather not. I started work at seven this morning. I'm frazzled, and I'm sure my hair is as well." She fingered her untamable curls.

"Don't worry about your hair. After it goes through photo editing, you'll have a new look." Sabrine gave Val a chance to change her mind, which she didn't. "Okay. No pressure."

Sabrine left to find an alternate photo-shoot victim. Val headed to the reception desk, where the woman who'd been watering plants on Tuesday sat. She looked about Bethany's age, mid-twenties, but her face had more makeup on it than Bethany wore in a month. The receptionist would have been pretty even without cosmetics, but false eyelashes resembling black caterpillars overwhelmed her good features.

She looked up from reading a fashion magazine. "Good afternoon. Are you here for a treatment?"

"No. I'm Val Deniston, dropping off some papers for Ron." Val held up a manila envelope.

"I believe he's in a meeting. You can leave that with me. I'll see that he gets it."

Val eyed the papers strewn around the desk and hoped Ron would get the envelope before it was buried. She'd made copies, though, so she could always try again. "If Chatty Ridenour isn't busy with a client, would you please tell her Val is here to see her."

Chatty emerged from the break room with a cup of coffee. "I heard your voice, Val. I don't have a client coming until three. I'll show you my lovely massage room." She led the way down the corridor.

Val could tell from her friend's jaunty walk that she had a head full of gossip bursting to be set free.

She led Val into a room with peaceful seascapes on the walls and a small indoor fountain that made soothing splashes. Whenever Val visited Chatty's treatment room at the club, one of them had to perch on the massage table because the cramped space allowed for only a single straight-backed chair. But here, in addition to the massage table centerpiece, Chatty's room included two comfortable chairs with a low table between them. She put her coffee on the table, brought Val water, and closed the door to the room. She apparently wanted privacy for whatever she was going to reveal.

Once they were both seated, Chatty wasted no time on chitchat. "We had quite the scene at the spa this morning. Leeann was in a rage. Last week she'd stocked a cabinet with syringes and injectibles. This morning she noticed that some syringes and vials of Botox were gone."

So the spa had a thief. Maybe Jane had recognized someone who'd escaped punishment for theft. "Surely the room with Leeann's wrinkle remedies is locked. Who would have a key to it besides Leeann?"

Chatty shrugged. "Ron, Leeann's nurse, and the cleaners who come after hours. I heard the lock was finicky and the cleaners didn't always manage to engage it. Patrick installed a new lock at the end of last week. The cabinet where the drugs are kept has a lock, but it's probably easy to pick with a hairpin or a pocketknife. It's not like a dead bolt."

Hmm. Did Chatty have experience picking such locks? Val decided against asking, not wanting to interrupt the flow of information. "Is anyone on the staff a suspect?"

"Not that I know of. There are other explanations for the missing vials. People invited to the soft opening have been wandering around yesterday and today. And Leeann might have mistaken how much she put on the shelf. According to the nurse who worked with her in another practice, Leeann is a perfectionist about appearance, but she isn't detail-oriented." Chatty sipped her coffee. "Ron also went on a tear. Remember the relaxation chamber I mentioned?"

"Ron's 'mind-enhancement room' with the floatation tank?"

"Uh-huh. Ron kept blaming Patrick because it wouldn't work right. Turns out it has a defective part. The manufacturer will replace the part, but it won't arrive until next week. Ron was fuming because he wanted to show off the tank at the open house. It's the one feature that sets this spa apart from others in the area." Chatty put down her cup and leaned back. "That's the latest news here. Have you learned anything about the fire and the frozen man?"

"Not yet. Do you happen to know what kind of cars Ron and Leeann drive?"

"I've seen Leeann in a beige SUV and Ron in a red sports car. Why do you ask?"

Val took a drink of water. She knew anything she told Chatty would be spread far and wide, so she made up a cover story. "I thought I saw them together in a big sedan, but I must have been mistaken." Maybe Ron had been driving his wife's SUV when he was run off the road instead of his little red car, which wouldn't have fared as well on uneven ground. "How does the staff here feel about Ron as a boss? He seemed nice enough to me when I interviewed with him."

"Most people think he's okay. If anything, he's too nice . . . to certain people."

Did that mean he favored some staff members over others? "Too nice to Sabrine? I caught her scowling at and skirting around Ron and Patrick, but I wasn't sure which of them she disliked."

"She's uptight when Ron's nearby. I think he's hitting on her, but she can't call him on it without risking her job. Becoming a marketing manager was a big promotion over her last position. Leeann offered her the job. The two of them were roomies when Leeann started practicing dermatology."

"Sabrine has no recourse." Could she have sent Ron death cards to get back at him without a direct confrontation? Receiving those cards might distract him from pursuing her, and sending them would make her feel less powerless. Or maybe he'd gotten on another staffer's nerves too. "Does anyone else have a problem with Ron?"

"Patrick and Ron are strictly business. From their body language, though, I'd say there's no love lost between them."

Maybe Patrick channeled his negative feelings into song. "Patrick sang a few lines from songs when I was talking to him. Have you ever heard him do that?"

"He stuck his head in here a couple times and sang 'Chatty, Chatty, Bang, Bang.' He has a good voice."

Various meanings of *bang* occurred to Val, including a gunshot sound. "You didn't take it as a soft-pedaled threat?"

Chatty rolled her eyes. "The song comes from a kids' movie. He turned *chitty* into *chatty*. He's just singing a tune, trying to be friendly."

Val wouldn't say the two songs she'd heard were friendly. She told Chatty about his substitution of *Leeann* for *Lola*. " 'Whatever Leeann wants, Leeann gets' sounded snarky to me. Why shouldn't Leeann get what she wants? She owns the place."

"He's got her number. She's laser-focused on getting what she wants. When she went husband shopping, she used a checklist longer than a weekly grocery list. Or so said the woman I massaged yesterday. She's known Leeann since college."

When Chatty massaged her clients, they relaxed,

lost their inhibitions, and spilled their guts. Val suspected Chatty spiked her oils and lotions with truth serum. "Did the woman say what was on Leeann's checklist?"

"For starters, she wanted someone with a post-grad education, a body mass index within a narrow range, and good looks. Leeann wants beautiful children. She also required a prenup that said any male offspring would have her surname, not her husband's. That was the deal-breaker for one almost-fiancé."

But not for Ron, who'd gone a step further, shed his own surname, and taken hers. Val thought of a reason he might have been willing to do that— a new name would help him disconnect from his past. "Did her friend say why Leeann demanded that?"

"She's close to her father. He was depressed because the family name would die out with him. Leeann came up with a solution that pleased him. She has some thickening around the middle. Looks to me like a baby's on the way."

Val couldn't fathom why continuing the family name mattered in a society without hereditary titles. "So Leeann married Ron for his looks and his willingness to adopt her surname. Why did he marry her?"

"Money. She's rolling in it. I'm not sure what else she brings to the table, and it doesn't look like a love match. You'd think a couple married less than a year would gaze fondly into each other's eyes now and then."

"You've seen them only at work."

"I've also seen his roving eye at work." Chatty glanced at the wall clock.

Almost time for her next appointment. Val took the hint and said goodbye.

On her way out she went by the reception desk. The envelope with the contract she'd signed was no longer there. The receptionist reported she'd given it to Ron when he came by the desk.

Val hurried to the parking lot. She looked forward to telling Granddad what she'd learned and hoped his visit to the Village had been as fruitful as her stop at the spa.

Chapter 14

When Val arrived home, Granddad was in his recliner with the book that had put him to sleep on his lap. Though she tiptoed through the sitting room, the creaking floorboards roused him.

"Sorry. I was trying not to wake you, Granddad."

"I wasn't sleeping, I was resting my eyes. How did your visit to the spa go?"

Val perched on the sofa and described her encounter with Patrick, including his songs with the tweaked lyrics. "Patrick has a car that resembles the one Jane's neighbor saw in the driveway before the fire broke out. It has a dent in it that he blames on someone who borrowed it. And he's doing work that's unrelated to his previous job."

"I looked him up online, where it says he's an audio engineer. His website says he's not available for any audio projects now, but the form to ask for his audio services is still there. He's keeping his irons in the fire in case his job at the spa doesn't pan out."

"Or he's taking time off while the weather's good and he can enjoy the outdoors, which is what he told me. Chatty said there was tension between him and Ron. I'm wondering if Patrick might have harassed Ron, sent him death cards, maybe even forced him off the road."

Granddad pushed up the bifocals that had slipped down his nose. "Could Patrick be the person Jane said got away with a crime?"

"Ron's a better bet because he changed his name, and you can't find any information about him online, no connection between his current name and his former one. It's like he's trying to keep his real identity a secret."

Granddad nodded. "And if Jane recognized him, he had a reason to get rid of her."

"So did Ron's wife, if Jane talked to her." Val told him about Leeann's search for the perfect partner and her prenup clause about the surname the couple's child would have.

"Hmph. Marriage didn't used to involve check-lists and contracts. Leeann shouldn't have let her father's hang-up control her life." Granddad locked eyes with Val. "I'd feel bad if you put off marrying because of what you think my needs are. When you marry, you'll set up your own house-hold. That's as it should be."

"That's what I'd like to do . . . if I ever marry." Though startled by the change of subject, Val was happy to hear Granddad's views. He'd settled something that had been on her mind. Marrying Bram, or anyone else, she'd have felt guilty about leaving Granddad. He'd just absolved her of any guilt. "Getting back to the Melgrems, Chatty believes Ron married Leeann for her money. That might be Chatty being catty, but she's probably right about the couple's lopsided assets."

"Sounds like the Melgrems each have what they wanted. Leeann got her boxes checked, and Ron got a fat checkbook. What's that got to do with Jane recognizing a criminal at the spa?"

"Think about this scenario. Leeann would have vetted Ron before marrying him, and he'd have explained away anything fishy as trumped up. She'd finally found her ideal mate, both a father for her children and a manager for her business." Val leaned back on the sofa. "Then Ron tells her that a woman who smeared him has shown up and might make baseless accusations again. If anyone believes that woman, Leeann's happily-ever-after dreams are threatened."

Granddad raised one eyebrow, as he usually did when he was skeptical. "Someone who got away with a crime once is more likely to commit another crime than a doctor who wants the perfect life." He drummed his fingers on the arm of his chair. "You haven't asked me what I learned at the Village today."

"I was about to do that. Did you get a chance to talk to Cassandra without Millicent trying to muffle her?"

"No, but I talked to Ned. He's going to help me keep an eye on folks at the open house. I didn't see the Rilke sisters, but Ned told me something juicy about Cassandra." He chuckled. "That's a pun."

Val didn't get it. The doorbell rang before she could ask him about his play on words. Val crossed the room to the hall and opened the door.

Cassandra rushed in. She wore the same gray athletic suit that she had for the rehearsals. Her red eyes suggested she'd been crying. "I need help. The police are talking to Millicent. I don't know what I'll do if she's arrested."

Arrested for what? Getting rid of her husband and putting him in the freezer? "Come into the sitting room." Val led Cassandra to an armchair, brought her a glass of water, and put it on a side table next to her chair. She looked as if she needed something stronger, but Val was afraid alcohol would make the older woman even less coherent than usual. She was babbling to Granddad about Millicent being innocent without saying what she was accused of.

Cassandra stopped talking long enough to sip the water. Then she took off her glasses, reached into her pocket for a small plastic container, and leaned her head back to put drops in her eyes. "The pollen makes my eyes burn."

She hadn't been crying after all, just suffering from allergies, and Val had seen her use eye drops during rehearsals. She sat down on the sofa near Cassandra's chair. "Where's Millicent now?"

"At the police station. This morning the police called and said they wanted to interview her at the Village. She didn't want the other residents to see her with the police. That would start everybody gossiping. I dropped her off at the station a few hours ago. She was supposed to call me when she was done, but she hasn't yet. Why would they keep her so long if they're not charging her?"

"What did they want to see her about?" Grand-dad said.

Cassandra bit her lip. "I'm not sure. Whatever else she did, she didn't kill anybody."

Val wondered what Millicent had done short of killing.

Granddad straightened his glasses. "Her husband owned the house Jane bought. He hasn't been seen for a few years. He's dead, isn't he?"

"He left for a warmer climate." Cassandra's instant response sounded rehearsed. She sipped her water and stared defiantly at Granddad. She straightened her back and, apparently, her resolve. "He was sick and in terrible pain. Millicent stopped him from committing suicide twice. He had multiple cancers from Agent Orange exposure in Vietnam."

Val's heart went out to the poor man and his wife. A better climate wouldn't change their grim situation. "I'm sorry to hear that."

"It's terrible what happened to the boys over there." Granddad frowned. "Are you saying Millicent let her sick, suicidal husband leave for a warmer climate and didn't go with him?"

Cassandra chewed her lower lip instead of answering his question.

Val tried a less confrontational approach than Granddad. "Your sister would never do that to her husband."

Again, no response from Cassandra.

Granddad folded his arms. "Let's cut to the chase. The police can identify the man in the freezer. No use pretending your brother-in-law ever left that house."

Cassandra's shoulders sagged. "Millicent did what he wanted. When he was sure the end was near, he put a foam pad and a pillow in the freezer. That's where he slept. He used a stepstool to get into it."

Granddad gaped at her, speechless.

So did Val. That story was too weird not to be true. Even the imaginative Cassandra couldn't have made it up. "Why did he sleep in the freezer?"

"He didn't expect to wake up in the morning. He was on so many painkillers, he might have overdosed by accident or on purpose. He told Millicent not to report his death. That way his disability checks from Social Security and the VA would still go into their joint account." Cassandra wrung her hands. "They'd depleted their savings and cashed in his insurance to pay for doctor bills and meds. Millicent needed the money. He convinced her the government was responsible for his illnesses and they owed his widow."

Granddad stroked his chin. "The Feds might go after her for fraud, but the local police have no jurisdiction. If the autopsy shows your brother-in-law died of natural causes, the police aren't going to arrest Millicent."

"I'm afraid they'll think she killed Jane to keep his death a secret." Cassandra's eyes filled with tears. "Jane didn't know about the freezer. Millicent paid her rent for the storeroom and kept it locked."

Bram's guess about the padlocks had been right. Val sensed an opening. In her distress, Cassandra might reveal what she'd previously kept to herself.

"The only way to make sure Millicent isn't blamed is to find out who killed Jane. She told you she'd seen someone at the spa who'd gotten away with a crime. The person she recognized might have killed her to keep that secret."

Granddad drummed his fingers on the chair arm. "Who is the criminal at the spa?"

Cassandra opened her mouth and then closed it. Her phone rang, saving her from having to reply. She pulled it out of her tattered straw bag, glanced at the caller's name, and answered. "Millicent! Are you okay? . . . Thank God . . . Yes, I'll be right over." She tucked the phone away. "They didn't arrest her." Cassandra stood up, rushed toward the hall, and banged the front door closed behind her.

Val hurried after her. She was sure Cassandra wouldn't now reveal the name of the person who'd gotten away with a crime. But she might have other information that would help Val make a timetable of what had happened in the days before the fire.

She caught up with Cassandra on the walkway from the house to the street and fell into step with her. "When did Jane tell you about this criminal at the spa? Was it last week?"

"No." Cassandra rubbed her forehead as if massaging her memory. "It was the previous week, on Friday, just before our first *Mousetrap* rehearsal. We were at Jane's house early, and that's when she told us."

"Were the Dernes there too?" When Cassandra nodded, Val pressed on. "When did Jane go to the spa for a job interview?"

Cassandra tugged open the door to her station wagon and hurriedly climbed in. "The day before that rehearsal."

Thursday, exactly two weeks ago today. Val turned back to the house as Cassandra drove off with a faint squeal of her tires.

Granddad was standing near the front door, looking out the sidelight. "That station wagon has to be at least twenty years old. Cassandra and Millicent have only one car between them. Money's gotta be tight for them."

"Selling the house to Jane must have given Millicent's bank account an infusion."

"She probably cleared enough to buy into an apartment at the Village, but the money from the house would dwindle if she has to pay the Village's monthly fees from it. I'd be surprised if the sisters get enough from their Social Security to cover those costs."

"What will happen to Millicent for not reporting her husband's death and taking government money she wasn't entitled to?"

"Most likely a steep fine, but it'll take years for the Feds to get around to it." He perked up at the idea that the government couldn't move swiftly to collect fines and taxes. "I'm ready for happy hour."

"I'll be there in a minute."

Val picked up a blank sheet of paper from the study and went to the kitchen, where Granddad was popping open a beer. She poured a glass of white wine from a half-full bottle in the fridge, grabbed a pencil from the kitchen junk drawer, and joined him at the small table.

He pointed to the paper she'd brought to the table. "What's that for?"

"I'm making a timetable of events related to Jane or the spa. I'll start with the day she interviewed at the spa two weeks ago."

"Good idea to pin down the order of events."

Val sipped her wine. "Can you think of any reason Cassandra won't tell us the name of the person Jane recognized at the spa?"

He shrugged. "Someone got away with a crime against the sisters. So they're planning to take justice into their own hands. An eye for an eye."

Val had seen nothing to suggest Cassandra was acting on a grudge. "Why do you think she's out for vengeance?"

"Because Ned told me what went on when the spa folks gave a presentation at the Village."

"When Ron drank punch he later decided was spiked?"

Granddad nodded. "Leeann was supposed to talk at the Village, but she didn't feel well. Ron substituted for her at the last minute. No one knew he'd be there or even that there would be punch."

"Then tampering with his drink wasn't premeditated."

"Right. After he finished his talk, Sabrine brought in the punch so folks would stick around longer and hear more pitches for the spa, but she didn't serve the punch. An aide at the Village ladled it from the punch bowl into the cups and left them on the table for people to serve themselves."

Val had filled in the first two lines of her timetable while he was talking. "Do you mean nobody could have messed with his drink?"

"Nah. Let me finish the story." Granddad took a swig of beer. "Cassandra brought drinks to the older folks who used walkers or wheelchairs. Ned said she also gave Ron a cup of the punch."

Val smiled. "Now I get your pun. That was Ned's juicy story about Cassandra. But she didn't know Ron would be at the Village. Are you saying Cassandra just happened to have a toxic substance with her that would dissolve in a drink?"

Granddad smiled like the cat that got the cream. "Yup . . . in her pocket. She always carries eye drops, a clear liquid with no taste. A little of it makes you sick. A lot of it can kill you. A few years back a woman was convicted of murder for putting eye drops in her husband's water over several days. Ron was lucky Cassandra only had a small container with her."

Chapter 15

Val stared across the kitchen table at Granddad. "Eye drops can kill you? Are they prescription drops?"

"No, you buy them over the counter. Most drops won't hurt you, only the ones that have tetrahydro-something in them. They're used to reduce redness, but if someone slips them into your drink, your blood pressure goes up, you feel nauseous, and you could have seizures. Swallow enough of it, and you're a goner."

Val sipped her wine. She could predict Chief Yardley's reaction to Granddad's theory—possible but not provable, unless a witness reported seeing Cassandra put eye drops in the punch she brought to Ron. "Do you know when Ron gave the talk at the Village?"

"Yup, a week ago Saturday. I saw it on the monthly activity schedule posted at the Village."

Val added a line to her list and showed it to Granddad.

Thursday two weeks ago: Jane has a job interview at the spa with spa director Ron.

Friday two weeks ago: Jane tells Rilkes and Dernes that she recognized a criminal at the spa.

Saturday two weeks ago: Ron feels sick after drinking punch at the Village, and his car goes off the road.

He glanced at the timetable. "When Jane told her friends about her job interview at the spa, she must have given them Ron's name."

"It's tempting to jump to the conclusion that Cassandra put eye drops in Ron's punch, but why would she do that? Just because Jane told her the day before that he was guilty of a crime?"

Granddad reached for a pretzel. "Maybe Cassandra or her sister was a victim of that crime."

Val swirled the wine around her glass. "But what *was* the crime? If it was something as serious as murder, Jane would have said she'd recognized a *killer* who'd gotten off scot-free. Yet Millicent said she and Cassandra are going to the spa's open house to look a killer in the eye and Nigel and Nanette should do the same."

"She mighta meant Jane's killer. Cassandra could be planning the same trick at the open house as she did at the Village, but with even more eye drops. I'm gonna ask Ned to watch her on Saturday night and to head her off if she tries to get near Ron's drink." He sipped his beer. "What's next in your timetable?"

"The harassment of Ron. Three days after he got sick at the Village, he received the tarot card in the mail." Val added more days to her timetable and passed the paper to Granddad.

Tuesday last week: Ron receives the tarot death card.

Wednesday last week: Nigel goes to the VIP night at the spa.

Thursday last week: Jane calls the spa for an appointment with Dr. Leeann.

Saturday last week: Jane dies in a fire at her house.

Tuesday this week: Ron receives the ace of spades.

Wednesday this week: Ron requests surveillance at the open house.

"Surveillance." Granddad gave her a thumbs-up. "I should put that on my business card as one of my services."

"I wouldn't do that. Surveillance usually means sitting in a car for hours on end. Really boring. You couldn't pay me to do that job." Val pointed to the timetable. "Look at when Ron received the playing cards. For him to get them on Tuesdays, they were probably mailed on Saturday and processed on Monday."

"That means Jane could have sent them, or one of her friends." Granddad peered at the timetable and frowned. "When Ron came to see me, he talked first about the punch at the Village reception, then about the cards in the mail, and finally about his car going off the road. If that happened the night of the reception like he said, he didn't put the events in order."

Val understood Granddad's point. Most people related what happened to them in chronological order. "So maybe Ron lied about when his car was run off the road because it happened near Jane's house on Saturday night. And that's why he didn't report it to the police. He wouldn't want them to know he was in the vicinity of the fire."

"Whoever ran him off the road knows where it happened. For sure, the Rilke sisters didn't do that. They have one car between them, and it probably has minimum insurance on it. They wouldn't risk their wheels and their driver's licenses by pulling a stunt like that."

"Millicent wouldn't, but I'm not sure Cassandra would think it through. Let's not leave out Nigel and Nanette. They have a sedan that resembles the one Jane's neighbor saw on the road just before the fire."

"Could the whole group of them be waging a campaign against Ron?"

Val shrugged. "A campaign might explain why they wouldn't say how they knew Jane. They don't want us to find out they're making Ron pay for his crime. Since they won't talk, the only way forward is to dig up what we can on him—what name he previously used and what crime he committed. The police could do that easily, but Chief Yardley had no interest in pursuing Jane's connection to the spa. And he'd accuse me of making assumptions—that Jane was telling the truth, that Cassandra was telling the truth, and that Ron is the one who got away with a crime."

"Those are pretty darn good assumptions." Granddad hit the table with the palm of his hand. "I've got an idea. Tomorrow afternoon before the rehearsal, stay in the study and eavesdrop like you did when Ron was here. When the Rilke sisters and the Dernes arrive early, as usual, they'll wait for the others in the sitting room. You can listen to what they say when they think they're alone. I'll be in the kitchen. If they don't talk about the spa, you call my cell phone. I'll poke my head into the sitting room and ask them if they're going to the open house. Then I'll go back to the kitchen."

Val didn't give his scheme much chance of success. "Suppose they don't come early? Even if they do, someone else in the cast might come early, and they won't feel free to talk."

Granddad shrugged. "I'll tell Bram and Bethany to be five or ten minutes late. Ryan's usually late anyway, but Bethany can pass on the word to him."

Val glanced at her watch. "Bram asked me to have dinner with him tonight. I have to shower and try to tame my hair before then." She stood up. "Sorry, I should have given you more notice that I wouldn't be here tonight."

Granddad waved off her apology. "No problem. I can fend for myself."

He'd probably rush out to the store for a steak, forbidden food on the healthy diet he was supposed to be on.

Instead of going to one of the restaurants on Main Street, Bram surprised Val by bringing her to the fixer-upper house he'd bought three months ago. The Cape Cod had undergone a face-lift with a fresh coat of white paint and a weed-free yard. When she first saw the inside, the only positive comment she'd made was that it had potential. What she hadn't said was how dreadful the kitchen and the upstairs bedrooms looked. She'd even had a dream about trying to cook in that kitchen and being chased away by an army of cockroaches.

Now, though, she was stunned by the kitchen's transformation. Everything was new—appliances, cabinets and counters, windows, and a glassed-in porch Bram had added to extend the small room. "It looks amazing, Bram." Like waking up from a nightmare.

"I asked you what you'd like in your dream kitchen, and it's all here. A refrigerator with a separate drawer for produce, an induction cooktop, a wall oven, and a dishwasher with drawers. Maybe I can tempt you to cook here."

"That's one temptation I won't resist." Val loved the kitchen at Granddad's, more for the memories than the equipment. Grandma had taught her to cook there. Bram's kitchen, hard and gleaming from the stainless steel appliances to the glass-topped table for two, lacked warmth. But that could be fixed. Pots of herbs on the windowsill, pictures on the walls, and colorful place mats would soften it.

Val was about to open the oven to check out its size when she realized it was warm. "Have you been cooking?"

He grinned. "Yeah. We're eating Italian, or rather your grandfather's five-ingredient version of Italian—baked rigatoni. I made the salad. The bakery made the cannoli. Let's sit in the sun porch and have wine and antipasto."

The porch had a view of a backyard. As they munched on cheese, olives, and melon wrapped with prosciutto, Val told Bram the identity of the man in the freezer and what Cassandra had said about how he'd chosen his resting place.

Bram's jaw dropped. "That's bizarre. What's going to happen to Millicent?"

"The police haven't arrested her for killing her husband, at least not yet. It might be true, as Cassandra claimed, that he died a natural death."

"I hope so for their sake." Bram reached for an olive. "Can you explain why your grandfather needs my help at the spa's open house? He hung up before I could ask what it's all about."

"It'll make more sense if I tell you what's happened in the last two weeks." Val fished the timetable she'd made from her shoulder bag. "This is a list of incidents involving Jane, the *Mousetrap* cast, and the spa. I'll tell you about the spa staff first and then go through the list."

When she finished, Bram topped off their wineglasses and set down the bottle. "I get why Ron's concerned about the open house. He might not realize it, but he's got more than one harasser. The punch spiker, the hate-card sender, and the road hog aren't the same person."

If that was Bram's imitation of a Sherlock Holmes deduction intended to awe his listener, she wasn't going to play the dumbstruck Watson. "Three different methods of harassment might mean three people or two or even one who's creative and versatile."

Bram considered this for a moment. "But the methods line up with the traits of the cast members. We got together three times before you joined us. I've had more chances to observe them than you. You already have a reason to think Cassandra gave Ron a cup of spiked punch. It was an impromptu act that fits her personality. She doesn't analyze before she speaks or acts."

Val wondered whose personality he'd match to the other threats. "Mailing Ron hostile cards a week apart isn't a spontaneous act. Granddad thought Jane might have sent them."

Bram shook his head. "Not her style or Millicent's. Jane was forthright and outspoken. Millicent focuses on reaching her goals efficiently. Neither would bother mailing cards with oblique threats. The payoff is too small." Bram put down his wineglass. "Nanette's fingerprints are all over those cards, figuratively speaking, and possibly for real. She nurses her grievances and enjoys complaining, but she wouldn't cross the line into something illegal. Instead of sending a threatening note, which the police might investigate, she sends playing cards."

Val conceded that Bram's reading of Nanette made sense. She could have learned about the ace of spades from Nigel, who'd been in the military, or from an *I Love Lucy* rerun. "By sending those cards, Nanette would feel she'd taken a stand against him."

"Forcing Ron's car off the road, though, is in a different league. It takes someone bold to do that." Bram stood up and paced. "Nigel comes across as bland, but that could be a façade. His wife mentioned they'd lived overseas. When I asked him what he did before retiring, he said he worked at embassies' commerce and trade offices, but he was vague about what his job entailed. Does that suggest anything to you?"

"According to Granddad, retirees who avoid talking about their former jobs are either ashamed of what they did or worked for the CIA. Nigel may be bolder than he seems, and he drives a sedan similar to the one Jane's neighbors saw the night of the fire. Of course, Ron said he was run off the road a week before that, but he might have lied about the date to cover up being on Jane's road that night."

Bram sat down and scrutinized the timetable. "The harassment against him started the day after Jane told her friends from the Village about her visit to the spa. You said Ron has a new name and an untraceable past. That makes him a good bet for the person with a criminal past."

"Yes, but why harass him instead of reporting him to the police?"

"I can think of two reasons. He was tried but not convicted, so double jeopardy applies. The police wouldn't bother investigating someone the law can't touch. Or the charges against Ron were dropped in exchange for his testimony against someone higher up the food chain."

That made sense to Val. She suddenly realized she'd seen no sign of Bram's post-fire-traumatic stress this evening. Analyzing puzzles was apparently therapeutic for him. "Good deduction, Sherlock. Jane and her friends couldn't hold Ron accountable even if they could prove him guilty, so they vowed to make his life miserable. After Jane's death, her friends were afraid he'd escape punishment again, so they're resorting to do-it-yourself justice. But they might be wrong about Ron killing Jane. I can't believe she would let a criminal who'd escaped punishment into her house."

Munching on prosciutto and melon, Bram took a moment before answering. "Maybe her door wasn't locked. He barged in, got her in a chokehold or smothered her, and then set the fire to her house to cover the crime."

That sounded more like one of Granddad's scenarios than a Sherlockian theory.

The oven timer dinged, telling them the pasta was ready. They cleared away the appetizers. As Bram opened the oven to take out the baked rigatoni, Granddad called Val.

"Quick!" he said. "Turn on the local news on TV. The anchorman promised he'd update the fire-and-ice news from Bayport after the commercial break."

Chapter 16

Val and Bram hurried into the living room and sat down on the new leather sofa. Bram pointed the remote at the television and tuned into the local station just as the commercials ended. The segment began with the news Granddad had anticipated.

"Bayport Police have identified the dead man found in a freezer after a house fire as Howard Docksteiner. The previous owner of the house, he died approximately three years ago."

Millicent's husband—not a surprise after Cassandra's visit today.

A reporter standing in front of Jane's house took up the story. "Police released a notarized statement found with the remains. It reads in part, 'I, Howard Docksteiner, being of sound mind and cancer-ravaged body, am aware that the massive amount of oxy needed to control my pain will kill me before long. I want it known that my wife,

Missy, previously foiled my attempt to take my own life and is in no way responsible for my death.' "

"Millicent and Cassandra are breathing easier this evening," Val said.

The reporter continued as cell-phone footage of the fire played behind her. "The medical examiner's office has determined that Mr. Docksteiner had end-stage cancer, but lethal levels of prescription narcotics probably caused his death. Police continue to investigate the death of Jane Johnson, who was the owner of the house at the time of the fire. First responders found her body in the kitchen while extinguishing the fire."

The anchor said, "Now, turning to other news—"

Bram clicked the television off. "Now, turning to dinner . . ."

Five minutes later, they sat down to dinner at the small, glass-topped table in the corner.

Val was pleased that Bram hadn't overcooked the pasta. She complimented the chef with sincerity. "The rigatoni is really good. It's chewy, and it soaked up the sauce well."

"Kudos to the recipe writer." Bram raised his glass to her.

He'd long since figured out that most of the five-ingredient recipes Granddad posted in his Codger Cook column were her recipes minus an ingredient or two. She would neither affirm nor deny Bram's deduction. "What other projects do you have in mind for the house?"

They were eating the last of the pasta on their plates by the time he finished detailing his plans for bathroom remodeling, window replacement, and landscaping. "And there's one other change that will make this house perfect." His eyes locked with hers across the table. After a long silence, he looked away. "But we'll talk about that some other time."

Perhaps in Paris? Or would it always be another time, another place with Bram? Val knew he was capable of making quick decisions. He'd chalked up his success with technical start-ups to seizing the moment when the market was ready for an innovation. But he put off making personal decisions, scarred by the engagement he'd drifted into and then ended a few days before the wedding. He'd never talked about what had gone sour in his relationship, but Val could tell the experience had left him commitment-phobic. She thought about the Melgrems' marriage and wondered if Bram had a checklist or should have had one before getting engaged.

She told him what Chatty had said about the Melgrems' relationship, Leeann's checklist for her ideal spouse, and Ron's simple criterion—money. "Chatty heard about the checklist from Leeann's longtime friend. At first, it struck me as peculiar to have a shopping list for a mate, but then I decided we all have ideas about what our mate should be like. In a way, we internalize our checklists. What do you think?"

Bram pushed the remaining rigatoni around his plate before answering. "You can start out with ideas about the perfect mate, but you can fall in love with someone who's nothing like the model in your mind. Or you find a person who meets your standards and realize later that your standards are wrong." He put his fork down. "That's when checkboxes turn into red flags."

Those flags could give Val hints about where their relationship was going. "What are your red flags?"

"Some of my ex-fiancée's dominant traits. I was attracted to Vanessa because she was beautiful, smart, and hardworking. But it took me a while to notice the negative side of those qualities. She spent a lot of time on her face and hair. Otherwise, she never did anything except work. She ate fast food because she was always in a hurry, and then she'd binge on salads to make up for the calories from the fast food. She was no fun to eat with."

Val didn't eat like his ex-fiancée, but she did work a lot. Managing a café, moonlighting as a caterer, and helping Granddad with his cookbook and the house kept her busy. Did Bram see her as a workaholic too?

"You make time for other things besides work," he said as if he'd read her thoughts. "You bike with me, play tennis with your friends, solve murders, and now you have a starring role in your theatrical debut."

Val laughed. "I have a lot of lines to read, though I wouldn't say I'm the star."

"I think of you as the star." Bram finished off his wine. "My relationship with Vanessa taught me something I never before realized. Marrying someone hitches you to a family. Her family didn't like me. They wanted her to marry a doctor or a lawyer. No matter how successful I was as a tech entrepreneur, they'd never accept me." He grinned. "I didn't care much for them either."

"You're right. The family matters." That was one box Val could check on Bram's list. Her parents had taken to him the first time they met him when they visited Granddad at Christmas. She, Bram, his mother, and Granddad made a congenial multi-generational foursome.

Val thought about why Bram appealed to her. He wasn't nearly as handsome as Val's cheating ex-fiancé, but handsome had become a red flag for her, or at least a pink one. But, of course, she wasn't going to say that to Bram. His boy-next-door looks and personality appealed to her. Smart, cheerful, and dependable, he was always ready to help, not just his mother with her start-up business, but also the local firefighters and a group of seniors putting on a play. And he was there whenever Granddad needed a hand.

As they cleared the table, Val's phone chimed. Bethany was calling.

"I've got bad news, Val. Ryan has to leave town. He's going to Florida because his father had a heart attack, and his mother needs moral support."

"I'm sorry to hear that." As soon as the words came out of Val's mouth, Bram came over to her with a look of concern. She added, "I hope Ryan's father recovers quickly." She saw Bram relax.

Bethany said, "No word on that yet. I have to call Millicent. She can tell the others in the cast. We're halfway through our scheduled rehearsals. I doubt she'll find anyone who can get up to speed and fill in for Ryan. *The Mousetrap* is toast."

Val had mixed reactions to the news. Once she'd gotten over the pressure of the first rehearsal, she'd begun to enjoy being in the play. "Millicent doesn't have to call Bram. I'll let him know."

After hanging up, she told him about Ryan's trip to Florida. "I guess tomorrow's rehearsal is off." Granddad would be disappointed that Val wouldn't get the chance to eavesdrop on the Rilkes and Dernes before the rehearsal.

"We'll have a rehearsal. Millicent will either scare up someone to take Ryan's part or play the role herself." Bram finished loading the dishwasher and turned his winning smile on her. "Phone calls over. Kitchen cleaned up. Missions accomplished." He enveloped her in his arms. "Now, how about some dessert?"

One long kiss later, her blood was pumping in high gear. "I get the feeling that the cannoli will be our second dessert."

"If we get around to it at all."

Bram had been right that the show would go on. Millicent sent an email to the cast on Friday morning, saying that Ryan had been called away indefinitely on a family matter, that she was working on finding a substitute for him, and that the rehearsal would take place at three thirty as scheduled.

Val texted Bram and Bethany to ask them to arrive five minutes late for the rehearsal. The Rilkes and the Dernes would come early as usual. The extra minutes would give them more time to talk among themselves before the rehearsal and gave Val a chance to listen to their conversation.

Chief Yardley came into the café at ten. After she served him coffee and a cranberry scone, she told him why the spa director had hired Granddad to make sure no trouble occurred at the spa's open house.

When she finished, the chief held out his coffee mug for her to top it off. "Let me get this straight. The spa director got sick after drinking punch at the Village. A few days later, he received a tarot card in the mail. The following week, the ace of spades arrived. He saw them as threats and decided his punch had been tampered with. Someone forced his car off the road, but he didn't report that, the so-called threatening cards, or his suspicions about the punch to the police." The chief sipped his coffee. "He doesn't want the police at the spa's open house, so he hires your granddaddy to protect him there. What am I supposed to do?"

"You could send an officer in plain clothes to the open house." *Or go yourself.*

The chief brushed scone crumbs from his lap. "I don't have the manpower. Ryan's gone. Another officer's just had a baby. On Saturday nights at this time of year, the town is full of traffic and tourists. Accidents happen. Folks drink too much and get rowdy. I can't spare anyone to send to the open house. Just what do you expect to happen there?"

"I have no idea, but I overheard Millicent Rilke say she was going to the open house to look a killer in the eye. She didn't say who the killer was."

"Millicent Rilke." The chief groaned. "She has a

dramatic streak. '*Looking a killer in the eye*' doesn't suggest she'll take action."

"But a killer might not welcome her scrutiny and take action. Her sister, Cassandra, has hinted that someone at the spa murdered Jane."

"Hints don't make a murder case. The autopsy report isn't final yet. Her low blood oxygen suggests death by asphyxiation, but she didn't have the carbon monoxide level typical of fire victims. She might have been suffocated before the fire was set, but that's hard to prove. Whatever was used to cut off her oxygen supply was destroyed in the fire." The chief drank the rest of his coffee, put money on the eating bar, and stood up. "By the way, Jane's ex-husband is due back from South America today. I'll interview Mr. Witterby tonight or early tomorrow."

As the chief left the café, Val wondered if he'd hear anything useful from Jane's ex. After being divorced for several years, how much could he add to what the police already knew about her?

Chapter 17

Half an hour before the rehearsal was due to start, Val moved her car out of the driveway and parked it around the block so the Rilkes and the Dernes would have no reason to think she was in the house when they arrived. Granddad shooed her into the study and closed the blinds to block anyone on the street or the path to the house from seeing her. He also cracked open the door between the study and the sitting room.

While waiting for the early-bird cast members to arrive, Val printed recipes for various smoothies so she and Bethany would have them handy at the open house. Then she searched for information online about Nigel Derne. Not that she expected to find any mention of a CIA background. The only references she found were from recent years and related to his position on the county council. She couldn't rule out that he had indeed been an intelligence officer.

When the doorbell rang, she closed the search

window on the computer. She could hear Grand-dad, Millicent, and Cassandra talking in the sitting room.

"I'll be in the kitchen finishing up the snacks for tea," Granddad said. "Make yourself comfortable. If you need anything, give me a holler."

"I'll open the door for the others as they arrive," Cassandra said.

Though Val couldn't see into the sitting room, she pictured Millicent in Granddad's chair, leafing through her notes, and Cassandra scrutinizing the bookshelves, as they had before other rehearsals.

The doorbell rang again a few minutes later. She heard Nanette's and Nigel's voices when they went into the sitting room.

Millicent greeted them and added, "I haven't seen you two at the Village the last two days. Have you been away?"

Nanette said, "We visited my mother in Baltimore for her ninety-fifth birthday. We wanted her to move into the assisted-living part of the Village here, but her gerontologist says she'd find the change disruptive. He says people her age get disoriented when their surroundings change."

"She's happy where she is, Nanette," Nigel said. "That's what counts."

"Did you get to see your daughter in Baltimore?" Cassandra's words hung in the air for a while as if she'd asked an embarrassing question.

"Yes, we saw her, but sadly not our grandson."

Remembering how emotional Nanette had been the last time she'd talked about her grandson, Val pictured the older woman holding back tears and clinging to her husband.

Millicent broke the silence that followed Nanette's statement. "I hope you've changed your mind about going to the spa's open house."

"We have not." Nanette now sounded combative. "You want to confront a killer? That's your business—but remember what happened to Jane after she did that."

"We don't know who's responsible for Jane's death." Nigel's quiet, calm voice contrasted with his wife's.

His comment got a rise out of Cassandra. "But we know who belongs in jail right beside Doctor Lazarin."

Val jotted down *Lazarin*, her best guess at spelling the name she'd just heard. She missed the first part of Nigel's response and strained to hear the rest because his voice was so low.

"Grubber was just as guilty. But nothing we do now can put him in jail for what he did previously," Nigel said. "We'll keep an eye on him. If he starts dispensing painkillers, we'll tell the police. But he won't do anything illegal at the open house. Too many eyes and ears for him to risk it."

Had Nigel called the man *the grubber* or was *Grubber* a name? Val wondered if the grubber could be a spa staffer she hadn't met. If he was the criminal, why was Ron being harassed? She thunked her forehead. Duh. Maybe his surname was Grubber, a name someone might be willing to give up because of the word's negative meaning.

Nanette changed the subject, describing the three possible outfits she could wear for the play and asking Millicent which would work best.

Val tuned out and turned back to the computer.

She had no success finding a Ron Grubber. Either her guess was wrong or Ron had gone off the grid entirely. Then she tried a name that sounded like the one Cassandra had mentioned—Doctor Lazarin. That got results. Val didn't have time to sift through the hits from her search before Bethany and Bram arrived. She seized her best chance for slipping unseen into the sitting room while Millicent herded the other cast members into the dining room.

Val took her seat, mumbling an apology for being late, as Granddad came in from the kitchen.

Millicent remained standing as the others took their usual places around the table. "In Ryan's absence, I've found a young man with acting experience to take the part of the policeman. I talked to him on the phone and discovered he'd played that role in a college production of *The Mousetrap.* Since the lines will be familiar to him, he'll get up to speed quickly." She glanced at her watch. "He arranged to leave work at three. He should be here any minute."

As if on cue, the doorbell rang. Val hurried to the hall. When she opened the door, she was startled to see Patrick.

He looked taken aback too. "Ms. Curiosity! What are you doing here?"

"I live here. Excuse my curiosity, but what are *you* doing here?"

"Maybe I have the wrong address, but I'm supposed to rehearse for a play."

"This is the place." Did Millicent have any idea that her latest recruit worked at the spa?

When Val led Patrick to the dining room, Millicent shook his hand and gave him a script. "This is Patrick Parenna, everyone. Take the empty seat, Patrick, and we'll go around the table, introducing ourselves by our real names and the roles we're playing."

As he sat down at the other end of the table, Bram mouthed the word *spa* to Val and pointed with his thumb at Patrick. She nodded. Until now, Bram hadn't heard Patrick's full name, though Granddad knew it because she'd given him a list of the spa employees. He pretended ignorance, though, asking Patrick to repeat his surname.

During the introductions, Patrick gave no sign that he'd ever met any of the cast.

The way he read his lines impressed Val. He made a better stage policeman than Ryan, the real officer, and could probably play any role. Could Patrick be playing a role at the spa? Applying for a position unlike his previous one and giving a vague answer about how he'd learned of the spa job suggested he might have an ulterior motive for being there.

During the reading, Val noticed Cassandra scrutinizing him. Patrick couldn't be the criminal she'd said was at the spa or her sister and the Dernes would have reacted to him too. Val itched to find out why Cassandra was staring at him.

After the play reading, Millicent announced that Monday's rehearsal and later ones would be at the community theater in Treadwell, where their *Mousetrap* production would take place.

"What time will that be on Monday?" Patrick said.

"Seven p.m. sharp. Does that work for everyone?" After they all nodded, Millicent continued. "We'll need at least two more rehearsals after that. Monday isn't our official dress rehearsal, but I'd like you to put on whatever you're going to wear for the performance. Then if your clothing doesn't go well with what the others are wearing, you'll have time to come up with a different outfit. Patrick, if you have a few minutes, I'll explain the stage setup and answer any other questions you have."

While Millicent conferred with Patrick in the dining room, Nigel and Nanette slipped out, Bram left for the bookstore, always busy on Friday evenings, and Bethany hurried to a bridal shower for her school's assistant principal.

Val approached Cassandra, who'd stepped into the hall to use her eye drops. "I noticed you watching Patrick during the rehearsal. Have you met him before?"

Cassandra shook her head. "He reminds me of someone, but I can't figure out who."

Val gave that response a fifty-fifty chance of being true. She'd noticed how nervous Cassandra was when withholding information, but now she seemed calm and matter-of-fact. "Maybe you've seen an actor who resembles Patrick."

Cassandra shrugged. "He looks like he could be a movie star. I might have seen him in a play in Baltimore."

"He lived in the Washington area before moving here. If he's really into acting, it's odd that he would take a job here instead of a city where more plays are produced." *Enough beating around the bush, Val.* "Patrick works at the spa."

Cassandra gaped at her. "I don't think Millicent

asked him where he worked. She was desperate to replace Ryan. How do you know Patrick?"

"I talked to him about where to set up my smoothie bar at the open house. He manages the spa's physical plant."

"Millicent and I will be at the open house. I've never had a smoothie, but I might try one from your booth."

With a vision of Cassandra pouring eye drops into a smoothie, Val said, "Bethany will be helping me at the booth. Granddad and Bram are going to the open house too." *In other words, Cassandra, many eyes will be on you.* "I'll tell them to look for you there."

"Please do."

After Patrick and the sisters left, Val joined Granddad in the kitchen. She reported what she'd overheard the Rilkes and the Dernes say before the rehearsal and handed him the paper where she'd jotted down the names they'd mentioned.

Granddad peered at it. "I'll go see if I can find these guys online."

"I got some hits when I searched for a doctor named Luварin. It might take you a while to go through them. Would you like me to start dinner?"

"Yup. I bought some chicken. I was planning to grill it."

Val checked the vegetables that were in the fridge and decided to make a dinner with Caribbean flavor—jerk chicken, baked sweet potatoes, greens, and slaw. She put the potatoes in the oven, made a marinade for the chicken, and chopped the cabbage.

By the time Granddad returned to the kitchen,

the potatoes were almost ready, and she'd turned on the gas grill to preheat it. "What did you find out about Lazarin and Grubber?"

"A bunch. I'll tell you after I grill the chicken. I'm hungry." He went out to the backyard.

Once they were seated at the kitchen table, Granddad dove into his dinner. "I like the chicken. It has a good flavor, something different. How many ingredients?"

"You'll have no trouble getting them down to five." She waited until the edge was off his appetite before prompting him to tell her what he'd found online.

He put down his fork. "Doctor Lazarin is notorious. He had a small practice in Baltimore, specializing in pain management. He was charged with overprescribing and dispensing drugs like oxycodone, morphine, and other opioids."

Val focused on the first drug—oxycodone. "The note Howard Docksteiner left in the freezer mentioned 'oxy' as something he needed for pain, though he expected it would kill him. Maybe he'd gotten his prescriptions from Lazarin."

"The case against him got tons of publicity in Baltimore. It took almost a year to go to trial. There were a lot of witnesses on both sides. Some folks testified in his favor. They said he helped them get through terrible pain. Others said he got them addicted, and they're still struggling with that. Two people with relatives who died from an overdose blamed Lazarin."

"And the verdict was . . . ?" Val prompted.

"Guilty. He was sentenced to seven years. He must still be serving it."

Val forked a piece of chicken. "Did you come across the names of any witnesses against him?"

"They came up in an article that summarized the case. The ones who talked about the harm Lazarin did weren't named, but his PA—physician's assistant—was. Patients would meet with the doctor the first few times and get a treatment plan. After that, they'd have follow-ups with the assistant, whose name was . . ." Granddad paused, leaving Val hanging as he sometimes did for dramatic effect. Then he continued. "Aaron Grubber."

Val sat bolt upright in her chair. "*Ron* is a nickname for *Aaron*. What role did Aaron Grubber play in the trial?"

"Lazarin's defense was that Grubber did it. He got patients hooked on pain meds by increasing the number or strength of the pills. Grubber testified that he consulted Lazarin when a patient needed more painkillers and that he just followed the doctor's orders. The jury believed him."

"Did you find any photos of Grubber?"

"Nah. There's not much online about him. There are some photos of Lazarin, including one with his defense team in front of the courthouse, but I didn't have time to look at them."

"I'll check them out after dinner." Val picked up her wineglass. "If Ron Melgrem is Aaron Grubber, he got off for the crime that put Lazarin in jail—overprescribing painkillers and addicting patients to them. Millicent might blame him for her husband's addiction and the painkillers that he was sure would kill him. Maybe she was a witness against him."

"I don't know, but once the sisters found out

that Grubber was in this area, I can see them trying to make him pay for what he did. If Jane told
them he was here, what did she have to do with
Lazarin and Grubber? I couldn't find anything online about a Jane Johnson connected with Lazarin
or Grubber."

Val sipped her wine. "That's just one of the
loose ends we have to tie up. The other one is how
Nigel and Nanette fit into the story. I'm going to
try to talk to Nigel tomorrow afternoon at the Village."

"Shouldn't you be getting ready for the open
house then?"

"The café closes early on weekends. I can fit in a
quick trip to the Village."

After dinner was over, Val searched for images
of Doctor Lazarin online. A photo in front of the
courthouse showed him to be a good-looking,
middle-aged man with receding dark hair. The
older man next to him, speaking into a microphone held by a reporter, was identified as Lazarin's lawyer. Both of them were in suits. Behind
them was an unidentified younger man with long
dark hair hanging down like curtains on either
side of his face. Because his morose expression resembled the doctor's, Val presumed the younger
man was related to the doctor.

She found another photo of the doctor, this
time with his lawyers flanking him. They and a
crowd of people were in front of the courthouse,
awaiting a verdict in the case. Val enlarged the
image and searched for the younger man in the
crowd. No luck, but a tall older man caught her

eye. He reminded her of Nigel, but he was so far back in the photo that she couldn't be sure.

Assuming she got to talk to Nigel at the Village tomorrow, should she bring up Lazarin and Grubber? Nigel might give her straighter answers than the Rilke sisters, but he could be more cunning and lead her astray.

Chapter 18

At noon on Saturday, Val was still pondering how to approach Nigel, when a big man carrying a gym bag came into the café. Fiftyish with a slight paunch, he had an owlish look. His large, round eyes and thick brows that just missed meeting over his nose were distinctive enough that Val was sure she'd never seen him before. He must be a new member. He looked around the café as though searching for a table. The only free one was in the corner, a table for six that Val preferred to save for a group.

"Come on in. The café's open for another hour. You're welcome to sit at the eating bar."

"Thanks. I'll do that." He dropped his bag on the floor and sat at the counter facing Val's food prep area.

She smiled at him. "What can I get you?"

"Something wet to start with. Tonic with lime and ice."

As she delivered his drink, she glanced at the blue,

yellow, red, and black bird on his T-shirt. Exotic-looking, probably tropical. Could this be Jane's birder ex-husband who'd come to Bayport to talk to the chief?

Val pointed to his T-shirt. "Is that a South American bird?"

The man looked at her with new interest. "Sure is. A paradise tanager. Only found in the Amazon Basin. I just got back from Ecuador. I wouldn't leave until I saw one, and I finally did." He smiled and sipped some tonic. "Unfortunately, I never saw a great potoo. They're hard to spot since they look like tree bark. You a birder?"

Possible answers raced through Val's brain before she said, "Who doesn't love birds? The most colorful ones I've seen around here are a scarlet tanager and a Baltimore oriole, but I wouldn't call myself a birder. South America was a lucky guess." The faster Val steered the conversation away from birds, the better. "I take it you're new here. I'm Val Deniston."

"Wally Witterby. Glad to meet you."

The chief had called Jane's ex Mr. Witterby. Before Val could think of how to get Wally talking about his ex, he'd downed half his drink and reached into his gym bag for a flask. He unscrewed it and topped off his tonic with a clear liquid. Was he making a gin tonic or a vodka tonic?

She pretended not to notice. She might as well nudge the conversation where she wanted it to go. "Are you related to Jane Johnson? Someone told me she was married to a man with a name that sounds like yours. If so, I'm sorry for your loss."

He shrugged. "Jane Witterby was my *ex*-wife. I

lost her a few years ago. I'm over it now." He guz-zled his drink.

Surveying the tables in the café, Val saw no cus-tomers ready for a check. She turned back to Wally. "I didn't know Jane well, but anyone who did thought highly of her. She contributed a lot to the community here with her volunteer work."

"She was like that in Baltimore too." Wally took another quaff. "She liked to think she was a good person. Mostly she was, except when it came to her marriage vows."

People who said that about their spouses usually meant they'd cheated, but maybe Wally consid-ered divorce a breach of vows. "I'm not married, but I can understand how a couple might grow apart after a while. They develop new interests not shared by the other person."

Wally laughed, more in sarcasm than amuse-ment. "She sure had a new interest I didn't share. A guy she worked with." He picked up his drink. "She kept my name for a couple of years after our divorce. I'm not sure why, unless she thought we'd get together again. Ha."

Val remembered the Rilkes saying that Jane had divorced her husband, not vice versa. Maybe he was claiming Jane had cheated to ease the pain of her ending their marriage because of his bird mania. Or maybe he'd cheated on her.

He downed the rest of his drink, held up the glass, and rattled the ice that remained in it. "I'd like a refill with a new slice of lime, but just give me half a glass of tonic."

Convinced he would reach for his flask again,

Val had qualms about refilling his glass, but she didn't want him to walk away yet. He knew more about Jane than anyone around Bayport, though he wasn't an unbiased source. And as a big man, he could probably hold more alcohol than he'd drunk so far, especially if he had some food in him.

She pointed to the menu on the blackboard. "Can I get you something to eat?"

He glanced at the board. "I'll take a ham and cheese on a baguette, mustard on the side."

Val made his sandwich and poured him more tonic than he'd wanted. She set his lunch on the eating bar. "You know, arsons are so rare around here that no one can figure out why an arsonist targeted Jane's house. Do you know of anyone who might have had a grudge against her?" *Besides you?*

"For sure." Wally pulled out his flask. "She was a whistleblower, turned in the doctor she worked for, a pain doctor. He went to jail for overprescribing narcotics."

Val heart sped up. Wally had just given her the missing link, the connection between Jane and Lazarin. Before Val got carried away, she'd better make sure there wasn't another jailed pain doctor in Baltimore. "I remember reading about that case. The doctor had an unusual name. Lazarus or something like that." She deliberately changed the final syllable so she wouldn't seem too knowledgeable.

"Lazarin," he corrected. "That's him."

After blowing the whistle on the doctor, Jane

must have been surprised to find his assistant, Aaron Grubber aka Ron Melgrem, running a spa. "What was Jane's job in Doctor Lazarin's office?"

"She handled insurance claims and billing. She got wind of the Feds looking into his records." Wally topped off his tonic from his flask. "His physician's assistant was also authorized to write prescriptions. He was the guy she was sleeping with."

Ron had been Jane's lover! Val looked down so Wally wouldn't see her surprise.

He stirred his drink and continued. "The PA was investigated for the opioids he prescribed, but he got immunity for testifying against the doctor. Jane had tipped him off so he could cover his tracks."

Val gripped the edge of the counter, her brain spinning. Wally had certainly tarnished Saint Jane's halo. Aware that he was peering at what must be her dazed expression, Val excused herself to wait on other customers.

Circulating around the bistro tables, Val thought about how Jane's sudden appearance would have affected Ron. He'd wiped out his history and assumed a new identity. Then along comes a former lover who not only knows all, but might tell all to Ron's newly acquired rich wife.

By the time Val returned to the counter, Wally had eaten most of his sandwich. He took a long swig of his drink. "I might not have sounded like it, but I'm really sorry Jane died in such a terrible way. She'd already gotten her comeuppance for cheating on me. Friends of ours told me that her

Prince Charming vanished as soon as Lazarin's trial was over."

So Jane was a woman scorned. Whatever rage or humiliation she felt must have been matched by Ron's anger at her. Though she'd saved him from jail, her whistleblowing had ended his career and driven him underground. No doctor would hire a scandal-tainted assistant. What's more, if Ron had kept his past a secret from his new wife, Jane was a threat. Fury combined with fear made a powerful motive for murder.

Wally picked up one of the flyers about the spa's open house. "Hey, this is tonight. Free drinks and food. I hope it's not too late to RSVP."

What would happen when Jane's ex-husband and her ex-lover came face-to-face? Nothing good. "I think it's too late to register for the open house," Val said as Chatty approached the counter.

"No, it's not." Chatty perched on the stool next to Wally and introduced herself as a spa employee.

He gave her a toothy smile, took off his glasses, and stammered, "I'm Wally. Nice meeting you, Chatty."

"I hope you'll come tonight. Val and I will both be at the open house. She's making smoothies, and I'm giving mini-massages."

Wally couldn't have looked happier if he'd just spotted a great potoo. "I wouldn't miss the open house for anything. How do I get there?"

Val left Chatty to give him directions and took checks to the tables where customers had finished eating. By the time she'd run the credit cards and cleared the tables, she'd convinced herself that

Wally wouldn't recognize Jane's former lover. Ron had a new name and a changed appearance. Jane had penetrated his disguise, but Wally had seen far less of the man, if he'd ever met him at all.

Wally paid Val in cash and, as he put his wallet away, she remembered Jane's neighbors saying that a man had visited her shortly after she moved in. "Wally, were you ever in Jane's house here?"

He nodded. "Right after she bought the place. I came because she had to sign papers so we could liquidate our stock holdings. Then I helped her shift some furniture around. I also made it clear we had no future together and she should go back to using her maiden name."

One mystery solved, though a minor one. The man Jane's neighbors had seen visiting her hadn't been her lover, but her ex.

Wally had given Val a new perspective on his ex. Though Jane had probably condemned Ron as a criminal to the Rilkes and the Dernes, she wouldn't have told them about her romantic history with him. And Val wouldn't tell them either, especially not Nigel. If she hoped to get any information from him, she'd better not even hint that Jane wasn't as perfect as he thought.

Chapter 19

After the guard at the retirement village raised the gate for Val, she drove along a winding street flanked by cottages. The small, one-story houses painted in shades of gray and brown had the same basic design, but the residents had stamped their personalities on the front yards. Some had picket fences and others low shrubs. A few houses had pocket-sized lawns with flower or rock gardens.

Bethany had told her Nigel and Nanette lived in a cottage rather than an apartment in the Village's main building. Their place was in the first set of cottages beyond the five-story building. Val parked in the lot in front of it and took the sidewalk to the cottages.

She spotted Nigel turning over the soil in a bed near the driveway, where his large sedan was parked. With hanging plants, vines, and a variety of shrubs, the yard resembled a miniature botanical garden. Two wrought-iron chairs in the center made it a peaceful place to sit.

Val called out to him as she approached. "Hi, Nigel."

He looked up. "Hello, Val. What brings you to the Village?"

"Bethany told me the grounds here are worth a visit. And it's a lovely spring day for a walk. Your garden is amazing. I bet it keeps you busy."

"Yes, but it gives me great satisfaction to grow things." He pulled a handkerchief from the pocket of his cargo pants and wiped his brow.

"I just got our tomato plants in the ground. Are you going to plant vegetables or flowers in that bed?"

"We grow vegetables behind the house. Nanette wants only ornamentals in front." He planted his shovel in the dirt and pointed to the chairs. "Have a seat. Can I get you anything to drink?"

"I'm fine, thanks." Once they were both seated, she said, "These are such charming cottages. You even have a place for your car just a few steps from the door." Val glanced at his dark sedan. "That reminds me . . . I was going to tell you something after our rehearsal yesterday, but I forgot. I was talking to Jane's next-door neighbors the other day. They said they saw your car go past her house not long before the fire started." *Or a similar sedan.*

He was taken aback. "I never met her neighbors. How would they recognize my car?"

"They have a view of Jane's driveway from their windows. They probably noticed your car when you parked there for *Mousetrap* rehearsals."

He wiped his hands on his handkerchief. "Come

to think of it, I *was* on Horseshoe Lane last Saturday evening. After I filled up at the Bayport gas station, I was listening to the news in the car, got distracted, and took a wrong turn. The country roads around here look much the same. I found a place to make a U-turn and went back to the main road."

That tallied with what Jane's neighbor had said about the sedan she'd seen. "The neighbors also saw a silver compact car in Jane's driveway. And it wasn't Jane's car. Did you see it?"

Nigel turned rigid. "Not in her driveway. The silver compact I saw was in a ditch on the side of the road. I drove by it."

Val immediately thought of Ron's story about being forced off the road. He didn't have a compact car, but if he was planning to kill Jane and set her house on fire, he wouldn't drive his distinctive red sports car. He'd rent a car that looked like a lot of others. "Did you happen to see who was in the silver car?"

"No. At first, I assumed the driver had run out of gas and left it. After I turned around to go back to the main drag, I saw the car in the same spot. It was moving, maneuvering to get back on the asphalt. It had tinted windows, so I didn't see who was driving it. What's your interest in that car?"

"Jane's neighbors roused my curiosity. They speculated the arsonist might have been in that car. It's too bad you didn't see who it was."

Nigel gazed at the patch of grass around his chair, leaned down, and wrenched a tuft of chickweed from it. "Weeds are evil. As Christie wrote, evil has to be fought, or we go down in darkness."

Val believed he would fight evil, but like beauty, evil was in the eye of the beholder. She wasn't sure what Nigel considered evil. "Besides the silver compact, did you notice any other cars near Jane's house the night she died?" When he shook his head, Val went on. "I met her husband at the café where I work this morning. He'd just returned from South America. I asked if he could think of anyone who would want to harm Jane. He said she had been a whistleblower for a doctor she worked for and might have made some enemies."

"It doesn't surprise me she was a whistleblower. She'd do what was right, even at her own expense. That's the kind of person she was." Nigel got out of the chair. "Excuse me. I need to finish preparing that bed before Nanette returns from petting dogs. She has seedlings to plant today."

"Bethany brought her dog to the Village pet-a-pet today. Such a sweet spaniel." Val stood up. "Thanks for sharing your garden with me, Nigel. See you at Monday's rehearsal."

She left convinced that Nigel hadn't told her the whole truth. He'd admitted driving near Jane's house last Saturday, probably because he thought someone had reported his car being there. Val didn't believe for a minute that he'd taken the wrong turn onto Jane's road. He must have had a reason for being there. Jane's neighbor had seen a sedan like his drive by, but that was before the fire started. They'd seen a silver compact in her driveway closer to the time when the fire broke out. Why had talking about the compact car in the ditch made him so tense?

The answer came to her in a flash—Nigel might have forced that car into a ditch, either accidentally or intentionally. But proving it would be impossible unless he admitted it, which wasn't likely.

Granddad was in the study, staring at the computer, when Val returned home.

She interrupted him. "Jane's ex-husband, Wally Witterby, came to the café this morning and revealed a lot we didn't know about her. Come to the kitchen and I'll tell you what he said. I'm going to make smoothies for my starter supply at the booth. You can cut up the fruit and vegetables."

"Sure. As long as I get to sample the smoothies." He followed her into the kitchen. "And I have some news too."

Val put the ingredients for four different types of smoothies on the counter—two with fruit and two with vegetables. As Granddad cut the tops off strawberries and peeled the mangos, she filled him in on her conversation with Wally that morning.

Granddad gaped when she told him about Jane's affair with Aaron Grubber and how she'd alerted him to an impending investigation. "That doesn't sound like the Jane I met."

"Who is the real Jane? I've been wondering that ever since the fire. The portrait of perfection her friends created never rang true to me."

"Her ex-husband is peeved. He has a reason to diss her. You believe everything he said?"

"He might be lying about which of them asked

for a divorce, but I can't see any reason for him to make up the rest of it. He could slam her without such an elaborate story." Val cut a banana she'd frozen that morning into four chunks and put it in the blender. "Wally is going to the open house tonight. He probably won't recognize Ron, but if he does, be prepared for unscheduled fireworks."

"You think he has a violent streak?"

"No. I meant verbal fireworks." Val added strawberries to the blender. "I don't judge Jane harshly for having an affair when her husband kept flying off to count as many birds as he could in a year. She fell in love and did what she could to protect Grubber, but he wasn't as good to her. After he testified, he disappeared."

"And turned up here a few years later as Ron Melgrem. It makes sense that Jane wouldn't realize before her job interview that her former lover was going to conduct it. But wouldn't he have seen her name and résumé before she came in?"

Val shook her head. "I doubt Jane would put on her résumé that she worked for the disgraced Doctor Lazarin. Her name wouldn't have told Ron anything. She went back to using her birth name when her divorce was final, but Ron had skipped town by then." Val started the blender and let it whir until its contents looked liquefied.

"Must have been a tense job interview, Jane spitting mad because he cut out after she saved his patootie, and him worrying she'd rat on him to his wife." Granddad took a spoon and helped himself to a taste of the strawberry-banana smoothie. He nodded his approval. "Ron probably gave Leeann a sob story about how his reputation was ruined 'cause he worked for a crooked doctor, but Jane knew he was just as guilty as the doctor."

Val poured the smoothie into a pitcher and snapped its lid on. "The day after the interview, she told the Rilkes and the Dernes that Ron had gotten away with a crime. From then on, he was harassed. Nigel might have been involved in targeting Ron." Val washed out the blender for the next smoothie and summarized her conversation with Nigel. "He admitted driving near Jane's house on Saturday evening and seeing a silver compact car in a ditch. I think he ran that car off the road, maybe by accident or maybe because he believed Ron was in it."

Granddad looked up from quartering an apple. "Didn't you say that Ron doesn't have a car like that?"

"Yes. His red sports car is flashy, easily traced if anyone spotted it near Jane's house. He'd want to use a more common vehicle. He could have rented a silver compact, or better yet, borrowed Patrick's. A rental leaves a paper trail." Val put the clean blender on top of its base. "Patrick's bumper had a dent in it. He said he lent it to someone who was responsible for the damage and would pay for repairs. Probably Ron dented the car when he went off the road going to Jane's house."

Granddad was quick to shake his head. "You gotta question what an actor like Patrick says. It coulda been him on the road near Jane's house."

"Jane's neighbors saw a silver compact parked in Jane's driveway just before the fire started. It makes sense that Ron was in that car. He had a reason to kill Jane. But Patrick didn't."

"Don't bet on that. It took some digging online, but I found a link between him and Doctor Lazarin." Granddad scraped carrots for a vegetable smoothie. "I went on one of those ancestor sites today, looking for the family of Doctor Zachary Lazarin. The site only gives names of people who have died. I lucked out because Doctor Lazarin's father had the same name. The father died when his son was about ten. I read the father's obituary, which listed the survivors as his wife, Elvira Lazarin, and one son, Zachary Lazarin."

Val grated ginger for the veggie smoothie. "I thought you were going to tell me what you learned about Patrick."

"Hold your horses. It's coming. Once I checked out the Lazarin family, I searched everything that's online about Patrick Parenna. Most of the links related to his audio work. And he got a mention in short articles about *The Mousetrap* and other shows he was in when he was in college."

That told Val nothing she didn't already know. "Finished with the carrots?" When Granddad handed them to her, she dumped them into the blender, along with an apple, lemon juice, grated ginger, and a bit of honey.

Granddad continued. "I went through more search pages. When I ran out of hits for Patrick Parenna, other people with that last name showed up. I saw a name that rang a bell in an obituary listing. It was for Patrick's mother. Guess what her first name was."

Val could guess a long time before hitting on the right name. "I give up."

"Elvira. Not a common name. The obituary said Elvira Parenna was survived by two sons, Patrick Parenna and Zachary Lazarin."

Val's jaw dropped. "She married again after her first husband died. That makes Patrick the half brother of the doctor who's serving time." Val thought about the photo she'd found online of Doctor Lazarin and a younger man in the background. Though not much of his face was visible, she'd noticed the resemblance between the two men. "There's quite an age gap between the doctor and Patrick, almost two decades. His mother must have had her first son when she was really young."

"And she died young, in her fifties. Elvira's obituary listed Patrick's father as a survivor. But he didn't survive long. His obit appeared a week after his wife's. When I entered both parents' names in a search box, I found a newspaper article about a really bad accident. A tractor trailer rammed the car they were in. The wife was killed instantly, and her husband died from his injuries a week later."

Val's hand flew to her mouth. "That's terrible. Poor Patrick. When did this happen?"

"Twelve years ago. Based on when he graduated from college, he must have been around fifteen when he lost his parents. I did some more digging and couldn't find any aunts or uncles who could have taken him in. A grandmother on his father's side was still alive but elderly. My guess is that Patrick's half brother took him in and became his substitute father."

"Then Patrick's only relative went to jail." Val

sighed. What a sad family story. "I feel sorry for Patrick."

"So do I. His troubles give him a reason to take vengeance on Ron, whose testimony put the doctor behind bars. And Patrick had a motive to kill Jane, the whistleblower who brought the law down on his half brother."

Val took a moment to digest Granddad's revelations. She made an effort to keep her sympathy from interfering with her thinking. "Nigel saw a car like Patrick's in a ditch that went off the road on Horseshoe Lane near Jane's house last Saturday. Let's say Patrick was driving his own car on that night. How did it end up off the road?"

"He mighta lost control of it. Plotting to kill someone can take your mind off your driving. Or else, Nigel accidentally ran him off the road. He doesn't want to admit that because his insurance rate would go up."

"Ron told you his car was forced off the road after he gave a talk at the Village. Was Nigel responsible for that too?"

Granddad shrugged. "Maybe, but remember, Ron is paranoid. He's spooked by an ace of spades in the mail. Maybe he was speeding in his sports car, lost control, and wants to blame someone else. What's important is we have two suspects who had motives to get rid of Jane. Ron, to protect his marriage, and Patrick, to get revenge. Either of them could have been driving the silver car a neighbor saw in Jane's driveway the night of the fire."

"Those are possible motives. We have no reason to think Patrick recognized Jane as the whistleblower, and we don't know for sure that Jane was a threat to Ron. If she planned to tell his wife about the illegal prescriptions, why did Jane wait a week before she called for an appointment with Leeann?"

Granddad stroked his chin. "Maybe she didn't intend to out him to his wife, but wanted to size up her competition by going in for, say, a Botox treatment."

Val slapped her hand on the counter. "Botox! That's what I forgot to put on the timetable. Chatty said Leeann pitched a fit about Botox vials that had disappeared. That was on Tuesday, the first day she was seeing patients. She'd stocked the shelves the previous week."

"But why should that go into your timetable?"

"I want to track what happened at the spa and to the *Mousetrap* cast, including Jane, during the week before and after she was killed. I'm going to look up Botox online. While I do that, would you load up the coolers with the smoothies I've already made and the ingredients to make more." She put the fruits and vegetables for the smoothies on the counter. "Please pack the blender too. I borrowed the giant blender from the café, but I might need two if the smoothies are really popular."

Val left him in the kitchen and sat down at the computer in the study. She looked up "Botox" on the National Library of Medicine site and found out the drug is made from botulinum toxin, the same substance that causes botulism food poisoning. Doctors inject the toxin in small doses, not just to smooth wrinkles, but also to treat muscle spasms and chronic migraines. Val followed a link to an FDA warning that in rare cases Botox had spread beyond the injection site with fatal results.

What would happen if someone received a larger-than-recommended dose? Val looked up botulinum and learned that it's the world's most lethal poison. Depending on the concentration, a mere drop could paralyze the body, including the muscles used to breathe, leading to death by asphyxiation.

Val's pulse quickened. Jane had died of asphyxiation. Could she have been injected with the Botox stolen from Leeann's office? Val read more about the drug. The vials doctors use for wrinkle treatments contain Botox in dry form, which then needs to be reconstituted. Using less liquid would presumably make a more concentrated version of the drug. A killer might also inject a large quantity of Botox from several vials.

Val returned to the kitchen and told Granddad her idea that Botox from the spa could have killed Jane. "Botox was stolen a day or two before she died."

Granddad closed the lid on one cooler. "The doctors look for injection sites on the skin when they do a postmortem, but with a burned body, they might not be able to find a spot. Who had access to the Botox?"

"Chatty said Leeann, Ron, and the cleaners had keys to the room where it was stored. The lock on the door was hard to engage, and Patrick put in a new one last week."

"He mighta made an extra key for himself when he did that." Granddad frowned. "I have to shuffle my team around. Someone needs to watch Patrick, and Bram's the only one who can keep up with him. I'll put Ned on Cassandra and Millicent. They won't move as fast as Patrick. I'm sticking close to Ron. The only person we can't cover is Jane's ex. He's got a big beef with Ron. What does he look like?"

"An owl. Roundish body, brown hair, thick eyebrows, big glasses. An inch or so above average height and light on his feet. He might bluster, but he doesn't strike me as the dangerous type." It crossed Val's mind that she could be wrong about that. "If either you or Ned needs another set of eyes, call me. Bethany can manage the smoothie bar without me for a while."

"Are you sure one of you is enough to handle the crowd clamoring for smoothies?" Granddad's eyes twinkled, suggesting he didn't believe the demand would be high.

"Making smoothies to order would lead to lines of people waiting, but we're not doing that. We'll make them in batches, pour them into cups, and set out a few flavors at a time. Then we'll replenish them as needed." Val checked her watch. "I should leave here by four. That'll give me time to fix any problems with the booth setup before the guests arrive."

"I'll go along with you. I want to see the layout of the place before Bram and Ned arrive. They'll be there around twenty to five."

"I talked to the chief on Friday morning and suggested he send an officer to the open house to deal with any trouble. He said he couldn't spare anyone. Maybe after he hears who Patrick is and how Botox kills by asphyxiation, he might be more interested in the spa. I wonder if there's a test that will show whether Jane had botulinum poison in her system." Val paused. "The chief would listen to you sooner than me. The two of you have been good friends for years."

"I want it to stay that way. The last time we went to a baseball game, he told me in no uncertain terms that he didn't want me mixing in police matters. And my client doesn't want any police at the open house. That's why he hired me."

"Your client, who doesn't want the police around, is the most likely person to have killed Jane. Though Patrick is our latest suspect, Ron is still at the top of my list. He previously broke the law. Patrick has had a hard life, but we don't have any reason to think he's turned to crime."

"We've figured out just enough to tell we still don't know a heck of a lot about any of these people. We gotta be double sharp tonight."

Chapter 20

When Val pulled into the spa's lot, she parked next to the catering company van. Patrick was piling boxes from the van onto a platform hand truck. His clothes were appropriate for casual Friday in an office, khaki pants and a button-down shirt, instead of the jeans and T-shirt he'd worn when she'd previously seen him here and at the rehearsal. Either way, he looked clean-cut and hardworking. The way he broke out in songs with changed lyrics had struck her as odd, but she was willing to cut him some slack now that she knew how alone he must feel without family.

He waved to her. "I'll come back and wheel your stuff to the tent as soon as I drop off this haul. Flyers with today's schedule are there." He pointed to a metal stand holding a brochure box.

"I'm sure glad to see him with that pushcart, even if he is a suspect," Granddad said. "It would take us three trips to carry the blenders, the bags of ice, and the coolers to the tent. I'll get the stuff out of the trunk."

Val went over to the brochure box near the path leading to the garden. She took out a flyer for herself and Granddad. The open house would start with a Meet and Mingle in the garden at five thirty. Activities would take place in the spa lobby at various times—Dr. Melgrem's presentations on nonsurgical medical treatments for a more youthful appearance, Sabrine's on spa treatments, and guided tours of the spa building. At the final event, a brief talk by Ron Melgrem at eight o'clock, five spa gift certificates would be awarded to members of the audience.

Granddad joined Val and scanned the schedule. "I hope this shindig won't last longer than a few hours. I'll be stuck here until everyone leaves after Ron's closing remarks and the prize drawing. You'll be stuck too since we came in one car."

"I don't mind waiting. We might finish around the same time if Ron will keep his talk short. The food tent is supposed to close at eight. Once it empties out, packing the leftovers and the blenders won't take more than fifteen minutes."

Patrick returned and loaded up the hand truck with Val's supplies. She'd planned to avoid him so he wouldn't sense a change in her attitude.

But he seemed to be waiting for her. "Come along and I'll show you where your smoothie bar will be." They took the path leading to the building and the tent on the lawn, Granddad following at a slower pace. "I found a heavy utility cart that you can use for your blenders. It has a shelf under it for storing ingredients."

"I appreciate that." Knowing he'd think silence from Ms. Curiosity odd, Val tried to make small talk. "I read the program for the open house. There's a lot going on, but I didn't see your name listed. Do you have a role to play?" *Aside from hiding your connection to the doctor Ron helped put in jail.*

"My job doesn't rate a credit in the playbill. I'll be on call to deal with any logistical or technical problems that come up."

And Bram would be watching him. "Hopefully, everything will run smoothly."

"If it does, I'll alternate with Sabrine giving tours." He pushed the hand truck across the lawn toward the tent.

Val was impressed with how festive the grounds looked. Soft spotlights illuminated the azaleas with their flowers in colors from deep pink to white. Helium balloons were tied to the tables and chairs on the lawn near the tent, the fountain, and the building. The balloons swayed in the light breeze, as if in rhythm with the soft new age music coming from loudspeakers around the property. "Great staging, Patrick. You're fortunate the weather cooperated." Warmer than-average temperatures for April meant the spa's visitors would be comfortable sitting outside in sweaters or light jackets.

"Rain's in the forecast, but not until after the open house ends." Patrick led Val to where he'd set up a spot for her to serve smoothies, midway down the longer side of the tent. "The table is adjustable. I set it up at bar height, but if you want it lowered, I can change it."

"It's perfect as is. Thanks for your help. My

grandfather and I can take it from here." Though Granddad still hadn't come into the tent.

"If I get some free time, I'll come by for a smoothie." Patrick skirted around the bistro tables and chairs in the center of the tent.

Val estimated the tent to be twenty by forty feet with tables in the middle that could seat about fifty people. Most of the hundred-plus visitors Ron expected would have to sit outside. She judged she could fit five different smoothie flavors, ten cups of each, on the bar surface. She had room to maneuver between the table and the utility cart, which was up against the side of the tent. An extension cord rested on the cart so she could plug in the blenders.

The caterers had set up their food on the opposite side of the tent. They'd pushed four tables together end to end and covered them with white tablecloths that reached the ground. Val moved closer to the tables to check out the food. There were platters with small sandwiches and bite-sized tortilla rollups, vegetable and fruit trays, and mini-desserts and cookies on tiered dessert stands. Near the entrance to the tent was a table with coffee, iced tea, water, and lemonade.

Granddad came in. "I scouted all the outdoor areas. The lighting's good everywhere except in the wooded area between the parking lot and the lawn."

He helped Val unpack the fruit and the blenders and set them on the utility cart. Then he left to meet Bram and Ned in the parking lot and make final plans for watching Ron, Patrick, and the Rilke sisters.

When Bethany came into the tent, she helped Val pour the smoothies from the pitchers into cups and arrange them on the bar. Val set out the name tags she'd made to identify the flavors.

Leeann stopped by the bar at five fifteen. She wanted to know the ingredients in each of the smoothies and to sample them. She was most enthusiastic about the mango one. Leeann found the strawberry, piña colada, and carrot and apple smoothies acceptable, but she didn't care for the Greek salad smoothie. Val promised to tweak the recipe when she made the next batch of it. Leeann told her not to bother because tweaking wouldn't save it.

As Leeann left, Bethany said in an undertone, "Just 'cause it's not to her taste doesn't mean other people won't like it."

The first hour of the open house passed quickly as Val and Bethany made smoothies that spa visitors snapped up, including the Greek salad one. Then Bethany and Val took turns visiting the caterer's buffet.

Halfway through the open house, Val's phone dinged with a message from Granddad. *Ron's going into the tent. Can you stay on him? I need a break.*

She texted him that she would. She spotted Ron just inside the tent opening. She'd seen him work the tent during the first hour of the open house. All smiles, he'd greeted and shaken hands with the spa visitors as they came in. Then he popped around to schmooze with groups of them, giving Granddad a chance to graze at the buffet. Ron looked less buoyant on this visit to the tent, and he wasn't making the rounds.

He spoke briefly with the head of the catering crew and then came up to the smoothie bar. "How's it going, Val?"

"Good. We've had a lot of customers coming back for seconds or to try a new flavor. Are you pleased with the turnout?"

"We have even more people than I expected." Yet he didn't seem elated. He fingered his beard and surveyed the smoothies on display. "Let's see what we have here. The orange one looks like it has carrots in it, not my favorite. What's in the pink one?"

"Strawberries and bananas."

"That's more like it." He took two cups of them. "See you later."

Val hoped he would sit down at a table inside the tent, but instead he walked out. She turned to Bethany. "Would you hold down the fort for a while?"

Bethany nodded, and Val hurried to keep Ron in sight as Granddad had requested. Her phone rang.

Granddad's friend, Ned, was calling. "I need backup, Val. Cassandra and Millicent went separate ways. I don't know which of them to follow."

"Where are they?"

"Cassandra is wandering around, checking out the flowers edging the lawn. She's near the wooded path to the parking lot. Millicent went toward the other side of the lawn near the patio and fountain."

"Hold on, Ned." Val looked around and saw Millicent in her red jacket at a table on the patio. "I have Millicent in my sights. Can you see Cassandra?"

"Sure can. I'll stay near her." Ned hung up.

Val hoped Granddad would return soon so she wouldn't have to keep track of two people at once. If Ron went inside the building, she'd have to follow him and leave Millicent on her own. She lost sight of him as he walked around a crowd of people outside the tent, but then he reappeared near the patio. Val's problem was solved when Ron sat down at the table across from Millicent.

Unfortunately, he also blocked Val's view of her. Val maneuvered around the crowd until she could see both of their profiles. They appeared to be having a serious conversation, each of them with a smoothie on the table near them, but neither of them drinking it.

A shriek came from the other side of the property. "Snake!" a woman yelled. "Oh, my God, it's a copperhead!"

As the word *snake* echoed around the groups on the lawn, Ron jumped up and ran around the fountain toward the area where the shriek originated. Val was about to follow him when Millicent slid her smoothie across the table and exchanged it for the one that had been in front of Ron.

Val couldn't believe what she'd just seen. Had Millicent slipped something into her own smoothie before swapping it for Ron's? Val could do nothing about a poisonous snake, but she could deal with a potentially poisonous smoothie.

She swooped down on the table where the drinks sat. "Hi, Millicent. These are the smoothies

Ron just picked up, right?" She didn't wait for a reply, but grabbed both cups. "Sorry about this. There was something wrong with this batch. A missing ingredient. I'll get you some new smoothies."

"Don't bother bringing me another. Too many calories. I'll just drink water." Millicent reached into a tote bag and took out an unopened bottle of spring water.

Val hurried in the direction Ron had gone. She dumped the smoothies in the first trash container she saw. Then she joined the cluster of people gathered where the lawn bordered a wooded area.

Granddad came up to Val. "Is this where the snake in the garden turned up? Ned called to tell me about it."

"I heard a shriek. I couldn't tell where it came from. I didn't know there were copperheads in this area."

"I haven't seen a copperhead for years. Black snakes are pretty common."

Val shuddered. "I'd just as soon not see any of them."

Ron emerged from the trees, flanked by two men. "We've searched the area and found no snakes. This was definitely a false alarm." He pointed to the men standing next to him. "I want to thank the volunteers who went snake-hunting with me. Now, everyone, please have something to eat and enjoy the rest of your visit."

Val fell into step next to Granddad, who was following Ron across the lawn at a discreet distance.

"Ned told me Cassandra was the one who yelled

snake," Granddad said. "She recovered quickly from her shock."

"Of course she did." Val had just figured out what the Rilke sisters had been up to. "There never was a snake. It was a diversionary tactic. Ron brought strawberry smoothies to the table for himself and Millicent. He sat down, and then Cassandra yelled. After he rushed to respond to the snake alarm, Millicent exchanged her smoothie for his."

Granddad was taken aback. "Did you see her put anything in her own smoothie before she switched it with Ron's?"

"No, I was watching Ron so I could tell you where to find him. But I made sure no one drank those smoothies. I dumped them."

Granddad frowned. "How did Millicent get Ron to sit down with her? The whole time I was watching him, I didn't see him go one-on-one with any guest at a table."

"She must have convinced him he couldn't ignore her, maybe telling him that she knew his real name. He wouldn't want her to bring up his past at the open house, so he agreed to talk to her."

"But how did she get him to bring two drinks to the table that looked exactly the same so she could pull off a switch?"

"Easy. He asks if she'd like a smoothie. She tells him she'll take whatever flavor he's having." Val thought more about the setup and came up with another scenario. "What puzzles me is why she had to switch the drinks. She could have tampered with *his* drink when he left the table to deal with the snake. I assume she'd told Cassandra what to do ahead of time and called her when Ron was coming back with the drinks."

As they rounded the fountain, Val saw Millicent and Ron at the same table where they'd sat earlier but without smoothies this time. Millicent was leaning toward him, grim-faced and talking. Without giving him a chance to say anything, she picked up her tote bag and left him alone at the table. He sat there, pale and rigid.

Val whispered to Granddad, "Millicent couldn't pull off the snake trick twice, but she might have another one up her sleeve. Ned asked me to keep track of her because he couldn't watch both sisters."

"She's walking in the direction where Cassandra was. They're probably meeting up." Granddad pulled out his phone. "I'll call Ned while I keep an eye on Ron."

"I'm going back to the smoothie bar in case Bethany needs help. If she doesn't, I'll search for Millicent."

The spa director squared his shoulders and headed toward the building, with Granddad following. He called Val just as she went inside the tent and told her not to bother searching for Millicent. Ned had both sisters in sight.

While Val was outside, Bethany had made more of the most popular smoothie flavors—blueberry, mango, and piña colada.

Val glanced at her watch. It was already after seven. "Why don't you take a break, Bethany? Tours of the spa start in front of the lobby. You'll get a chance to see Chatty's massage room."

"That'll be fun. When the tour's over, I'll come back so you can take a tour too."

As Bethany left, Val noticed Jane's ex, Wally Witterby, filling a plate from the caterer's buffet. He was dressed as he'd been that morning, in cargo pants and a bird T-shirt, but he'd added an accessory—a serious pair of binoculars hanging from his neck. He sat down at a small bistro table in the tent and tackled his food.

Fifteen minutes later, he greeted Val at the smoothie bar. "Hey, I'm glad to see a friendly face. I don't know anybody here except you and Chatty."

"Did you get your mini massage from her?" He gave her a thumbs-up. She pointed to his binoculars. "You brought those to look at the birds in the garden?"

"And the woods around it, where there are quite a few birds, but none I hadn't previously seen." He pointed to the cups. "What's on offer here?"

"Smoothies. The bright yellow one is mango, the purplish one is cucumber with blueberries, the white one's piña colada—"

"That's what I want," Wally said. "Does it have hard stuff in it, or is it non-alcoholic like the other drinks in this tent?"

"No alcohol, just fresh pineapple, pineapple juice, banana, coconut milk, and ice. Help yourself to one."

He moved the cup to the side of the bar, took out his flask, and splashed a colorless liquor into the smoothie. "This isn't rum, which belongs in a piña colada, but vodka never hurt any drink."

Was the vodka left over from this morning or had he refilled his flask since then?

As he sipped the drink, Millicent and Cassandra came up to the bar and studied the array of smoothies.

Val said, "I can tell you what's in each of them, if you'd like."

Wally held up his smoothie. "This one's delicious. I recommend the piña colada to you ladies." He showed them his flask. "And if you want to give a little kick to it, I'll share some of my private stash."

Millicent smiled. "Thank you, but we'll drink our smoothies straight."

"Speak for yourself," Cassandra reached for a cup of piña colada and held it out to Wally. "I'll take up this nice man's offer."

He poured some vodka into her cup. "I'm Wally Witterby, by the way."

The sisters gaped at him. They must have recognized his surname as Jane's married name.

Millicent's glance at the bird on his T-shirt would have eliminated any doubts she might have had about his identity. "You must be Jane Johnson's ex-husband. We miss her greatly. She was in our book club."

Cassandra added, "We also knew her in Baltimore. She told us you were an avid birder."

He stared into his cup. "I'm surprised she mentioned me at all."

"Of course she did." Millicent picked up a mango smoothie. "You were an important part of her life. Her death must have upset you. Come and sit down with us outside."

Behind his glasses, Wally's eyes glistened. "Thank you."

Val was sure those weren't crocodile tears. She watched Wally and the Rilke sisters leave the tent together. Would Wally reveal how Jane helped put her boss, the pain doctor, in jail and got his assistant, her lover, off scot-free? Probably. He hadn't held back those details when talking to Val this morning. She couldn't predict how the sisters would react. Would they brush off Wally's report as bogus or accept it as the truth? Though his story could taint their glowing image of Jane, they might still view her as a good woman who was seduced by a bad man. That would give the sisters another reason to give Ron a hard time.

Chapter 21

After Val replenished the smoothies on the bar, she slipped out of the tent and spotted Wally at a table with the Rilkes. The three of them appeared locked in a deep discussion. Val was sadly too far away to eavesdrop, and there was no way to move closer to their table and escape their notice. She returned to her post.

Bethany was smiling when she came back to the tent fifteen minutes later. "Patrick was leading the tour. I spent more time looking at him than at the rooms. By the way, I saw Bram in the lobby. I thought he was going on the tour too, but he'd already taken the previous one Patrick led. I suggested he come and have a smoothie. Did he?"

"Not yet." Val figured he was sticking close to Patrick, as Granddad had asked him to do. But Bram couldn't take more than one tour without making himself conspicuous. He was hanging around waiting for the tour to end. Then he'd go back to keeping Patrick in sight.

Bethany opened the coolers. "Looks like we have enough smoothies to last until the open house ends."

"I agree. Two of us don't have to stay here. If you want to cut out early, Granddad and I can manage packing up the leftovers."

"Before I go, you should take a break. Why don't you walk around the garden or go on the spa tour? When you come back, I'll head home."

"Thanks. I wouldn't mind some downtime." Before leaving the tent, Val stopped by the caterer's buffet and piled up sandwiches and cookies on a plate for Bram.

When she got outside the tent, she was surprised at how overcast the sky had become. The wind had picked up, and the balloons that had swayed gracefully in the breeze were now doing a mad dance. Patrick was picking up paper cups and plates that had blown off the tables onto the lawn. Bram was sitting in a lawn chair half-hidden by the shrubs near the fountain.

Val went up to him and held out the plate of food. "Here's a little something for you to munch on."

Bram stood up and hugged her. "This is just what I need, not only for my stomach, but as a change from doing nothing but watching Patrick. I don't know how detectives spend hours on surveillance. It's more boring to be a 'tec than a techie."

Val chuckled. "Better boring than exciting, at least from Granddad's point of view. He's grateful for your help. Bethany's minding the smoothie bar, and I'm going to catch the next spa tour."

"I'll see you later." He looked at his watch. "Less than an hour to go."

She left him munching on a sandwich, headed toward the building, and found the group waiting for the next tour. She counted two middle-aged couples, four women middle-aged or older, and three younger women. Sabrine arrived to lead the tour, taking them first to the Wellness Emporium, the name of the shop selling diet supplements, organic cosmetics, and homeopathic pills and potions for assorted ailments.

Sabrine handed out discount coupons for the emporium and led the group to the corridor where the spa treatment rooms were. A tall, older man with a thick, droopy mustache joined them.

Val thought there was something familiar about him, but she couldn't get a good look at him because he was always behind her. He was the last to go into Chatty's room, where she enumerated the various types of massages people could enjoy. Val turned around and caught a glimpse of him. Not much of his face was visible between his mustache, his tinted glasses, and the driver's cap that came down low on his forehead. He was among the first to go into the room next to Chatty's. Val could see only the gray hair on the back of his head. Like the others on the tour, he was facing Sabrine, who stood near the hot tub in the room.

"We expect to have an outdoor hot tub very soon," she said. "It will accommodate six or eight on a first-come, first-served basis. Anyone who books a day at the spa will be able to make use of it at no extra charge. Here we have a smaller hot tub that's more private. It can be reserved for half an hour by one person or two who know each other. There's a nominal fee for the use of it."

"I have a question," one of the older women on the tour said. "I find most hot tubs too hot, so I don't go in them. Since this tub is for private use, can I choose the temperature I want?"

"You can change the temperature on the thermostat here." Sabrine pointed out the mechanism on the side of the hot tub. "But I assure you this tub will not have very hot water. Our dermatologist, Dr. Melgrem, tells her patients that really hot water is bad for the skin. Our spa director has very sensitive skin. He checks the temperature of this hot tub by climbing into it himself every night. If there are no other questions, we'll continue the tour."

As the group followed Sabrine down the hall, Val lingered in the corridor, hoping to get a better look at the man with the mustache. When he finally emerged from the hot tub room, two minutes after the rest of the group had left, he turned back toward the lobby, in the opposite direction from the sauna room. Val barely glimpsed his face before he skipped out on the tour.

By the time she joined the group in the sauna room, Sabrine was winding down her talk about it. "The next room has our floatation tub in it. You can achieve complete weightlessness in the tub and feel as if you're floating in space. It's not up and running yet, so there's no point in my showing it to you. We'll visit the rooms farther down the hall, our salons offering hair, nail, and facial treatments."

Val decided she'd been gone long enough from the smoothie bar. When she went outside, she noticed Ron talking to the man with the big mustache. Granddad was sitting on a nearby lawn chair. She was glad he had a chance to get off his feet for a while.

She went up to him. "Does the man with Ron look familiar to you?"

Granddad studied the two men. "He reminds me of Sean Connery in *Murder on the Orient Express.*"

A hazy image of the actor popped into Val's mind. Yes, there was a superficial resemblance. "I thought he looked familiar, but not because of that movie."

As a couple approached Ron, the man with the mustache turned on his heel and headed for the path to the parking lot.

Val gave him a thirty-second head start. "Be right back." She speed-walked to the path and jogged along it. When she reached the parking lot, a car was pulling out onto the road at the far end. A large, dark car like Nigel's. Could he have come to the open house in a simple but effective disguise?

After retracing her steps, she told Granddad she suspected the Sean Connery look-alike was Nigel. Granddad couldn't come up with any reason for Nigel to hide his identity unless he was up to no good. But as far as Val could tell, the open house was going smoothly. Nothing bad had happened . . . yet.

At ten minutes before eight, Ron's voice came through the speakers that had been piping music outside. He spoke loudly enough that Val could hear him in the tent. He invited everyone to come to the lobby for the gift-certificate raffle and a champagne farewell. The twenty or so people snacking in the tent cleared out quickly.

Leeann came in and surveyed the buffet tables. "There's more food left than I expected. Lots of veggies, sandwiches, and rollups, but not many desserts."

The head of the catering team approached her. "What would you like me to do with the leftovers? We can put them in the coolers with dry ice, and you can eat them tomorrow."

As long as you don't mind soggy sandwiches. Val kept that thought to herself.

Patrick slipped into the tent and came over to the smoothie bar. "Glad I made it in time for a smoothie." He picked out two flavors and sauntered away.

"Are you sure the food won't spoil overnight?" Leeann said to the head caterer.

"Ten-pound bricks of dry ice last for twenty-four hours in the cooler. We picked up the ice five hours ago. If you'd rather not deal with it, we can also take the leftovers away and dump them."

"I don't believe in wasting food. Load it into coolers. I'll take it to the homeless shelter tomorrow morning." She reached into her wristlet wallet and gave him a check. "Here's a tip for your team."

"Thanks, ma'am. Keep us in mind for your next event."

Leeann crossed the tent to talk to Val. "Our guests seemed to really enjoy the smoothies. I appreciate your doing this on short notice. Here's a tip for you and your helper."

Val smiled. "Thank you from both of us."

"You're welcome to join us in the lobby for a toast."

And for Ron's final pitch. Val wouldn't rush there for that. "Thank you. I'll go to the lobby as soon as I pack up the blenders and the leftover fruit."

While she did that, the caterers put their leftovers into two coolers and took champagne bottles from a third cooler. They carried the bottles toward the lobby. Val followed them and was surprised at how many people had stuck around for the grand finale. She estimated that sixty folding chairs had been added to the more comfortable sofas and armchairs in the lobby. Granddad was sitting in one of those chairs just inside the door where she'd come in.

"Are your helpers here?" she asked him.

"Ned went home. Millicent and Cassandra left, so he didn't need to stay. Bram's standing along the wall halfway down this side. He has a view of everyone in the audience."

Val didn't see any empty seats. She moved until she was standing by the wall a few yards from Bram. Scanning the room, she noticed Wally sitting at the end of a row of folding chairs. Though someone blocked her view of his face, his cargo pants and bird-adorned T-shirt made identifying him easy.

At the far end of the lobby, Leeann announced the raffle winners and asked them to see her when the program ended to claim their gift certificates. She held out the microphone to Ron.

His voice boomed through the lobby. "I'd now like to introduce the team who worked so hard to make the open house a success. I'll ask them to stand up when I announce their names and their job titles." Starting with Sabrine and Patrick, Ron went on to those who'd staffed the spa's treatment rooms for the touring visitors. The audience applauded each of them, but they clapped for Chatty longer and louder than the others. Her mini-massages had been a hit.

As Ron was introducing the employees, the caterers circulated with trays of plastic flute glasses, each with enough champagne to fill two shot glasses. Val thought serving a small amount of champagne was a good idea, given that the guests would soon be on the road, but those guests had probably expected more than a mere two ounces of champagne. A few glasses had a deeper yellow liquid in them, probably sparkling cider.

"That takes care of the introductions." Ron raised his mini-cup. "I'd like to propose—"

"Wait!" The shout came from the audience. Wally stood up. "Why don't you introduce yourself? By your *real name—Aaron Grubber*? Tell them how many lives you've ruined pushing painkillers, how many people died of overdoses because of you."

Chapter 22

Wally's outburst stunned the lobby into si-lence, but only briefly, before the murmurs began. Leeann looked aghast at her husband. Ron avoided eye contact with her and said something to Patrick, who took out his phone and poked at it. Before Val could signal Bram to get Wally out, Bram was already on his way.

He made it to Wally in two strides and spoke quietly to him, though Val was close enough to hear. "Sir, you might want to leave quickly before the police escort you out. I think a spa staffer is calling them."

"I'll leave when Grubber tells the truth," Wally roared. He pointed at Ron. "He's a money-grubber *and* a wife-grubber!"

As Leeann stepped toward Ron, he handed the microphone to Sabrine, making sure that what-ever his wife had to say wouldn't be amplified through the room. Half the audience gawked at them and the other half at Wally. The buzz in the room grew louder.

Bram leaned closer to Wally. "You've made your point, sir. It's time to go."

It took Sabrine half a minute to realize she should use the microphone to claim the audience's attention. "I'm sorry about this interruption, but we'll continue as planned. Let's raise a glass to toast everyone who has made the open house such a success, not just the staff, but all of you in the audience, our wonderful guests."

Patrick held the phone to his ear as he made his way through the chairs to reach the disrupter. Tucking his phone away, he loomed over Wally. "If you don't want to be charged for being drunk and disorderly, you'll leave right now. Come with me please."

Wally eyed him with suspicion and pointed to Bram. "I'll go with him."

Val wondered if Wally mistrusted Patrick because he worked for Ron or because Bram sounded less hostile . . . or both. Wally followed Bram to the exit, with Patrick the caboose in the three-car train.

Val told Granddad she'd be back in a minute and went outside. The building entrance was well lit, but the patio and lawn beyond were illuminated only by feeble path lights. When Val's eyes adjusted to the dim light, she made out Bram and Patrick flanking Wally as they walked toward the path to the parking lot. Ron burst out of the lobby, nearly knocking Val down, and trotted after the three men.

They stopped when he caught up with them. After a moment, Bram started back toward the building.

Apparently, Ron had relieved him and taken over the job of getting Wally off the premises. Wally unleashed a string of curses at Ron. The thought of him near Jane's ex made Val nervous.

She hurried toward Bram. "The loudmouth is Wally Witterby, Jane's ex-husband. He knows the truth about Ron, and so did Jane. I think Ron killed her to keep his past a secret, and he won't be gentle with Wally."

Bram raised his hands, palms up. "What do you want me to do?"

"Go back and convince Ron to return to his guests. Unless he can stall them, they'll leave and hear more of Wally's yelling in the parking lot."

"Okay. And if Wally is too drunk to drive, I'll take him to where he's staying."

Bram sprinted after the three men. As she watched them, Granddad joined her.

"Where's Ron? I should be watching him."

"No worries. Bram's with him." She told Granddad what was going on and soon saw what she'd hoped for. "Ron's on his way back."

The door from the lobby opened, and a dozen spa guests came out. Ron cut them off as they walked along the path toward the parking lot. He shook hands with each of them.

Granddad said, "I'm guessing the guy who stood up and denounced Ron was Jane's ex-husband, Wally." When Val nodded, he said, "How did he recognize Ron as Aaron Grubber?"

"Millicent and Cassandra must have told him. He talked with them for a while."

People started leaving the building in waves, making it impossible for Ron to stem the tide. He kept his head down as he approached the building, slipping by Val, Granddad, and the last of the guests.

Granddad frowned. "I gotta make sure Ron's okay with me leaving. Also, I'd like him to pay me now."

"I'll go inside with you and find a place to sit. I've been on my feet all day."

As they started toward the door to the lobby, Granddad said, "Patrick's coming back from the parking lot. Are we gonna need his hand truck to haul your smoothie stuff to the car?"

Val shook her head. "It weighs much less than when we came in. I used up most of the ingredients, and the smoothie jugs are nearly empty."

Patrick trotted toward them. "Hey, Val. Bram's driving the drunken loudmouth's car, taking him to his bed-and-breakfast in Bayport."

Val frowned. "Is Bram coming back or leaving his car here until tomorrow?"

"He'll call and let you know whether he can get a lift back here tonight. I was surprised that almost the whole cast of *The Mousetrap* was at the open house. Millicent and Cassandra, Bram, plus the three of us." Patrick crooned, "*Three blind mice, three blind mice, see how they run.*" He went inside the building.

His singing set Val's teeth on edge. The recurring tune of "Three Blind Mice" heralded the murders in *The Mousetrap*. It was the killer's signature song. She shivered as a cold gust swirled around her. Then a rumble of thunder made her jump. The song, the wind, the thunder—three bad omens.

Granddad looked up at the dark sky. "I sure hope that storm isn't coming this way."

"Me too. I can't figure out why Patrick mentioned the *Mousetrap* cast being here." When Granddad shrugged, Val continued. "Maybe because it gave him a chance to creep me out with his crooning."

"What, you didn't like his serenade?" Granddad winked.

They went into the lobby, now empty of spa visitors. The caterers were collecting the small, plastic wineglasses. Patrick had gone to the far end of the lobby, where Ron, Leeann, Sabrine, and some of the spa employees, including Chatty, were drinking champagne. Their glass flutes held far more than the plastic glasses given to the spa guests. Patrick popped the cork on an unopened champagne bottle.

"If you want talk to Ron, Granddad, you're going to have to crash the party. You'd better hurry, though. He just guzzled his champagne and is going for a refill."

"It won't be the first party I've crashed." He crossed the lobby.

Val sank into a plump armchair next to a tall fig plant, which would mostly hide her from the champagne drinkers. She leaned back and closed her eyes. She opened them when she heard her name.

Chatty stood over her. "Sorry for waking you."

"Whenever I say that to Granddad, he insists he wasn't sleeping, just resting his eyes. That's my story, and I'm sticking to it."

Chatty grinned. "I was surprised by Wally's outburst. He was so friendly and easygoing when I gave him a massage. All he talked about was birds. Then he comes here and accuses Ron of drug dealing. What's that about?"

It wasn't about anything Val wanted to tell her gossipy friend. "That was the vodka talking. He put it in his tonics at the café and in his smoothies here, possibly also in whatever he drank in between. Bram's driving Wally to his B&B." Val glanced across the lobby. Ron was refilling his glass again. It was a good thing he could walk home, rather than drive. At least he had his wife to lean on . . . or maybe not. Leeann had disappeared from the lobby. "Where's Leeann?"

"If you hadn't been resting your eyes, you'd have seen her go out. She told Ron she was going home because she was tired. If you ask me, she was upset about what Wally was yelling at Ron. He claimed it was drunken nonsense and told her he'd be along later, after a relaxing soak in the hot tub. By the way, I heard good things about your smoothies. If you have any left, I'd love a taste."

"I have some in the tent. Do you want a sample now?"

"I need a few minutes to straighten the massage room and set it up for clients. Then I'll go to the tent. Does that work?"

"That's fine."

As Chatty hurried into the spa wing, Val turned her attention back to the celebration across the room. Granddad and Ron were facing each other, but reading their body language, Val doubted they were having a friendly talk.

Two minutes later Granddad ambled across the lobby toward Val. "I'm officially off duty."

"Everything go okay?"

Granddad lowered his voice. "He was grumpy. He said it was my job to make everything run smoothly, and I should have noticed the crazy drunk guy before he made a scene. I told him it was my team member who got to the guy first and coaxed him to leave. And my team member's driving him home. Otherwise, the guy might get pulled over for DUI and tell the police he got drunk at the spa."

"What was Ron's response to that?"

"He said I should have introduced him to my team so he'd recognize them."

"So it's still your fault," Val said. "What a jerk. Did he pay you?"

"He told me to send him a bill. Let's pick up the smoothie stuff from the tent and go home."

As they left the spa building, Val felt a raindrop hit her face, and then another, and another. Before they reached the tent, the rain was light but steady. The caterers had gone, leaving only bare tables and the coolers holding their leftovers. While running the smoothie bar, Val hadn't noticed the lights strung along the tent's perimeter. She was grateful for them now. Without them she'd need a flashlight inside the tent.

Granddad moved away from the tent opening when sheets of rain came down. "If this keeps up, we're not leaving anytime soon." He sat down at a table near the smoothie bar.

Val looked up as the rain hammered the top of the tent. "Fingers crossed that the electricity stays on and the tent doesn't collapse on us."

Granddad adjusted his hearing aid. "I gotta

turn the volume down. The sound of the rain is deafening."

No use trying to talk until the storm let up. Val pondered what she'd learned about the two men with the best reasons to kill Jane. The outgoing, friendly spa owner had shown his ugly side this evening, apparently enhanced by champagne. Patrick, whose brother was in jail because of Jane's whistleblowing, once again showed his passive-aggressive meanness through an unnerving song.

After ten minutes Granddad looked up at the tent top. "The storm's quieting down."

"It's raining less hard, but we can't leave yet. We'd be soaked by the time we got to the parking lot."

She was startled to see someone at the tent's entrance, covered from shoulders to knees with a plastic trash bag that had armholes cut in it.

Patrick came toward them carrying several empty plastic grocery bags. His hair and shirt sleeves were wet. "Do you have leftover ice?"

Val shook her head. "I used most of what I brought and dumped the rest."

He pointed to the two foam coolers the caterer had left. "Any ice in those?"

"A couple of ten-pound dry-ice bricks in each one. The caterer put them there to keep the left-over food from spoiling."

Patrick opened and rummaged around in the coolers. "One of these should be enough to keep the food cold in a cooler." He looked at his hands. "You're not supposed to touch dry ice. Do you happen to have paper towels or a cloth of some kind?"

"I do." Val had brought dish towels so she could dry the blenders after rinsing them. She fished out two towels from her tote bag and gave them to him.

He wrapped them around the ice bricks, which he dropped into plastic bags, and then returned her towels. "Thanks a lot." The walking trash bag left.

Granddad stroked his chin. "What's he gonna do with that ice?"

"Keep the leftover champagne chilled?"

Bram called Val to say that Dorothy would drive him back to the spa and that Wally was safely in his room at the B&B. Val relayed the message to Granddad.

Chatty ran into the tent and folded her small umbrella. "I'm glad you're still here. I didn't want to leave until the rain let up a bit. This umbrella was no match for it." She sat down at the table with Granddad. "I'm ready for a taste of the famous smoothies."

"Blueberry banana or cucumber lime?"

Chatty chose the cucumber, and Granddad asked for blueberry.

Val poured drinks for them, but not for herself. She'd OD'd on smoothies today by sampling each batch she'd made.

Chatty sipped her cucumber concoction. "Delicious! You two left the building at the right time, before Ron went ballistic."

"He wasn't in a great mood when I talked to him," Granddad grumbled.

"He's been under a lot of pressure," Chatty said.

"He went to unwind in the hot tub and became furious because the water was too hot. He bawled out Patrick for setting the temperature so high. Patrick said a spa visitor must have fiddled with the thermostat."

The man with the mustache, probably Nigel, was Val's candidate for that visitor. He'd stayed behind in the hot tub room long enough to fiddle with the controls. "So did Ron relax his temperature standards or do without his soak?"

"I'm not sure. When he asked how long it would take for the water to cool down to its usual temperature, Patrick said several hours. Then Ron demanded he bring some ice to chill it faster."

"That's why Patrick came here for ice," Granddad said. "Were you in the room when they were talking?"

"No, but there's a paper-thin wall between my massage room and the hot tub room. When I heard Patrick say, 'Here's your ice,' I got ready to leave. Patrick was right behind me. He locked the entrance to the building."

"Was he still wearing his makeshift black plastic raincoat?"

Chatty nodded. "Even that couldn't spoil his looks." She drank the rest of her smoothie. "I'm heading home. Nice seeing you, Mr. Myer. Thanks for the smoothie, Val. It perked me up."

Granddad had just finished his smoothie when Bram arrived. The three of them managed to carry the coolers and blenders to Val's car in one trip.

Half an hour later, she was fast asleep.

* * *

Val went to the kitchen at eight the next morning to make coffee and warm up day-old muffins. With her assistant manager handling the café, Val planned a leisurely day of gardening, reading, and spending time with Bram later. She might fit in some baking too.

The doorbell interrupted her thoughts. It would surely wake Granddad, whose bedroom was near the front door. She hurried to the hall.

She was surprised that the doorbell ringer was Chief Yardley. He came to the house now and then to visit Granddad, but only once before had he shown up this early. And that was to break the news that a woman they knew had been killed in an apparent accident.

Why was he here now?

"Good morning, Chief." She opened the door wider for the barrel-chested man to come in. "You're just in time for coffee."

"I could use some coffee . . . and some help from you and your granddaddy."

Granddad had emerged from his bedroom at the end of the hall in time to hear the chief's comment. "Good morning, Earl. What kind of help do you need?"

"I want to hear what happened at the spa's open house." He turned to Val. "You were right that I should have stationed an officer there, though I don't know that it would have changed what happened. A dead body was found there this morning."

Chapter 23

A dead body at the spa! Val's stomach roiled. Her first thought was that Wally had returned in his drunken state to confront Ron again and had paid a price for that. "Who's dead?"

"Ron Melgrem."

Val exchanged a look with Granddad and suspected he was thinking what she was. Which of the people who hated Ron had killed him?

"There's no sign of foul play," Chief Yardley added, as if he'd read their thoughts. "But Mrs. Melgrem is convinced that a maniac who disrupted the open house and made false accusations against her husband killed him. Before I go talk to her, I wanted an independent view. Were either of you there for that disruption?"

"Yup. Both of us." Granddad sniffed. "Coffee's ready. Come to the kitchen, and we'll fill you in." Granddad led the way. "How did Melgrem die?"

"The medical examiner isn't sure. He saw no trauma to the body. Melgrem's wife said he was healthy, in good shape for a man in his forties, with no history of heart disease or any other condition that might have caused his death. She showed us a report of a physical he'd had six months ago. It confirmed what she'd told us."

"A prenuptial physical," Val muttered as she took out coffee mugs.

The chief continued. "The estimated time of death is between nine and eleven last night. An autopsy will tell us more, but we won't have the results for a few days."

An autopsy hadn't been able to explain what had killed Jane. Could Ron have died from the same cause? He'd been Val's pick as Jane's murderer, but Granddad's pick, Patrick, could step into that role now. Val would push back on that assumption. Ron's death didn't rule him out as Jane's killer.

Granddad handed the chief a mug of coffee. "Who found Melgrem's body?"

"His wife. When she woke up around six, she saw that he hadn't slept in their bed and he was nowhere else in the house. He'd told her he was going to soak in the hot tub before turning in. That's where he was when she found him."

Poor Leeann. She'd married her perfect man only months before he died. "That must have been devastating for her," Val said.

"Yes, and people who are grieving often try to find someone to blame for a loved one's death. Mrs. Melgrem is blaming the troublemaker at the open house, but she doesn't even know his name. She'd never seen him before."

Val took the muffins from the oven. "It's Jane's

ex-husband, Wally Witterby. He'd been drinking, but his accusations against Ron were largely true."

Chief frowned. "I talked to Witterby on Friday. He didn't strike me as a maniac. Mrs. Melgrem didn't tell me what he was ranting about."

Granddad said, "We will."

Val brought the plate of muffins and the coffee-pot to the dining room. Granddad sat at the head of the table. Val and the chief faced each other on the sides.

After Granddad paraphrased Wally's accusations against Ron, Val told the chief Ron's real identity and his previous job in Baltimore. "His boss, Doctor Lazarin, is in jail now, convicted for overprescribing painkillers. Ron testified against him, though he was probably guilty of the same thing."

As she talked, the chief was writing in a small notebook. "I should be able to get hold of the full case file. How did you find out all this?"

Val focused on buttering her muffin. "Before our last rehearsal, I overheard the cast members from the Village talk about someone named Aaron Grubber. They said he deserved to be in jail like Doctor Lazarin."

Granddad nodded. "Then I looked online for the doctor and Grubber. I read a long article about the case."

"And Wally told me about Jane's part in the story." Val summarized it for the chief. "When Jane showed up at the spa and recognized Ron as her former lover, she was a threat to his new business and his marriage to a wealthy woman."

The chief reached for a muffin. "So he had a

reason to get rid of her. Now he's dead too. And we don't know who or what killed either of them. Do you know of anyone who might want both of them dead?"

"Yup," Granddad said. "Patrick Parenna, the half brother of the jailed doctor, also works at the spa. I figure he took a job there to get at Ron for testifying against the doctor. And along comes Jane, the whistleblower who sicced the law on the doctor. Patrick's got a motive for both murders."

"But, Granddad, he was there with Ron last night when almost no one else was left at the spa. Patrick would have to be stupid to kill Ron at that time, and I don't think he's stupid." She turned to the chief. "My friend, Chatty Ridenour, who works as a massage therapist at the spa, overheard the two men talking in the hot tub room last night. They wanted to cool down the water so Ron could take his nightly soak. She can fill you in on what they said and pin down the time when Ron was still alive."

The chief asked for Chatty's contact information and jotted it in his notebook. "Anything else I should know?"

Val nodded. "Chatty also told me about a theft at the spa. Several vials of Botox disappeared from the cabinet where Dr. Leeann Melgrem stored it. It was there before Jane died, but not after that. I looked up Botox online. It's short for *botulinum toxin.* Injecting it can cause death by asphyxiation. You said Jane died of asphyxiation. Maybe Ron did too."

The chief didn't look convinced. "The medical examiner would routinely check for an injection site. He might find one on Ron's body, but probably not on Jane's because of burns. Though Botox isn't part of a standard tox screen, there might be a specific test for it." The chief stood up and pointed to the muffins. "Mind if I take one of those for the road?"

"Help yourself," Granddad said.

"You've both been really helpful. And thanks for breakfast."

As Val walked him to the door, she remembered a fact she hadn't mentioned. "By the way, Patrick owns a silver compact car. Jane's neighbors saw one like it in her driveway the night of the fire. Of course, it's a common car, but it might be worth checking out."

"Got it. If you think of anything else, call me."

When Val returned to the dining room, Granddad was clearing the table. "I sure wish Ron had paid me last night. It'll be harder to get the money now, and I owe Bram and Ned."

"You wouldn't want to send your bill to his widow just yet, but you can do it in a couple of weeks. You have a contract that proves Ron hired you, right?" When he nodded, she continued. "Ron had so many enemies that it's hard to believe he died a natural death, but he might have."

Granddad raised a skeptical eyebrow. "You're right that it would have been smarter for Patrick to wait for a better time and place to kill Ron, but rage could have made him lose control. If he had a way to kill Ron that leaves no trace, he has no worries. Police make a case against criminals by finding trace evidence at the crime scene—fingerprints, hair, fibers. But that's not going to be evidence against Patrick. He had a reason for being in that room."

Val finished putting the breakfast dishes in the dishwasher. "I'm going out back to check on my tiny tomato plants. I hope they survived last night's downpour. What's on your schedule today besides church?"

"I'm taking Dorothy to the four o'clock Orioles game. She needs a day off. Bram's managing the bookshop. Are you going to call and tell him about Ron?"

"Yes, but not until later. This morning he's riding on the Oxford-Easton bike loop. It's thirty miles long. He had to start early so he'd be back in time to open the bookshop at noon. I'll call Bethany to tell her about Ron." Val wouldn't need to call Chatty. If her antenna hadn't already picked up the news of Ron's death, the chief would soon tell her.

Val and Granddad had just finished lunch when the doorbell rang. Val went to the hall and opened the door to the Rilke sisters dressed in their Sunday best. Millicent wore a bright purple jacket over her black top and pants, and Cassandra had exchanged her gray sweat suit for a gray pantsuit. Val was sure their visit wasn't a social call. Outside of rehearsals, the only time either of them had shown up here was when Cassandra feared her sister would be arrested and had asked for their help.

Taking them into the sitting room, Val asked if they would like something to drink. They declined. The sisters perched on the edge of the sofa, Cassandra wringing her hands. Val sat down in an armchair at right angles to the sofa. Granddad joined them, sinking into his recliner.

Millicent got down to business. "We have friends who stayed longer at the spa's open house than we did. They told us a man was escorted out after he went on a tirade. Based on their description of him, we guessed he was Wally Witterby. Did either of you hear him?"

Granddad nodded. "Nothing he said would have surprised *you*. He announced that Ron Melgrem's real name was Aaron Grubber. You already knew that, and so did we."

Millicent didn't bother to deny it. "We heard rumors at the Village that Grubber died after last night's open house. We thought you might know something about it."

Cassandra piped up, "He was alive when we left."

Val suppressed a smile at Cassandra's attempt to show that she and Millicent couldn't have killed him. "He was found dead this morning. The police don't yet know the cause of his death."

"Let's hope it was *not* sudden and painless," Cassandra mumbled.

Millicent turned to Val. "You were watching when I was at a table with him last night. I'm afraid you might have misinterpreted what you saw."

"You mean when you substituted your drink for his?"

"Yes, but it's not what you think. I'll tell you the full story."

Granddad said, "Start with how you got him to

sit down with you. I didn't see him at a table with any other guests last night."

"He was going around shaking hands with everyone. When he shook mine and introduced himself as Ron Melgrem, I didn't give him my name. I said I recognized him as Aaron Grubber and knew what he'd done when he worked for Doctor Lazarin. He suggested we sit down so he could explain what I'd gotten wrong. Then he went for drinks for both of us. I thought he might have slipped something into my smoothie, so I switched the drinks when he left the table. If he keeled over, it would be nobody's fault but his own."

Granddad peered around Millicent to catch Cassandra's eye. "You pulled the snake ruse to get him away from the table."

"Millicent called me when he went to pick up the drinks and told me what to do." Cassandra gave her sister a sidewise glance. "It would have been easier just to knock over the drink he gave her."

Millicent shook her head. "That wouldn't have stopped him. He'd have gone to get another smoothie to tamper with. Besides, if he drugged my smoothie, he deserved to drink it himself."

Granddad scratched his head. "Why did you think he was carrying something to slip into your drink?"

"The man was a drug dealer before he was a spa manager." Millicent spoke through clenched teeth. "He sold painkillers directly to patients when their prescriptions would have raised overdose flags at the pharmacy. Even if he didn't have a pocket full of pills, he was steps away from his office, where he doubtless had them. Nigel went to the spa's VIP soiree the week before last. Ask him what he learned about painkillers while he was there."

Val made a mental note to do that this afternoon. "I don't understand why you confronted Ron."

"To tell him that people around here knew his history and they would be watching him. If he ever pushed addictive drugs again, the police would hear of it immediately. We couldn't do anything about what he'd done previously because he had immunity for that crime, but we'd make sure he didn't do it again."

Looking impatient, Granddad trained his eyes on Millicent. "Ron is the person Jane said committed a crime and didn't get punished. Was your husband addicted to painkillers because of Ron and the doctor he worked for?"

Millicent closed her eyes and took a deep breath. "My husband had several health problems. He needed painkillers, but not as many or as strong as the ones they put him on."

"Did you testify against the doctor?" Granddad said.

"No. Witnesses with more powerful evidence took the stand. They told the jury about younger people who'd become addicted. Some of them died of overdoses because of him."

"Nanette was a witness, and she did a wonderful job," Cassandra added.

Granddad's eyebrows rose. "Nanette testified?"

Val was equally surprised. She'd underestimated the woman's courage.

"It was probably the bravest thing she ever did," Millicent said. "Her daughter was in a terrible car accident and became addicted after Doctor Lazarin and his assistant prescribed drugs for her. She got clean, but then relapsed. She was fired from her job. Her husband divorced her and won full custody of their son."

Sympathy for the Dernes and their daughter flooded over Val. She remembered Nanette on the verge of tears twice at the mention of the grandson she rarely saw. And Nigel, who often dismissed his wife's concerns, had comforted her. "Did Nigel testify?"

Millicent shook her head. "He wanted to, but the prosecutor chose Nanette to tell their story. Nigel would have stated the facts and nothing else. To sway opinion, an emotional appeal works better. Nanette gave such moving testimony that there wasn't a dry eye in the courtroom, not even the judge's."

Cassandra added, "I'm sure it swayed the judge to impose the maximum sentence."

Based on their brief acquaintance, Val wouldn't have described Nanette as brave and sympathetic. Yet those traits had emerged under pressure. She didn't have the acting skills to fake them, but her emotions were never far from the surface. Her stiff-upper-lip husband rarely showed any emotion, but he had as much reason to hate the opioid supplier as anyone. Nigel might have gone to the spa in disguise last night to reconnoiter and plan his revenge on Ron.

Val turned to the sisters. "Did you get to know the Dernes and Jane during the doctor's trial?"

Cassandra nodded. "The two of us and the Dernes sat in the gallery every day of the trial. Jane wasn't there except when she had to testify."

"And for the doctor's sentencing hearing," Millicent added. "A few months after the trial ended, we ran into her again at a couple of charity events and got to know her better."

Val wondered if the sisters had changed their high opinion of Jane after listening to her ex. "I never met Jane. I know her only through what you and the rest of the *Mousetrap* cast have said about her. Wally painted a very different picture of her. I assume he told you about her connection to Grubber. Did you believe what he said?"

Cassandra got up and crossed the room to the shelves around the fireplace, apparently reluctant to answer. She took a book down and opened it to a random page.

Millicent spoke up. "We believed part of what Wally said. He wasn't exactly a perfect husband. I can understand her having an affair with Grubber, but I don't believe she helped him escape justice. He avoided going to jail only because the prosecutor cut him a deal to get his testimony against the doctor."

Val persisted. "Why would Jane's ex lie about her tipping off Grubber?"

Millicent shrugged. "As a defense mechanism. To deal with rejection and losing her, he had to convince himself that she wasn't the honest, good-hearted woman he married."

The explanation made sense to Val. "People believe what they want to believe." She'd done it herself when she ignored the first signs that her former fiancé was cheating on her.

Millicent stood up. "I hope we've clarified some issues. Let us know if you learn anything more about the death at the spa. We'll see you at tomorrow evening's rehearsal."

Val walked them to the door and returned to the sitting room. "The sisters visited us to learn more about Ron's death and keep me from telling the police about their drink switch scheme."

"And to convince us they still had faith in Jane's goodness and wouldn't have killed her." Granddad hadn't budged from his chair, though it was time for him to put on his Orioles T-shirt, jacket, and hat. "We need to think outside the box about Jane's death. It's easy to blame Ron for killing her. Millicent and company have manipulated us so we would reach that conclusion."

Val knew from experience that his out-of-the-box scenarios were usually off the wall. She decided to tease him. "You have a new theory. Let me guess. The four Villagers hated Ron for hooking their loved ones on painkillers. They found out that Jane had slept with the enemy and helped him stay out of jail. So they killed her and tried to frame Ron."

Granddad frowned in concentration, apparently giving her ridiculous theory serious thought. "Nah. It wasn't in their interest to kill Jane. Her death meant attention on the body in the freezer. The Rilke sisters didn't want that. I wouldn't rule out Nigel or even Nanette killing her, though the folks at the spa are better suspects. No matter who killed Jane, the Rilkes and the Dernes decided Ron should take the rap. Every time they talked to us, they scattered bread crumbs to put us on his trail. We have to cut our own path."

Chapter 24

Val settled down on the sofa. She couldn't reject Granddad's theory out of hand. He could be right that Millicent and Cassandra were doing their best to make Ron look guilty of killing Jane, and maybe the Dernes were in on it. "What are these bread crumbs you say they left for us?"

"First, Cassandra whispered a vague hint: '*The spa's the key.*' The next time, she added an intriguing detail: '*Jane saw someone at the spa who got away with a crime.*' Her sister was always hushing her. That made us even more curious. They led us down the garden path step by step, until finally they spoke the criminal's name right in this room." Granddad took off his glasses and polished them on his shirt. "The four of them live in the same community and could have held their private conversations there. Why here? Because they assumed you'd overhear them."

Val was about to protest when she glanced into

the dining room. The first time the older cast members had come here for a rehearsal, she'd listened to their conversation, pressing herself against the wall between the sitting room and the dining room. From there she could barely see them and hadn't caught them looking in her direction. But Nigel on the sofa and Millicent in Granddad's chair might have noticed her creeping across the dining room toward the wall.

"You could be right, Granddad. It's possible that the Rilkes and the Dernes pegged me as an eavesdropper from the start. Even so, why would they bother leaving bread crumbs for us?"

"They know I'm friends with the chief. They're counting on us to put the bug in his ear. Now they're in an even better position to frame him because Ron can't defend himself."

"I'm going to follow up on Millicent's latest bread crumb, though it was more like hitting us over the head with a hard roll rather than a crumb. She said to ask Nigel what he learned about painkillers at the spa's VIP night." Val had other questions for him about the evening Jane died and about last night's open house. She stood up. "I'm going to whip up a batch of cookies for Nigel and Nanette."

Granddad gave her a thumbs-up. "Good idea. Cookies open doors and mouths. Put aside a few for Dorothy and me to have after the Orioles game." He glanced at his watch. "Time to put on my fan gear. I'm supposed to pick up Dorothy in fifteen minutes."

* * *

As Val drove by the Dernes' cottage at the Village, she spotted Nigel pruning a Japanese holly near his driveway. She pulled up to the curb and climbed out of the car with a gift bag of cookies.

He stopped trimming the shrub as she walked up the path to his cottage. "A visitor, but not a surprise one. Millicent told me you or your grandfather might contact me. Perfect timing. I'm ready for a break."

Perfect timing for Val meant talking to him without his wife interrupting. "I brought you and Nanette some cookies."

"She'll be leaving soon for her Sunday bridge game. Have a seat in the garden. I'll tell her you're here." He took off his gardening gloves and put his pruning shears on the table between the two wrought-iron chairs.

"Thank you." Val put the bag of cookies down next to the shears.

Nigel went inside and came out a minute later with Nanette. She wore a neon-pink pantsuit and looked more cheerful than Val had ever seen her. He pointed out the bag of cookies Val had brought.

Nanette sat down in the other garden chair and took a cookie. "Thank you for the sweets. This is a bittersweet day for us. Millicent said you know what the spa director did in his former life. I'm not sorry he's dead, but I'd rather have seen him miserable in jail. I'm going to make sure Doctor Lazarin serves out his full term."

Nigel stood behind her chair and massaged her shoulders. "When the doctor came up for parole a month ago, Nanette contacted the victims we met at his trial. She encouraged them to write to the parole board to oppose his release. Some of them went with her to the hearing to speak against letting him out of jail early."

"And I'll do the same the next time he comes up for parole." Nanette took another cookie and stood up. "Please excuse me. I'm off to my bridge game." Munching the cookie, she strolled toward the Village's main building.

Nigel folded his lanky frame into the chair she'd just vacated. Though the chairs were in the shade, he kept his reflecting sunglasses on. Too bad. Eyes could reveal more than words or even belie them. Unless he shed his glasses, Val would miss signs of evasiveness like rapid blinking, a downcast gaze, and a far-off look.

Two could play that game. She put on her sunglasses so her eyes wouldn't reflect any suspicion she had of him.

"Have a chocolate chip cookie," She offered him the bag, and he took a cookie. "Millicent mentioned you heard about painkillers at the spa's VIP night."

He chewed a bite of the cookie before he responded, "When Jane told us Grubber interviewed her for a job, she said she believed he'd turned his life around. She didn't intend to expose his previous crimes. I disagreed with that. People who get away with wrongdoing once have little incentive to change. At the VIP night, I discovered Grubber hadn't changed." Nigel stretched out his long legs. "The spa's shop was open that night. I saw a shelf of homeopathic pain relievers, told the clerk those products hadn't worked for me, and asked if the spa could offer other remedies for pain. She suggested booking massages and talking to the director. He'd told her to send him anyone who needed stronger pain relief than the shop offered. Grubber was going to get up to his old tricks."

Val wasn't sure how that could happen. "He's no longer a physician's assistant. He can't prescribe painkillers now."

Nigel flicked his wrist. "He doesn't need a prescription pad. He could get those drugs through his old connections. He previously dispensed what he called '*samples of painkillers*' for a price."

"Did you tell Jane what the shop clerk said?"

"Of course. I called her the following morning to prove that Grubber hadn't reformed."

The schedule Val had made flashed into her mind. The morning after the VIP night was Thursday. "The day you told Jane he hadn't reformed, she made an appointment to see his wife." Val paused to let that sink in. "Do you think Aaron Grubber killed Jane so she wouldn't tell his wife about his drug dealings?"

"I can't say what his motive was, but I've no doubt he killed her." Nigel took off his sunglasses and polished the lenses on his shirt. "Before the fire broke out at her house, he was pumping gas. I'd previously seen him driving around town in his red sports car, but at the gas station, he was in a smallish silver car. I assumed he had a second car. I ran some errands in town and as I was driving back to the Village, I saw the silver car turn onto Horseshoe Lane."

"Where Jane lives." He'd previously told Val

he'd seen that car in a ditch. Had he put it there? "You followed the silver car?"

Nigel nodded. "I didn't want him near Jane. I could think of only one way to stop him." Nigel glanced toward his sedan in the driveway. "My car can intimidate a driver in a smaller car. I pulled up alongside him."

"On that narrow, two-lane road?"

"There was no oncoming traffic. I scared him off the road, but the car wasn't damaged enough to keep him there. I'll never forgive myself for failing to keep him away from her." Nigel's jaw clenched. "I'd taken my best shot. If I tried again, he'd have the chance to identify my car and possibly read my license plate."

"There are a lot of silver compact cars. Are you absolutely sure Ron was in that car on Horseshoe Lane?"

"The tinted windows kept me from seeing him, but it was the same make of car he was filling at the gas station."

Ron had mentioned being run off the road to Granddad, saying the incident had occurred the previous week. That would have been before Jane died. Either Ron was lying about the timing or Nigel had used his big car as a weapon more than once. "That wasn't the only time you forced Ron off the road, right?"

After a moment of silence, Nigel put on his sunglasses again. "I should get back to pruning." He stood up.

Val took that as a *yes*. Nigel had dodged, but not denied, a sign that lying didn't come easy to him.

Val had one more matter to raise with him. It just might tempt him to lie. "You must have had a thorough look at the spa during your VIP visit. I was wondering why you went back there for the open house last night."

He picked up his shears. They were four inches long, sturdy and sharp. "Who said I did?"

Val hesitated. Her college friend who couldn't remember faces identified people by their walk. Though Val hadn't paid attention to Nigel's gait last night, he wouldn't know that. "You were on the spa tour with me. You didn't look like yourself, but I recognized you by your walk."

He trimmed the holly's wayward stems ruthlessly. "I went to the open house in disguise so I could talk to Grubber without him recognizing me the next time he saw me. I couldn't get near him at first. I bided my time, took the tour, and visited the shop again. When I finally caught him alone, I told him several people in Bayport were aware of what he'd done and that if he pushed drugs here, he'd be arrested. I warned him to assume that anyone who went to him for painkillers could be recording him and conducting a sting."

Eying his shears, Val framed a reply she thought he'd like. "You were trying to keep him from ruining any more lives. Bravo." Nigel's story didn't cover all that he'd done last night. "While we were on the spa tour, I noticed you stayed behind in the hot tub room after the others on the tour had moved on."

Nigel shrugged. "Call of nature. All those former motel rooms have facilities, and I didn't want to walk back to the restrooms off the lobby."

That sounded like a prepared statement to Val. Maybe he had another reason to stay behind—to turn up the temperature on the hot tub, a small act of sabotage bound to get under Ron's skin.

She stood up. "I won't keep you from your gardening any longer, and thanks for putting up with my questions."

"Thank you for the cookies. Before you go, I have a question for you. Why are you so interested in the spa director?"

"His connection to Jane is my only interest. Her death shocked my grandfather. He wants to see justice done and the person responsible for her death and the fire held accountable."

"Grubber will never be held accountable now."

Nigel sounded angry that the man had escaped punishment. Was the anger genuine? Or was it Nigel's ploy to suggest he wouldn't have killed Ron even given the chance?

On her drive home, she mulled over what a perfect suspect the older man would make if the spa director had been murdered. Nigel had a strong motive, blaming Ron for his daughter's addiction and for Jane's death. Val would have suspected Nigel of fiddling with the hot tub wiring if Ron had been electrocuted, but he hadn't. In any case, Nigel couldn't have known who'd be the next person in the hot tub. But he might have returned to the spa in a different disguise and hidden in an empty treatment room or the restroom, hoping for a chance to get at Ron. Could he have had military or CIA training in how to kill a man without leaving a mark?

Val stopped herself from speculating any more

about Nigel. First of all, no one had said Ron was murdered. Secondly, she'd detected no sign Nigel was lying. He just ignored any questions he didn't want to answer.

As she pulled into Granddad's driveway, Chatty called her.

"You must have heard Ron was found dead in the hot tub this morning." When Val didn't contradict her, Chatty continued. "The spa will be closed until Tuesday. I'm baking bread to take to Leeann tomorrow and express my condolences. I figure she's too upset to talk to anyone today. Do you want to go with me?"

"Yes. I'll bring her something she can heat up for dinner. Anytime after two works for me."

"I have a few appointments at the club tomorrow morning. I'll meet you in the spa parking lot at two fifteen."

Val thought of a question her friend would answer truthfully, unlike others who might have a reason to lie. "Was anyone else in the spa building when you and Patrick left last night?"

"As far as I know, only Sabrine was still there. She was waiting out the rain in the staff kitchen. Patrick called out to her to say that he was leaving and that the rain had let up. She said she was in the middle of texting and would head out when she finished."

Maybe she'd had some unfinished business with Ron, her boss who'd been hitting on her, according to Chatty. "Did you see her after that?"

"No. You sound as if you think there's something fishy about Ron's death."

"I have no reason to believe that. But if it looks suspicious, the police might want to talk to you, Patrick, and Sabrine as the last people in the building. Could any open house visitors have stayed behind and hidden in one of the treatment rooms?"

"The wing with the offices and medical treatment rooms was closed off during the whole open house. In the wing where my massage room is, we're responsible for locking our doors whenever we're not in our rooms. One of the beauticians or nail artists might have forgotten, especially after drinking champagne. Patrick should have checked all the doors, but I don't know whether he did."

Even if he had, Patrick might say he hadn't locked the doors to suggest someone other than a spa staffer could have killed Ron. Val knew a couple of outsiders who might have returned to the spa to act on their grudges against Ron—Nigel and Wally. But was Wally in any condition to drive back to the spa after Bram left him off at his B&B? She'd ask Bram when she met him tonight for dinner.

Chapter 25

Val and Bram went to the Bugeye Tavern for dinner. Housed in a brick building on Main Street, it was named for the type of boat used to dredge oysters in the nineteenth century. Bram wanted to eat in the glass-enclosed front porch, but it had no empty tables. Fine with Val. This evening she preferred the tavern's narrow back room. Lined with booths, it offered a more private place to talk about murder suspects.

They passed up several empty booths on their way to one at the far end. The tavern had recently added weekly international dishes to spice up the menu. This week's special was shrimp paella for two, which they ordered, along with salads.

When the server left, Bram said, "I heard rumors at the bookshop this afternoon that the spa director was found dead. No one had any details, but I'm guessing you spent the day scrambling to get them."

"I didn't have to scramble. All I had to do this

morning was answer the doorbell." She told him what Chief Yardley had said. "The cause of Ron's death is still under investigation, but there was no sign of violence or trauma to suggest anything but a natural death. He was on the young side for a heart attack or a stroke."

Bram shrugged. "But it sometimes happens."

"Millicent and Cassandra were the next people to show up on our doorstep. They said Ron worked for a doctor convicted of pushing painkillers and that the two men were responsible for addicting their patients. Some of them OD'd." Val paused for the server to deliver their drinks. When he left, she told Bram about the Dernes' daughter. "Nanette testified that her daughter became addicted and lost custody of her child. That emotional testimony was one reason the doctor got such a stiff sentence."

Bram looked pained. "That's really sad. I understand now why Nanette's so unhappy. I'm sure Nigel feels the same way. He just doesn't show it."

"Does that mean he's a good actor?"

"The only role I've seen him play is a man like himself. Not much acting ability required." Bram sipped his beer. "Men of Nigel's generation were raised to keep their emotions in check. For him it's a habit, not acting."

"Speaking of acting, do you think Wally might have faked his drunkenness and driven back to the spa last night?"

"He was really drunk. I don't think he could have kept his car on the road much less get into the spa without anyone noticing him."

The server brought their salads to the table.

While they ate those, Val told him that Patrick was the pain doctor's half brother, that Jane had blown the whistle on the doctor's prescription practices, and that Wally claimed she'd had an affair with Ron. Then she recounted what Nigel had said about the silver car on Jane's road. "If Nigel's telling the truth, it's likely Ron was responsible for Jane's death and the fire."

Bram stabbed lettuce leaves with his fork. "Did Nigel say he followed the silver car from the gas station to Jane's house?"

"No, and he didn't say how much time elapsed between when Ron filled his tank and when the silver car turned onto Horseshoe Lane." Val saw the point of Bram's question. "Since the car was out of Nigel's sight for a while, someone could argue that he couldn't know for sure that Ron was still in the car."

"Exactly." Bram sipped his wine. "Who was the last person to see Ron alive, and when was that?"

"Patrick's the last person I know of. Chatty was waiting out the rain in her massage room. It's next to the room with the hot tub. She heard Ron demand Patrick bring ice to cool down the water because the thermostat had been set too high."

Bram shook his head in disbelief. "It takes a lot of ice to cool down a hot tub."

"The caterers had left dry ice in the coolers with leftovers. Patrick took some of it to Ron."

Bram's eyes widened. "Dry ice. How much did Patrick take?"

"Two ten-pound bricks."

The server set down a huge flat pan of rice stud-

ded with big shrimp. He spooned a generous helping onto each plate and left.

"That is a beautiful dish." Val took a forkful of
rice. "And it tastes wonderful too."

"It does. Should we go to Spain instead of
France?" Bram grinned.

"No. I'm sure you can eat paella in France, but
you can't see the Eiffel Tower in Spain. We'll go
there or maybe to Italy on our next trip to Eu-
rope."

"I like the sound of 'our next trip,' but we
should plan the upcoming one first. When I was at
the bookshop today, I sold myself some guide-
books to France. We can go to my place after dinner to comb through them."

Val lifted her wineglass. "I'll drink a toast to
that. But I'd like to ask one more question, Sherlock."

"Fire away."

"What do you think happened to Ron?"

Bram didn't hesitate. "Most likely, his death was
an accident. But there's a chance someone—his
wife, Patrick, Sabrine, Nigel, or even someone we
don't know—committed the perfect crime."

A perfect crime intrigued Val. "Why do you
say—?"

"Uh-uh. You promised only one more question."

Val might have talked him into answering another question, but two of her café regulars
greeted her as they sat down in the neighboring
booth. So much for privacy. "Now tell me about
your day, Bram. How was your long bike ride?"

"I enjoyed it. It's a really scenic ride. I think you'd like it too, if you can work up to biking thirty miles. Or we can just do half the trail."

For the rest of the meal, he described the historic towns the trail went through, including St. Michaels, where he visited the maritime museum, and Oxford, where he'd taken a ferry across the river, enjoying the wildlife along the way. Val made up her mind to train for a fifteen-mile bike ride.

After their meal, they adjourned to Bram's house to plan their trip to France, a welcome break from the subjects that had obsessed her ever since the arson at Jane's house.

When Chief Yardley stopped by the café, it was usually for coffee and a muffin or scones. But on Monday he didn't come in until after the lunch crowd at the café had dwindled. He must have been working all morning because he was ready for a late lunch. Val served him a club sandwich with his coffee at the eating bar.

He wolfed down most of his sandwich in silence. When the last customer left, he looked up from his plate. "You get a gold star for your hunch about the Botox."

She licked her thumb and mimed putting a star on her shoulder. "That almost makes up for all my wrong hunches." She'd had plenty of those in the last two years.

"Asphyxiation due to botulinum toxin killed Jane. Botulism from food sources would have shown up in the initial autopsy, and it didn't. The only way that much toxin could have gotten into her system was by injection."

"So that narrows down who could have killed her to the people from the spa who had access to the drug. Ron and Leeann had keys to the room where it was stored. Patrick changed the locks on that room and could have made himself a spare key."

The chief shook his head. "Like other drugs, Botox is trafficked. A couple of people died after injecting a black-market version of it, which was more concentrated than what the doctors inject."

"Okay, anybody could have done it, but each of those three had a motive to get rid of Jane." Val had at least found the cause of one mysterious death. One to go. "I suppose it's too early for autopsy results on Ron."

"The report is still pending, but I got the crime lab to prioritize him. Two people who knew each other died under mysterious circumstances one week apart. That's a reason to act fast, in case a third death is in the offing."

Val's heart skipped a beat. "A *third death*? You're worried about a serial killer?"

"I'm less worried now that I got the test results." The chief sipped his coffee. "Serial killers tend to use the same murder method each time. After the botulinum showed up in Jane, I asked the lab to test Ron for it. He had no trace of it. It's possible he drowned, but medical examiners won't list drowning as the cause of death until they've excluded other possible causes."

Val had assumed water in the lungs was enough to reach that conclusion. "But what else could have caused his death?"

The chief shrugged. "Anything that interferes with the flow of oxygen to the brain. Gases and poisons do, but a routine tox screen doesn't test for them, just for the drugs people often abuse. There are ways to test for almost any substance, but you have to know what you're looking for. We wouldn't have known what killed Jane without your tip on botulinum." He finished the last bite of his sandwich.

"The Rilkes and the Dernes are convinced Ron killed Jane. Nigel saw Ron in a car like the one Jane's neighbors said was in her driveway the night she died—a silver compact." Val expected her news to come as a surprise, but it got no reaction from the chief.

He sipped his coffee. "I know about that. Ron was supposed to pick up champagne for a brunch his wife was giving the next day. His car had a flat, so he borrowed Patrick's."

Ron clearly hadn't bought champagne at the two places where Nigel had seen the car—the gas station or along Jane's road. And a flat tire was a lame excuse to borrow a car. "Ron couldn't put on his spare tire or borrow his wife's car?"

The chief chuckled. "You think like a cop. I asked the same thing. Ron's sports car didn't come with a spare tire. His wife was out getting supplies for her party. Patrick was at the spa mowing the lawn on his day off so it would be perfect for her party. He was willing to lend his car as long as Ron put some gas in the tank because it was low."

"What time did Ron bring back the borrowed car?"

"Patrick didn't know. He doesn't wear a watch, and Ron left the keys under the mat. Luckily, your friend Chatty has a watch that she checks frequently. She gave me an account almost down to the minute of what happened at the spa after the open house ended." The chief downed the rest of his coffee and put the money for his lunch on the eating bar. "You can pass on what I said to your granddaddy, but I don't want it going any further until we make a public statement." He headed out of the café.

Val called Granddad to update him on the case.

"I'm surprised those test results on Ron came in so quickly," he said. "A possible third murder sure lit a fire under the crime lab folks."

"It's not clear yet that there was a second murder. Ron could have died by accident, but the evidence against him for Jane's death and the arson is pretty strong." Val noticed Chatty in the club's reception area outside the café entrance. "Chatty and I are going to visit Leeann today when I finish here. Do you want to join us?"

Granddad said nothing for a moment. "Nah. I'm too busy to do that today. I don't think Leeann will miss me since I never even met her. I'll pick up a pizza for us so we don't have to fuss about dinner before tonight's rehearsal."

Granddad hung up before Val could ask him what was keeping him busy. On any other Monday he'd have been testing recipes to meet the deadline for his Codger Cook column, but this week he'd already submitted recipes for smoothies based on the ones Val had made for the open house.

As customers drifted into the café for coffee, iced tea, and snacks, Val pondered the case against Ron. He'd had the motive to kill Jane. He'd had the means to do it with access to his wife's Botox and maybe even to the black-market version of it from the drug dealers Nigel claimed Ron knew in Baltimore. Ron not only had motive and means, but he'd had the opportunity to commit the crime, driving to Jane's house in Patrick's silver compact car. If he'd been in either his own or his wife's car, he'd have parked it farther from the house, but he had no reason to do that in the silver car. By parking it in Jane's driveway, he wasn't implicating himself.

What time had he returned to the spa in the silver car? Patrick hadn't known when Ron brought the car back, but maybe Leeann did. Val wondered how she could insert that question into a condolence visit with Ron's wife.

Chapter 26

When Val met her friend in the spa parking lot, Chatty was all smiles. "I got to help in an investigation. You and your grandfather probably talk to the police chief a lot, but I don't. It was fun."

"Hardly anyone enjoys talking to the police." But Val was gratified that the chief had taken her suggestion and interviewed Chatty.

"It was easier than talking to a widow after her husband's sudden death is going to be. I never know what to say to someone who's grieving."

Val had never seen Chatty at a loss for words, but this was one time when she couldn't fill silence with the latest gossip.

As they crossed the spa's lawn toward the building, Val shivered in a chill wind. She would have zipped up her windbreaker except that she needed both hands to carry the spinach quiche she was bringing to Leeann. "It looks gloomy, a big change from Saturday night, when people were enjoying themselves around the garden, eating and talking."

Chatty said, "I spent most of the open house in my treatment room, so I didn't see it looking lively."

Today the lobby, where the staff and visitors had gathered for champagne on Saturday night, was empty except for the receptionist.

Chatty approached the desk and said, "We came to offer Leeann our condolences, if she's up for visitors."

The receptionist nodded and picked up her phone. "I'll ask Sabrine if it's okay for you to go back."

A minute later, Sabrine emerged from the wing where the medical and administrative offices were. She greeted them with a subdued smile rather than her usual dazzling one. "Hey, Chatty. This isn't the opening day we anticipated, is it?"

"No. How's Leeann doing?"

"She's still in shock, but she's coping. She's had calls and visitors, so she hasn't been alone. We plan to be open fully tomorrow. I suggested she delay the opening a few more days, but she said work would keep her mind off her troubles."

Val nodded. "Staying busy helps the day go by." But probably not the nights.

Chatty sighed. "It'll be hard for her to manage the first day without Ron. On top of everything else, she'll have to find a new spa director."

Sabrine smiled briefly. "I'm the new spa director, at least for now."

Looking startled, Chatty took a moment to respond. "Congratulations on your promotion."

Val remembered Chatty saying Sabrine's position as marketing manager was a huge step up from her last job. As the spa's new director, Sabrine had gone up a whole flight of stairs in a single bound. "We came to give Leeann our condolences. We brought food too." Val held up her covered pie container. "I made a quiche, and Chatty brought her terrific homemade bread."

"Just leave them on the receptionist's desk. I'll put them with the other food Leeann has received. Let me ask if she's up for more visitors."

She stepped away from them to talk on the phone and gave them the go-ahead half a minute later. As they followed her down the corridor, they passed the office where Val had interviewed with Ron. His nameplate had been replaced by Sabrine's. A fast change, good for Sabrine, who needed respect as the new boss. It might also be good for Leeann, who'd otherwise see her dead husband's name every time she walked by.

Sabrine took them into Leeann's offices, mentioned the quiche and the bread they'd brought, and hurried away.

Behind the desk with folders stacked neatly on it, Leeann sat tight lipped. "Thank you for coming and for the food. Please have a seat." She pointed at the two straight-backed leather chairs in front of the desk.

Val sat down. "I was sorry to hear about Ron. My condolences to you and your family."

Chatty nodded. "He was a fine man. The staff will really miss him."

"I appreciate that. Even people I hardly know have brought meals. Of course some of them came only because they're nosy, but most have been very kind."

Val glanced sidewise at the nosiest person in Bayport, and admitted to herself that she was the second nosiest, though she didn't gossip as much as Chatty. "We have a tradition in this area to feed people who are grieving. It's one less thing for them to deal with at a difficult time."

"It was so sudden. Focusing on the opening is easier than dealing with his death. I haven't arranged any memorial yet."

Chatty spoke up. "You're really busy with the spa going into full gear this week."

"Ron did so much with very little help from me. Hiring staff. Getting the grounds and the building ready for the VIP event, a brunch for my friends, and then the open house. He spent time in the hot tub every night since it was installed. It relaxed him so he could wind down and fall asleep." Leeann sighed, shifted the folders on her desk, and picked up her pen.

She looked ready to go back to work, but Val wasn't ready to leave. To keep this visit from ending too soon, she'd give Leeann information and hope for some in return. "Ron had other worries in the last few weeks—harassment and some potentially dangerous incidents. That's why he hired my grandfather's security crew to watch for trouble at the open house."

Chatty stared open-mouthed at Val. She hadn't known about the incidents or Granddad's gig.

Leeann frowned, the only lines in her doll-like face that Val had ever seen. "The drunk who made a scene at the open house was certainly harassing

Ron. I didn't hear about any dangerous incidents. What exactly happened?"

Val told her about the punch Ron drank at the open house and his car being run off the road.

Leeann gaped at her. "He didn't tell me. He must not have wanted me to worry. Someone vandalized his car too, punctured his tire."

Val faked surprise. "Gosh, when did that happen?"

"Ron noticed the flat Saturday evening a week ago. He had to borrow Patrick's car to pick up the wine for my brunch and the dinners I ordered from the Tuscan Eaterie. For health reasons, I eat at the same time every day. So He needed to be back by six with dinner."

"Did he make it on time?" Val hoped that didn't sound too nosy.

"With a few minutes to spare." Leeann's eyes welled with tears. "He was always sensitive to my needs."

Val made a mental note to ask the chief when the 911 call about the fire had come in. The answer would tell her whether Ron's errands that evening could have included a detour for arson.

For the last few minutes, Chatty had been in sponge mode, soaking up juicy details to pass on, but now she turned to Val. "Why did Ron ask your grandfather for help instead of the police?"

To avoid any scrutiny into his past. "He couldn't prove that his drink had been spiked or his car run off the road. And he didn't want police around at the open house."

Leeann pursed her thin lips. "The local police do not impress me. They have no idea what killed

Ron. I'm afraid he might have pushed himself too hard the last few weeks to make the business successful. And now he's not here to see the fruits of his labor." Leeann patted her stomach. "My only consolation is that I'm pregnant. I'm expecting a boy. I hope he'll be just like Ron."

Be careful what you wish for. "Congratulations. That's wonderful news," Val said.

Chatty nodded. "And a good reason for you not to push yourself."

"Sabrine said the same thing. She's taking everything she can off my plate. I don't know what I'd do without her."

Chatty stood up. "We don't want to intrude on your busy day any longer. If you need anything, let me know. I'm happy to help any way I can."

"Thank you."

As they went back to the lobby, Val spotted Patrick talking to the receptionist. Once they were outside, Chatty gave Val a disgruntled look. "Why didn't you tell me Ron was being harassed?"

"He confided in my grandfather, not me." Val dropped the sore subject. "Sabrine moved up quickly into a really responsible position. Do you think Patrick will resent her shooting to the top?"

Chatty shrugged. "She'll be easier to work for than Ron. And Patrick is lower on the totem pole. He couldn't expect to be Ron's replacement."

Val remembered Chatty saying that Sabrine and Leeann had been roommates years ago. It was still a startling promotion to go from marketing manager to director of a new business. "Is Sabrine married?"

"She's single. That's all I know about her private life. She doesn't talk much about it."

Val gave Sabrine credit for figuring out that anything private wouldn't stay that way if Chatty knew about it. "It's a good thing Ron survived long enough to give Leeann a male offspring. Now she doesn't have to dust off her checklist and find a new perfect husband. If he'd lived longer, she might have given birth to more than one little Ron."

"Could still happen. Leeann plans ahead. I wouldn't be surprised if there are frozen embryos of future Melgrems."

The short visit with Leeann had given Val food for thought on her drive home. All along she'd assumed that if Ron had been murdered, his death was linked to his former career and his relationship to Jane. If that was true, the Rilke sisters, the Dernes, and Jane's ex had reasons to hate Ron and take revenge. But none of them had easy access to the hot tub room. Motive but no opportunity. But what if his death was based on the present, not the past?

The person who'd gained the most from his death was Sabrine. She'd gotten a promotion she could only dream about. And Chatty had commented that Ron was hitting on Sabrine. Val remembered the look of hatred the marketing manager had directed at him. She had good motives and the best opportunity to get rid of Ron. After Chatty and Patrick left on Saturday night, Sabrine was the only person besides Ron in the building.

A good theory, but Val doubted it would convince anyone that Sabrine had killed Ron. Bram believed Ron died by accident or by a perfect murder, but the police had found no evidence of foul play. And Granddad was interested only in who killed Jane.

Chapter 27

Granddad took two slices of pizza from a box on the counter and brought his plate to the kitchen table, where Val and a salad were waiting for him.

He sat down across from her. "You find out anything at the spa related to Jane's death?"

She nodded. "The evening she was killed, Ron had a flat tire from a deliberate puncture. He might have done it himself so he could drive Patrick's car, rather than his own, to Jane's house."

"Or Patrick could have punctured the tire because he wanted people to see Ron running errands in the silver compact. After Ron brought the car back to the spa, Patrick coulda driven it to Jane's house. When Nigel spotted the silver car on Jane's road, he didn't see who was driving it, right?"

"That's true, but I came up with a way to figure out who was in the car when the fire started. Leeann said Ron was back from his errands before six o'clock, their hard-and-fast dinner hour. Once we find out when the 911 call for the fire went out, we can figure out if Ron had time to set the fire and arrive home when Leeann said he did."

Granddad took a bite of pizza, chewed it, and drank some beer. "A couple of minutes one way or another wouldn't make a big difference. Unless Leeann was looking at the clock exactly when Ron came back with the car, you can't pin down when he got home. And the time of the 911 call won't tell you when the fire started. It could have been going for a while before the neighbors noticed and called it in. The arson investigators might be able to estimate when it started, but probably not down to the minute."

Val hid her disappointment. So much for sewing up the case against Ron by proving when he was in the silver car, but another timing issue suggested he was the killer. "Jane died two days after she set up an appointment with Leeann. Ron wouldn't have wanted his wife to hear what Jane knew about him. No one else had any reason we know to attack Jane on that day."

Granddad shrugged. "I wouldn't put much store by the date of the arson. That could have been random."

"Other evidence also points to him—her death from a drug he had access to and the fire in her study, which would destroy any records connecting Ron to her."

"Patrick also had access to Botox and would have wanted to burn any records that showed Jane worked for and blew the whistle on his brother."

Val conceded that Granddad was right. Though

he'd shot down all her theories so far, she went ahead and told him her latest one. "I came away from the spa with a new idea about Ron's death. Sabrine hated Ron and now she's taken over his job as the spa director. She was handing out glasses of champagne on Saturday night and could have put something into Ron's to make him drowsy. Maybe he dozed off and slipped under the water, or she could have given him a little help going under. The two of them were the last people in the building."

"Sabrine had no reason to harm Jane. You believe Ron killed Jane and then someone killed Ron?" When she nodded, Granddad continued. "We've had a few bad apples in these parts in the last few years, but never two different folks committing murders a week apart."

"There's a first time for everything, but okay, maybe there wasn't a second murderer. Bram thinks Ron died by accident."

"Mighty convenient accident. No reason to look for Jane's murderer if he's dead. Case closed." Granddad stuck his fork into a lettuce leaf. "Let's say Ron didn't kill Jane and he didn't die by accident. That means the same person might have killed both of them. Two nearly perfect murders. No trace of evidence to point to the killer. No way to tell how the victims died. Even the experts didn't know what killed Jane until you made that lucky guess about the Botox—"

"Are you referring to my brilliant, educated guess?" Val winked at him.

"Call it what you like. You know what worries me? Folks who get away with two murders might think they're invincible and commit more. You could be right that Ron killed Jane and then died by accident. But what if you're wrong? Someone else may die."

His words echoed dialogue from *The Mousetrap* about staying one step ahead of the killer or there would be another death. "You know what worries me, Granddad? That going after the murderer might make *you* the next victim. Just tell the chief what you suspect and pass on any clues you dig up to him." Maybe Granddad had already been digging for clues and that's what had kept him busy today. "What did you do today?"

"Went to the Village in the morning. Spent some time talking to Millicent and Cassandra. Then Nigel and Nanette joined us."

"Did Jane's or Ron's death come up in the conversation?"

Granddad hesitated. "We talked mostly about tonight's rehearsal. After lunch we all went to the theater to look at the setup. I met the college students who are going to handle the sound effects and the lights. I got to see all the different types of lighting you can use."

Val could understand the director and the stage manager scoping out the theater ahead of time, but why the others? "You *all* went to the theater this afternoon? Not just Millicent and Cassandra, but you, Nigel, and Nanette?" When Granddad nodded, she continued. "Why weren't Bethany, Bram, and I invited?"

"Because the three of you work and the rest of us are retired."

"What did we miss by not being there?"

"Nothing you need to know." Instead of savoring the dinner as usual, Granddad wolfed down the rest of his pizza. "I want to get there early, and I still have to change clothes for my role."

"I haven't picked out my outfit. What are you wearing?"

"A black shirt and a white scarf. Millicent can give me tips on how to tie the scarf so I look Bohemian."

Val glanced around the kitchen at the small mess that even a simple meal like pizza and a salad left. "You go ahead. I'll clean up here and catch a ride with Bram or Bethany. See you later, Granddad, on the big stage."

As Val finished her meal, she thought about Leeann having her dinner at six sharp, probably eating food people had given her along with their condolences. Company would comfort her more than food. Though she'd been married to Ron only six months, it would be difficult for her to eat alone. Or would family members or Sabrine join her? Before long, Sabrine might even move into the big house with Leeann, roomies once more.

Val went upstairs to choose the clothes most suitable to her role in the play, a young woman on a limited budget trying to make a good impression on paying houseguests. She ended up with a gray skirt, a white blouse she hadn't worn since leaving her office job in New York, and a green cardigan sweater her mother had left the last time she visited Granddad.

By the time Val called Bram for a ride, he was already near the theater in Treadwell.

"I left early to pick up a few items on my way

here," he said. "If Millicent okays it, I'm going to demonstrate something I learned from doing magic shows. I think we can use it for dramatic effect in *The Mousetrap*."

Val was intrigued. "How would a magic routine fit into *The Mousetrap*?"

"I don't have time to explain now. Just do me a favor. While I demo it, keep an eye on Nigel and Patrick. See you later, Val."

She put the phone down. What did Bram have up his sleeve?

Chapter 28

Val hitched a ride to the rehearsal with Bethany. They were the last two cast members to arrive. After dropping their jackets and bags on the theater's front-row seats, where the others had left their belongings, they climbed the steps to the stage.

Eight chair-height stools were set up in a shallow half-circle. They took the two empty stools on stage right, with Val on the one closest to the audience and across the stage from Bram.

While Millicent and Cassandra stood onstage conferring, Val checked how everyone was dressed. Next to her, Bethany wore a black blazer over gray slacks, perfect for her role and a change from her usual bright colors. Granddad's scarf set him apart from the other men in jackets or sweaters. Millicent, playing a young man, wore a knitted vest and a bow tie. Nanette's large peacock-blue shawl and matching bucket hat made her the most striking cast member. Her clothes were a bit flamboyant for the prim, uptight woman she was playing. She hadn't dressed for her role, as Millicent had instructed. How would the director react to that?

To Val's surprise, Millicent raised no objection. "Good clothing choices, everyone. I've guided you through the early rehearsals when we focused on the script reading. The stage manager is in charge of the action in the theater. Cassandra will explain how we'll use the stage and backstage. And I'll put on my actor hat or, rather, my actor glasses." Millicent perched a pair of rectangular glasses, oversized with dark plastic frames, on her nose.

Cassandra faced the cast, holding a clipboard and looking confident. "The curtain will rise on an empty stage. You'll follow the stage directions in the script when you exit and enter." She pointed to the upstage and downstage entrances from the wings on both sides.

Millicent pulled off the glasses she'd just donned, still the director and not the actor. "At a rehearsal last week, I said most of you would exit before the scenes when the murderer attacks the one person remaining onstage. We decided to clear the stage for another dramatic scene. It's in the second act when Val and Bram will be alone on stage, the scene when the married couple suspect each other of being the killer. A subplot in the play is whether their marriage can survive murder, so this is a tense and significant scene."

Cassandra added, "If you're not in that scene or the other scenes when the stage is cleared, you can stretch your legs and get a drink of water, but silence is essential backstage. If you want to talk, even during intermission, please go outside by the stage door. Follow me, and I'll show you where that door is and how the backstage is laid out."

They trooped after her. Val was surprised at how cramped the area behind the stage was. Connecting the wings was a narrow passage, what Cassandra called the crossover, allowing the cast to get from one side to the other. The men's dressing room and bathroom were on the right, next to the stage door, and the women's rooms were on the other side. Val noticed a metal staircase to a catwalk above the stage.

As Cassandra led the group back to the stage, Nanette spoke up. "After I'm murdered in Act One, I'm supposed to stay backstage during the second act, but there's no place to sit."

Millicent looked sympathetic. "I'm sorry about that. The green room, the cast lounge where you'd normally be able to wait, is full of props for the Treadwell Players' next production. But I'll check if there's a chair in that room that we can borrow for our show." She hurried backstage.

Cassandra continued the tour and pointed out the black curtain separating the stage and the backstage. A few feet in front of it was a white gauzy curtain. She fingered it. "This is the scrim. It will be the backdrop for our show. When the light hits it from the front at an angle, it looks like a solid white wall. But it turns semi-opaque, like a sheer curtain, if it's lit from behind. That lets the audience see what's behind the scrim, though it's fuzzy. Bright light from the front makes the scrim transparent so the audience can see what's behind it as clearly as what's in front of it."

Since all the action took place in one room, Val

couldn't figure out when the scrim might be used in *The Mousetrap*. "Is the scrim going to look like a wall during our entire show?"

Cassandra shook her head. "No. In Christie's stage directions, the policeman presses his face against a window before his entrance, frightening the people inside. We'll get a similar effect by changing the lighting while Patrick peers through the scrim." She walked between the scrim and the black curtain a few feet behind it. "I'll position Patrick here just before his entrance in Act One. Other than that, we won't be using this area."

Millicent rejoined the group. "I found a folding director's chair for Nanette. It's so tight backstage that the best place to set it up is behind the scrim." She turned to Nanette. "The light will be dim where you'll be sitting. You won't be visible. Do you want to sit there so you can watch the second act?"

Nanette nodded. "If you're certain I won't be seen."

Cassandra pointed to the back of the theater, behind the last row of seats. "Jamal will make sure of that. He's our lighting technician. He's handled the lighting for his college productions."

The young African American man at the lighting console grinned and waved to them.

Cassandra waved back and turned to the cast. "Our sound technician couldn't come to this rehearsal, so I'll be playing the sound effects from the wings. Lights, please, Jamal." Instantly, the lights onstage became more intense, the scrim turned into a white wall, and Cassandra nodded approval.

"If you'll take your seats again, I have a few announcements to make." Millicent remained standing as the rest of the cast sat down. "We'll have at least one person in the audience for tonight's rehearsal, but that won't distract you. As you can see, the auditorium looks like a black hole when you're onstage."

Val peered into the black hole and noticed a sliver of light around the door into the auditorium as it closed. Someone must have come in to watch the rehearsal, but Val didn't catch even a silhouette.

Millicent continued. "The artificial snow we were going to sprinkle around as the characters come onstage may not be delivered in time. Bram had an idea for a different way to suggest the foul weather that maroons the characters at the guesthouse. He and Cassandra will demonstrate it for us."

Bram carried his stool upstage and set it between Nigel and Patrick, the two men he'd asked Val to watch. He went into the wings and brought out a bundle wrapped in a towel. "Let's say the snowstorm in *The Mousetrap* is followed by a thick fog. As the characters arrive, we can show the fog creeping into the room."

Cassandra emerged from the wings with an electric kettle and put it on the stool as if she were a magician's assistant. "The water's hot."

"Thank you, Cassandra." He opened the towel and raised the lid on the kettle. "Now I'm going to add chunks of dry ice to the water."

Nigel barely glanced at what Bram was doing, apparently lost in his own thoughts. Patrick and the other cast members appeared transfixed as a cloud of dense fog arose from the kettle.

Bram explained how the fog might be used during *The Mousetrap*. Cassandra, standing just off-stage, would drop ice in the kettle. With the help of a fan, the fog would swirl along the floor as each new arrival came onstage.

Bethany craned her neck as more fog arose from the kettle. "My first graders would love that! What makes the fog, Bram?"

"Dry ice is solid carbon dioxide. It doesn't melt in water but turns into a gas. With this small amount of ice, the gas disperses quickly, especially in a large building like this. But don't do this with a lot of ice in a classroom unless you can open the windows. Carbon dioxide could displace the oxygen you're breathing." Bram turned from Bethany to gaze into the auditorium as though his real audience was there. "There was a case a few years ago when dry ice tossed into an indoor pool killed three people. They died of asphyxiation."

Val gasped. So dry ice in hot water could explain Ron's death. Granddad exchanged a look with her. He too understood the meaning of Bram's demonstration, and maybe Bram expected whoever was sitting in the audience to make the connection too. But what about Nigel and Patrick, whose reactions Bram wanted her to watch?

Nigel had shown little interest in the demo, possibly because he was aware of the effects of dry ice in water, but Patrick was the one who'd brought the dry ice to the hot tub room. He'd reacted to Bram's demo no differently than the other cast members.

* * *

"Thank you for the fog demonstration," Millicent said. "I'm going to hope that the artificial snow arrives before our performance, Bram. It's less trouble than making fog. For this rehearsal, I'd like you all to focus on getting your entrances and exits down pat. If I have comments on your reading, I'll save them for the end."

Cassandra took over. "Let's begin the rehearsal. Everyone, please clear the stage."

Once they were all in the wings, the stage went dark. She then played the opening sound effects—the whistled tune of "Three Blind Mice," a piercing scream, police whistles, and a voice over a staticky radio reporting a woman's murder in London.

When the stage lights came up, Val went onstage and took her seat. The radio announcer's warning of snow and ice on the roads was Val's cue to read her opening lines.

She was surprised at how quickly the first act went by with no interruptions from Millicent. The dramatic scene at the end of the act worked well. All the cast members except for Nanette exited the stage. Val waited in the wings for her cue to enter. Sound effects suggested a door creaking open, someone whistling "Three Blind Mice," and the click of a light switch as the stage went dark. Noises suggesting a struggle ensued and then the thud of a body hitting the floor. Val felt a chill. She'd heard those sound effects at earlier rehearsals, but in total darkness they sounded more ominous.

Cassandra tapped Val's shoulder to tell her to

enter. As the lights came up, Val spotted the victim and screamed. Her scream had improved, but it still sounded forced to her own ears. The stage lights dimmed for the intermission.

Val grabbed a bottle of water backstage, caught Bram's eye, and pointed to the stage door. They went outside. She led him a few yards away from the door so anyone else going in or out wouldn't hear them. "Your demo of what killed Ron was great, but that doesn't prove someone intended to kill him. It would be hard to prosecute anyone for murder."

"I still think it was probably an accident, but I wanted to know if Patrick or Nigel looked nervous."

"Neither did. Nigel didn't pay much attention. Patrick, like the others onstage, seemed fascinated by the fog cloud." Val spotted Patrick coming from the parking lot toward the stage door with his phone to his ear. "Speak of the devil."

He approached them. "Looks like you both needed fresh air too. I got a chance to stretch my legs as well, but you might not. Intermission should be over in another minute." He opened the stage door and went inside.

Val barely finished her water before Cassandra poked her head out and said it was time to go back onstage. When they followed her inside, she went up to Nanette. "I set up the chair for you behind the scrim. You'll have to be in place before Act Two starts."

Nanette slipped behind the scrim as the rest of the cast filed onstage. The lights were dim until they were all seated. Then the stage went dark for a few seconds. Through the scrim, Val glimpsed Nanette briefly in the director's chair.

"Sorry about the lighting glitch," Jamal said from the back of the auditorium as he lit up the stage and the scrim turned into a solid wall again.

Act Two had more tension and less comedy than the first act. The dialogue centered on which of the characters could be a murderer. Midway through the act, five of the actors exited, leaving Val and Bram alone. They hurled accusations of secrecy and lying at each other across the stage. Val hoped she and Bram would never talk to each other like that for real.

During Bram's longest piece of dialogue, the lights went off, as they had just before the murder in Act One.

Except this blackout isn't part of the script. Had Jamal accidentally flipped a switch again?

The only light was a weak one coming from behind the scrim. Sitting on the dark stage, Val had an indistinct view of Nanette in the chair and of a man coming up behind her, one arm extended toward her in a thrusting motion. Another man appeared behind the scrim on the opposite side. He held a gun.

None of this is in the script! A scream caught in Val's throat.

"Stay put, Val. I'm coming over to you." Bram's whisper was amplified by the microphones near the footlights.

Val could just make out his shadowy figure as he crossed the stage toward her.

Nigel's voice rang out from behind the scrim. "If you make a move, I'll shoot, and this isn't a prop gun."

Is he going to shoot Bram? Fear paralyzed Val for a second. Then she jumped up.

An instant later, Bram's arms closed around her. His body blocked her view of the scene behind the scrim. She peered around him.

The light brightened, making the scrim totally transparent. Nanette was slumped to the side on the chair. Patrick stood frozen behind her with Nigel pointing a pistol at him.

Val shouted, "Nanette's hurt! Call 911."

The auditorium lit up as it would for an intermission.

Val turned and saw Chief Yardley rushing down the center aisle. "Police! Stay where you are!" he roared and charged up the steps to the stage.

Millicent emerged from the wings. "This way!"

The chief followed her backstage and appeared behind Patrick a moment later.

Granddad hurried toward Val from the other side of the stage. "It's okay, Val. Nanette's safe in the women's dressing room. That's a dummy dressed in her clothes behind the scrim."

She stared at him. "What? You mean this whole rehearsal was a setup?"

Granddad's eyes twinkled. "It was a mousetrap."

Chapter 29

The mouse was trapped between the chief and Nigel. Nanette appeared behind the scrim and moved next to her husband.

Patrick looked from the dummy to the real Nanette. "My brother's still in jail," he bellowed, "because of you! He's on a suicide watch, and it's your fault!"

Nanette hid behind Nigel. He stepped toward Patrick and raised the gun as if taking aim.

Val cringed and clutched Bram even tighter.

Two uniformed police officers rushed past Nigel, apparently after entering by the stage door. At first Val thought they were actors because she didn't recognize their uniforms. Then she realized they were Treadwell police. The theater was in their jurisdiction, not Chief Yardley's.

He pointed at Patrick. "Cuff him and take him to the station." While the officers handcuffed Patrick, the chief added, "Send over some techs to process the scene here. They might find evidence relating to a crime we're investigating in Bayport. I'll talk to your chief and tell him what's going on."

Patrick continued his tirade against Nanette as the officers marched him backstage. The stage door banged shut and soon drowned out his rage.

"Third time wasn't the charm for Patrick," Granddad muttered.

Behind the scrim, the chief turned to Nigel. "Give me the gun, Mr. Derne."

Nigel handed it over. "It's not loaded. And I have a permit."

"I'll check that before I give it back to you, but that won't happen tonight. I'll be here until the Treadwell detectives take over."

With the gun in the chief's hands, Val's tension eased.

Bram relaxed his hold on her. "When I saw the gun, I was afraid Nigel had lost his mind and was going to shoot us all."

And he'd put himself between her and Nigel. *He risked his life for me.* What if Bram had been shot? Tears welled in Val's eyes at the thought of losing him. "I love you, Bram," she whispered. She'd never said that before.

"I love you too." Another first. He bent down to kiss her.

They were reminded they weren't alone by Cassandra's plaintive voice from on high. "Can I come down yet?"

Her sister looked up. "Yes, but be careful." Millicent turned to the others onstage. "Cassandra was stationed on the catwalk. She could see what was happening below, behind the scrim, and texted Jamal when to turn the lights off and on."

As Cassandra joined the cast onstage, the chief addressed the group. "I'd like you all to vacate the stage, backstage, and auditorium. If you have business to conduct, do it in the lobby."

"We're sure glad you came," Granddad said.

The Villagers nodded their agreement. Val wondered how Granddad had convinced the chief to attend the rehearsal.

"Good show," he said. "I'll buy a ticket to find out who Agatha Christie's culprit is. By the way, Ryan's flying back from Florida tomorrow. You'll have a replacement for the actor you just lost."

Bethany's eyes lit up. "That's wonderful news!"

Once they were all in the lobby, Millicent announced they were free to go and that the next rehearsal would be in the theater at seven on Wednesday night.

She approached Jamal and thanked him for his superb handling of the lights. They couldn't have pulled off the hoax without him. He declared it had been fun and headed out.

Bethany put her hands on her hips. "I'm not leaving until someone explains what happened behind the scrim. I saw part of it from the wings, but it made no sense."

Bram added, "And I'd like to know *how* it happened."

While glowing from his declaration of love, Val still wondered about his role in the hoax. "So you weren't in on any of it, Bram?"

Before he could answer, Granddad did. "Nope. Us old folks did it on our own."

Val glanced at him, the Rilkes, and the Dernes. "So that's why the five of you spent hours in the theater this afternoon. You were rehearsing your play within a play."

Nanette went over to Granddad and hugged him. "I thought your scenario was crazy and nothing would happen after we went to the trouble of setting up the trap. I was wrong. Thank you for figuring out how to snare the man who wanted to kill me."

"It was a group effort." Granddad looked from the Dernes toward the Rilke sisters. "You all played your parts to the hilt. And you did it with only one rehearsal."

Nigel shook Granddad's hand. "If we hadn't given Patrick the perfect opportunity to kill Nanette, he'd have tried when we didn't expect it."

Millicent nodded. "We prevented a murder, and Jane's killer is in custody."

Val smiled at the well-earned display of elder pride.

Bethany waved her hand like an impatient student. "Patrick killed Jane and tried to kill Nanette? Why? And what was going on behind the scrim?"

Millicent patted her on the back. "Sorry to keep you in the dark. Sit down, and we'll fill in the blanks for you." She pointed toward two long benches at right angles in the far corner of the lobby.

Bethany, Granddad, Val, and Bram sat on one bench, the Rilkes and the Dernes on the other.

Granddad explained how Patrick, Ron, and Jane were connected to a doctor serving time for overprescribing painkillers. "I believe Patrick applied to work at the spa so he could take revenge on Ron for testifying against his half brother, Doctor Lazarin. Then Jane showed up, another person high on Patrick's hit list. She'd reported the doctor to the police. So Patrick devised a scheme to kill her and frame Ron for it."

Bethany frowned. "Okay, but how on earth did you figure out that Patrick would go after Nanette next?"

"*The Mousetrap* gave me the idea. A vengeful killer gets away with two murders and goes for a third, with 'Three Blind Mice' playing right before each murder. Patrick sang it on Saturday night." Granddad sat forward on the bench. "Ron died that night, exactly one week after Jane did."

Bram spoke up. "Ron's death could have been accidental."

"Or not," Val pointed out. "Patrick was in the tent when the caterers told Leeann they'd pack the leftovers in dry ice." Though he'd pretended not to know about it when he came to the tent for ice. "And he was in charge of setting the hot tub temperature. But producing the ideal conditions for Ron's death doesn't mean Patrick can be tried and convicted of murder."

Nanette spoke up. "Ron was fated to die. I sent him some serious bad luck cards, and they worked." She paused and then laughed. "Just joking. I'm not superstitious. I mailed him death cards to make him squirm."

"Told you so," Bram whispered in Val's ear.

Cassandra pointed to herself. "I did more than that. The eye drops I put in his drink at the Village turned him green."

"Just like I said," Granddad whispered in Val's other ear.

Val wondered who else would vie for the honor of having made Ron suffer the most. Nigel would beat the death-card sender and the punch spiker, but he was smart enough not to confess to forcing cars off the road intentionally. And Millicent had her story about the smoothie switch down pat, either because it was true or because she was a good actress.

Bethany tapped her foot. "I still don't understand why Patrick targeted Nanette and how your trap worked."

Granddad said, "It occurred to me that Patrick, like the *Mousetrap* killer, could have a third victim in mind. I didn't know who that might be. Then I remembered Cassandra saying Nanette's testimony led to Patrick's brother getting the maximum sentence."

Nanette added, "I also waged a campaign to deny him parole."

Nigel patted her on the shoulder. "You did well."

Millicent said, "Once we realized Patrick might go after Nanette, we came up with a ruse to catch him in the act. I borrowed a dummy the Treadwell Players used in a production last year. Nanette and I picked out a distinctive shawl and hat that we could put on the dummy quickly. Before the rehearsal started, I told everyone that Nanette would be behind the scrim during Act Two, basically a sitting duck. All of us, including Patrick, saw her there right before we went onstage for the second act."

Nanette smiled. "When you all started reading your lines, Cassandra and I dressed the dummy and put it in the chair behind the scrim."

Cassandra nodded. "Jamal lit up the scrim so it looked like a wall, and no one could see what we were doing. During the scene when Val and Bram were the only ones onstage, Millicent made sure everyone backstage kept away from Patrick. He couldn't resist temptation. You know the rest. I signaled Jamal when to change the lighting, and Patrick was caught in the act. I just hope he doesn't get off on a technicality."

"He definitely stuck something in the dummy." Nigel imitated Patrick's arm motion. "And he shouted out his motive when the police arrested him. His acting skills deserted him."

Millicent smiled. "The rest of us put on quite a good performance tonight."

During the Rilke sisters' explanation of the ruse, Val had tamped down her annoyance, but now it bubbled up. "Excuse me, Millicent, but I wasn't performing when Nanette was attacked and Nigel brandished a gun. I was quaking in fear. Why did you keep the plan a secret from three of us?"

"We kept you, Bethany, and Bram out of the game because we needed some cast members to behave naturally, rather than anticipating the trap and tipping off Patrick."

In other words, Millicent doesn't trust our acting abilities.

Nigel added, "The details about the operation were shared on a strictly need-to-know basis."

Bram winked and whispered to Val, "Like a top-secret military plan."

"Now I understand what happened." Bethany stood up. "School starts early, so I'm going to head home. Good night, everyone." She turned to Val. "Do you want a ride back to Bayport?"

"No, I'll drive back with Granddad."

The rest of the cast was ready to leave too.

On the way out of the theater, Granddad said to Bram, "Come over to the house for a nightcap and bring your mother. With her love of Agatha Christie, she'll enjoy hearing how we sprang our mousetrap."

And Granddad would want to impress her with the success of his scheme.

Chapter 30

Val and Granddad were about to get into the car when Chief Yardley hailed them in the theater parking lot. "The Treadwell police and their tech team have taken over. I thought you two deserved to know that a hypodermic needle was stuck in the dummy. The lab should be able to determine what was in that needle."

"Huh," Granddad grunted. "I thought Patrick would go after Nanette with a pocketknife or try to strangle or suffocate her. Why would he bring a loaded hypodermic needle to a rehearsal?"

Val remembered Patrick coming to the stage door from the parking lot. "He didn't, until he learned Nanette would be alone and unseen behind the scrim. He went out to his car at intermission. He must have felt safe hiding a hypodermic and maybe even Botox in his vehicle. If they were ever found, he'd say that Ron had left them there when he borrowed the car."

Granddad nodded, "Patrick reckoned he could

use them again on his next victim. Why not? He got away with it once."

"It's easier to find evidence once you have a good idea who committed a crime," the chief said. "Though attacking a dummy won't get Patrick convicted of murder, other evidence has turned up. When we searched Ron's office after his death, we found Botox in the back of the closet. The fingerprints on the vial weren't Ron's, but they might match Patrick's. And if the syringe he used tonight had Botox in it, we've got a connection to Jane's death that the lab may be able to prove. I'll keep you two posted. Have a good night."

As he turned to go, Granddad said, "Thanks, Earl, for listening to my idea and trusting the cast to carry it through."

"I didn't expect your ploy to work, but on the off chance it did, I needed to be here. The hardest part was convincing the Treadwell police to cover the stage door while we waited for Patrick to take the bait."

"That explains how the police got here so fast," Val said. "Good night, Chief."

Val climbed behind the wheel while Granddad opened the passenger door of his car. The glare of headlights bothered his eyes, so he preferred that she drive at night. While he buckled his seat belt, she enjoyed a view of the full moon through the windshield.

Once they were on the road, Val congratulated Granddad. "You were right about who killed Jane, and I was wrong. For Leeann's sake, I'm glad Ron wasn't the murderer." She expected Granddad to crow about his detective skills. When he didn't, she continued. "You and Millicent set a perfect trap for Patrick. It was poetic justice. He fell for an illusion after he created the illusion that Ron had killed Jane. Patrick made sure Ron was seen driving the silver compact and told me that he'd lent the car to someone who put a dent in it. He planted Botox in Ron's office in case the police figured out what killed Jane. He might have erased Jane's appointment with Leeann so it would seem Ron had done it to keep her away from his wife. Or maybe Ron erased the appointment. We'll never know for sure."

Granddad didn't respond. She glanced sideways at him. As usual, when she was driving him, he was taking a catnap.

Five minutes after Val and Granddad arrived home, Bram and Dorothy came to the door.

She'd brought a bottle of champagne. "I always have champagne in the fridge in case there's a celebration. Bram said we should have one tonight, but he didn't say why."

Val locked eyes with Bram. Was the champagne to toast Granddad's triumph, or would there be something else to celebrate?

Granddad broke into a wide smile. "Thank you. I'll open the bottle and get some glasses."

Val reached for the bottle. "Bram and I will do that. You sit down with Dorothy and tell her what happened at the theater."

Once Bram and Val were in the kitchen, she

filled a divided serving dish with pretzels and veggie chips. "Did I ever tell you that my grandmother
taught me to cook in this kitchen?"

"I think your grandfather mentioned that."
Bram went over to the window that looked out on
the backyard.

The kitchen was Val's happy place not only because of its connection to cooking. It also repre-
sented the love her grandparents had shared there
and showered her with. Her parents' marriage was
equally loving. She wanted that kind of marriage
for herself.

The next move was hers. She joined Bram at the
window. "It's a beautiful night with a full moon.
Let's have a sip of champagne and then go for a
walk."

He smiled as if that was the best idea he'd ever
heard. "I'll drink to that."

He kissed her and popped the cork on the champagne. A minute later they were clinking glasses
with Granddad and Dorothy. He'd told her what
had happened at the theater. She proposed a toast
to Granddad for figuring out how to trap Jane's
killer.

He grinned. "Thank you. I have to give credit to
the Rilke sisters and the Dernes. They took my
idea and ran with it."

Dorothy sipped her champagne. "I'm surprised
none of them recognized Patrick from the doctor's trial."

"They told me Patrick wasn't there for the trial."
Granddad adjusted his glasses. "He was probably
away at college. His online bio says when he gradu-

ated from a California university. It was about the same time his brother was sentenced and jailed."

"Cassandra thought he looked familiar when he came to his first rehearsal," Val said, "but she couldn't place him."

Granddad nodded. "When I told her who he was, it jogged her memory of a young man who was with the doctor the day he entered a plea and posted bail. She said Patrick looked a lot different then, unshaven with long hair down to his shoulders."

Dorothy sighed. "So sad, a young man ruining his life. I keep thinking about that Robert Frost poem. It starts, 'Some think the world will end by fire, some by ice,' and it ends with 'I know enough of hate to say that ice is nice and will suffice.' At first we thought Jane's life ended by fire, but the ice of hate was what really killed her."

And ice had killed Ron too, not just figuratively but literally. Val put down her champagne. "I could use some fresh air."

"Me too," Bram said. "Let's take a walk."

They hurried to the hall before Granddad or Dorothy could suggest going along. Val grabbed a windbreaker from the hall closet, opened the front door, and slipped out with Bram.

Five minutes later they were on a path along the river, a popular walk for locals and tourists on weekends. But on a Monday night, they shared it only with an occasional couple and some dog walkers. Bram was uncharacteristically silent as they strolled.

With no one in sight, they stopped where the

river widened on its way to the Chesapeake Bay. The moon's reflection made the river sparkle like diamonds.

Bram put his arm around her shoulder. "It's not the Seine River, and you can't see the Eiffel Tower, but this is a beautiful spot."

"Yes, and it's peaceful, no traffic noise, no pollution." Had he brought up Paris as a lead-in to postponing their trip again? Val steeled herself for the bad news.

Bram stared at the water. "You can't step into the same river twice. Nigel's gun-waving impressed that on me. Putting off what you've decided to do is crazy because you might not get the chance to do it." He swung her around to face him. "We met just six months ago, but we know each other well. We love each other." He took a deep breath. "I can't think of a better way to say this than the straightforward one. Will you marry me?"

Val was stunned into silence. For half a second. "I can't think of a better answer than *yes*." She saw the joy in his face and remembered the news she'd anticipated. "We're still going to Paris, right?"

He nodded. "We'll seal our engagement with a kiss under the Eiffel Tower."

"Let's do that right now under moonlight. The time is perfect—or, as the French would say—it's *parfait*."

Acknowledgments

Like many other mystery writers, I'm inspired by Agatha Christie, the best-selling fiction writer of all time. Besides eighty mystery novels and short story collections, she wrote twenty stage plays. They include *The Mousetrap*, the longest-running play in the world, with seventy years on the London stage. It's also a staple of community productions, like the one in *A Parfait Crime*. I've seen the play twice and remember its scary moments and its stunning ending. To avoid spoiling that experience for anyone who hasn't yet seen the play, I revealed the minimum about the plot and nothing about Christie's culprit in scenes where my characters rehearse the play and try to solve the murder of a cast member.

I'd like to thank the people who shared their expertise with me as I wrote *A Parfait Crime*. James Gifford, Ph.D., drew on his experience acting in and directing plays, including Readers Theater productions, to give me enough information to write the rehearsal scenes in my book. Despite being busy with a six-course teaching load at a college, he kindly took the time to review the theater scene at the end of the book for accuracy. I'm grateful for your help and for our long friendship, Jim.

I consulted books and blogs by D.P. Lyle, M.D., for information on the availability and forensic detection of the substance used by the murderer in *A Parfait Crime.* As he did for earlier Five-Ingredient Mysteries, Dr. Lyle kindly responded to a question about the murder method in my book. Thank you again for your help, Dr. Lyle.

My son, Paul Corrigan, who has worked in wildland fire management for two decades, gave me information about the operation of volunteer fire departments and the Critical Incident Stress Debriefings (CISDs) that help firefighters deal with the trauma of a fatal fire.

Any mistakes in *A Parfait Crime* related to theater, forensics, or fires are inadvertent, the result of my misunderstanding of what the experts told me. Though my book is a work of fiction, I did not invent the fatal effects of the substances that kill characters in this book. I was inspired to put them in a mystery after reading newspaper reports about deaths at an indoor swimming pool and instances of rare but fatal complications from a drug that's safe when properly used. The characters in my book cite those same accounts.

It takes a community to catch a killer in *A Parfait Crime.* Likewise, it takes a community to bring a book to publication. I'm grateful to everyone who helped me while I wrote the book, in particular my mystery-writing critique partners, Carolyn Mulford and Helen Schwartz. They brainstormed the plot with me, gave me feedback on each chapter as I finished it, and edited the full manuscript on a tight deadline. Thank you for your advice and for your friendship.

I also owe thanks to the reviewers of the book's first draft, whose feedback made the story better. They include Cathy Ondis Solberg, Elliot Wicks, as well as my daughter, Nora Corrigan, and my husband, Mike Corrigan.

Mike helped me through the whole process of writing this book and the previous eight in the series. His knowledge of birds was useful as I developed one character's backstory in *A Parfait Crime*. Like the character in the book, Mike took a birding expedition in Ecuador. Thank you for all the ways you support me, Mike. I love you.

Thank you to my agent, John Talbot, who brought the Five-Ingredient Mystery series to Kensington Books. I appreciate the work everyone at Kensington puts into bringing my books to market and making them a success: my editor, John Scognamiglio; publicists Larissa Ackerman and Jesse Cruz; and the design, production, marketing, and sales teams.

I'm also grateful to mystery readers and fans. I'd especially like to thank Dru Ann Love for all she does to support writers through her blog devoted to mysteries, Dru's Book Musings, and her talks at mystery conventions. You have an awesome ability to bring writers and readers together, Dru. I appreciate all the work you put into that. Readers who buy mysteries, those who request them from their libraries, and those who review books keep mysteries alive and encourage authors to continue writing them. Thank you all.

The Codger
Cook's Recipes

Grilled Jerk Chicken

Cooking this dish doesn't take long, but you have to marinate the chicken for at least half an hour before grilling it. This recipe is adapted from one on the McCormick spice company site. The flavor varies depending on which spice company's jerk seasoning you use, but most of the time the spices include garlic, thyme, allspice, nutmeg, and red pepper.

2 tablespoons jerk seasoning (more if you like
  spicy food)
3 tablespoons vegetable oil
2 tablespoons soy sauce
1 tablespoon cider vinegar
2½ pounds bone-in thighs or legs, or 1½ to
  2 pounds boneless chicken tenders

To make the marinade, mix the jerk seasoning, oil, soy sauce, and vinegar in small bowl. Place the chicken in a glass dish or a large resealable plastic bag. Add the marinade and turn the chicken to coat it well. Refrigerate the chicken for a minimum of 30 minutes. The longer it stays in the marinade, the stronger the flavor will be. Turn the chicken halfway through the marinating time.

Remove the chicken from the bag or dish and discard any remaining marinade. Grill the chicken over medium heat on an outdoor grill, turning the chicken to ensure even cooking. For chicken tenders, the grilling takes 5 to 7 minutes. Make a small cut in each tender to check that the chicken is cooked.

For bone-in thighs or legs, sear the chicken for 10 minutes, and then grill at a lower heat for 15 minutes or until the chicken is done. The internal temperature should be 165 degrees.

Makes 4–6 servings.

Baked Rigatoni

This easy pasta dish is like a deconstructed lasagna. The dish works best with short squat pasta that holds sauce well, like rigatoni, ziti, or penne rigate. Though the recipe makes a vegetarian pasta dish, you can stir in cooked ground beef or sausage before baking it. You can easily double or triple the recipe, but you'll need to use a larger pan or casserole dish than the recipe specifies.

8–10 ounces rigatoni, plus ¼ cup of the water in which the pasta cooked
1¾ cups marinara or spaghetti sauce
1 cup cottage cheese
1 egg, whisked
1 cup shredded cheese (mozzarella, cheddar, Parmesan, or a mix)

Preheat the oven to 350 degrees.
Cook pasta al dente in salted boiling water and drain it, reserving ¼ cup of the pasta water.
Mix the sauce, the cottage cheese, the egg, and half the shredded cheese (½ cup).
Add the cooked pasta and reserved water to the mixture.
Put the mixture into a medium-sized pan or casserole dish (9x9 or 7x11 inches). Sprinkle on the remaining cheese.
Bake for 30 minutes.
Serves 4.

Adapted from a recipe by Kristen Chidsey, A Mind "Full" Mom website.

Baked Fish with Basil Pesto

This recipe combines salmon, basil pesto, and a crust of bread crumbs and Parmesan cheese. The pesto blanket on the salmon adds moisture and flavor while the fish is cooking. The recipe makes enough fish for two and is easily doubled or tripled. The recipe also works for other fish, like grouper, bass, and halibut.

10–12 ounces of salmon filet (or *fillet*, if you like that spelling better!)
2 tablespoons fresh, frozen, or store-bought basil pesto
¼ cup bread crumbs
¼ cup finely grated Parmesan cheese

Preheat oven to 400 degrees.
Line a baking pan with foil or parchment paper, and place the salmon filet on it.
Mix the bread crumbs and cheese together.
Spread the pesto on the salmon. Top with the bread-crumb mixture.
Bake for 10 minutes or until done to your likeness. The baking time will vary depending on the thickness of the salmon and your own taste.
Serves 2.

Berry Smoothie

This recipe makes fourteen ounces, enough for two medium smoothies or one large one. You can use an immersion blender to combine the ingredients. It's easy to double or triple the recipe, but you'll have to make the smoothies in a standard blender.

10 ounces of raspberry sorbet
⅓ cup 2-percent milk (or any kind of milk or a vegetable-based milk alternative)
4 ounces of plain Greek yogurt
⅓ cup fresh or frozen raspberries
⅓ cup fresh or frozen blueberries

Put all the ingredients in a blender.
Whirl them until the smoothie is the consistency you like.
Pour the mixture into glasses and serve.

Tiramisu Parfait

Though tiramisu is usually made in a large pan, this recipe makes 6 to 8 individual servings for glasses, jars, or cups. The number of servings depends on the size of the cups or glasses.

1 cup espresso or strong coffee, cooled
¾ cup cold heavy cream
8 ounces mascarpone cheese
3 tablespoons Kahlúa or coffee syrup
12 crunchy ladyfingers (1 package Savoiardi Italian ladyfingers)
Optional: Unsweetened cocoa powder or shaved chocolate for garnish

Note: The sweetness in this dessert comes from the liqueur or coffee syrup. If you leave out that ingredient or if you have a sweet tooth or usually drink sugared coffee, add ¼ to ½ cup of confectioners' sugar to the cream when you beat it.

Make the coffee and set it aside to cool.

Beat the cream in a small bowl (adding any sugar you want to include) until it forms stiff peaks. Set the cream aside.

In a different bowl, beat the mascarpone and the Kahlúa or syrup until the mixture is soft.

Fold the whipped cream into cheese mix.

To assemble a parfait:

Cut one ladyfinger in half, dunk it quickly in the coffee, turning it once, and place it in the bottom of a glass. Add additional pieces of the ladyfinger as needed to cover the bottom of the glass. Spoon a layer of the cheese mixture over the ladyfinger. Dunk another halved ladyfinger in the coffee and add it on top of the cheese mixture in the glass. Spoon another layer of cheese on top. If you have really tall glasses, you may need to add other layers. Always end with the cheese mix on top.

Repeat the assembly instructions for each parfait glass.

Refrigerate the parfaits for at least 4 hours. You can keep them in the fridge for as long as two days. To make the parfaits prettier, you can add shaved chocolate or sifted cocoa powder on top before serving.